After graduating in chemistry and physics from London University, he worked in pharmaceutical research for a few years before joining a well-known international computer company in sales and marketing.

He has worked in the computer industry for over eleven years in several African countries, such as Ethiopia, Zambia, Botswana and South Africa.

During his time in Zambia in 1973–75, he drove from Lusaka to successfully climb Mount Kilimanjaro. He obtained a private pilots' licence in 1974 at the Lusaka Flying Club and went on to be an instructor.

He has a strong interest in music, particularly jazz.

He has a keen interest in classic cars and owns a Triumph TR4A.

As a result of working abroad, he enjoys travel, especially to places of historical interest in Europe and Africa.

He is thoroughly committed to his family (four children, nine grandchildren) and to his local C of E church.

Over the last ten years, he has written articles for the local Parish News on subjects such as: the Ark of the Covenant, the Knights Templar, the Cathares, the Battle of Agincourt, the Scramble for Africa.

A keen sportsman, he still plays squash and jogs, with a strong interest in most sports, particularly at international level.

He was a crew member on 42ft yacht in 2002 from Menorca to Split, Croatia. In 2004, he again was a crew member taking 44ft yacht from Southampton to Split.

His close relative's involvement in WWII stimulated him to write historical novels based to some extent on the relative's experience in the Intelligence Services.

To all those courageous people who used their 'small ships' to successfully evacuate many thousands of soldiers from Dunkirk in May–June 1940.

To all the British, French and Polish service personnel who gave their lives in the Norwegian campaign as they attempted to prevent the German occupation of Norway in April–June 1940.

Mike Walsham

DOING ONE'S DUTY

AUSTIN MACAULEY PUBLISHERS™

LONDON ★ CAMBRIDGE ★ NEW YORK ★ SHARJAH

A CIP catalogue record for this title is available from the British Library.

ISBN 9781398416680 (Paperback)
ISBN 9781398416697 (Hardback)
ISBN 9781398416703 (ePub e-book)

www.austinmacauley.com

First Published (2021)
Austin Macauley Publishers Ltd
25 Canada Square
Canary Wharf
London
E14 5LQ

The people at the National Archives in Kew, London, greatly assisted me in my research.

Members of the Newhaven Museum gave me an invaluable insight into the activities of the Newhaven Port and its involvement with the hospital ships, particularly during the period of the evacuation of Dunkirk in May–June 1940.

To my wife, Sandra, and all our family.

Chapter 1
Monday, 13th May 1940

Andrew Williams was in his boss' office in St James in London; he had been summoned there following his return to England by boat from Marseille the previous week. He had written a detailed report for the intelligence service's file that Charles Compton-Browne had already read, but he still wanted to hear Andrew's version in full.

"You have mentioned quite clearly that you stayed with Pierre for a couple of weeks in Aramon, near Avignon and that he was to contact Claude, who was to assist you with an exit from the port of Marseille. We don't know Claude, but we certainly thought we could trust Pierre to cooperate, that's why we gave you his contact details. You strongly suggest, however, that Pierre and Claude collaborated and were prepared to hand you over to the French police? That's a very serious allegation, Andrew, one that could well jeopardise our chances of using Pierre again."

"I realise that, Charles, but I'm not sure how else to explain it; I definitely saw Pierre in the police car coming out of the docks. In addition, when I had been standing on the ship's deck, Pierre and another man – presumably Claude – were in the car at the time the police were remonstrating with the woman that had taken me to the boat."

"We will obviously have to follow that up with one of our other agents before too long or perhaps send someone else to check them out.

"Anyway, Andrew, you got back to England safe and sound, and not just a little thanks to the ship's captain being Danish!"

"I have to say, Charles, it was certainly a stroke of luck. There was me using a Danish passport, being able to speak Danish and in a disguise that just about resembled the identity in my Danish papers! Captain Hansen couldn't have been more helpful."

"It will be written up in your records, but I must tell you that everyone in the Service that knew of your mission is most impressed with what you and George achieved: the sabotaged railway line disrupted the movement of heavy armament to Leipzig for several weeks.

"Have you been able to get up to speed with what's happening in the British Parliament and, in particular, with the prime minister, since you got back?"

"Yes, I have. I heard that Churchill has been invited to replace Chamberlain by the king and that the Nazis have invaded Belgium, Holland and Luxemburg. If those three countries do surrender, it only really leaves France before they think about invading England. I don't like the sound of it at all, nor will most people in this country.

"What I feel I really ought to do, and soon, if you'll allow me, is to go and visit my wife and new son: his first birthday was last Saturday and I haven't seen them since the two days I was with them at Christmas. I did manage to phone my wife on Saturday to wish Alfred a happy birthday and I did tell her that I hoped to be back home for a few days during this week."

"I'm not sure we like the idea of you contacting your wife without first getting clearance from the Service. I have to remind you that you must not call your wife out of the blue. She must have been very surprised to hear from you. Didn't she ask you where you were?"

"You are right, it was very foolish of me. Fortunately, she didn't ask too many questions."

"On the other hand, Andrew, it sounds like a good idea; you deserve some time off. I suggest you leave for home on Wednesday and come back to London on Monday, at a time convenient to you. I also recommend that you wear Royal Navy uniform so that she thinks you are really still in the navy!" Charles said with a smile. "I suggest a naval rating's kit rather than an officer's one. Go over to our establishment in Broadway, they'll sort you out."

They continued to discuss Andrew's recent mission and his report and, as there was nothing new on the horizon of immediate concern, he was allowed to take some leave while he could. The future very much depended on what Mr Churchill and his new cabinet decided to do in response to Hitler's invasion of the Low Countries. Charles also mentioned that Denmark had been overrun by the Germans and that the situation for the British and French expeditionary forces in Norway was looking dire.

Just before Andrew left Charles' office building, he had a quick chat with Helen: the very attractive receptionist lady that he had met several times before. He reckoned he might have time to take her out for lunch the following week, as she said she might be available. Andrew went back to his Service's flat and told his flatmates that he would be away until Monday evening. Even after what Charles had said, he thought it would be best not to surprise his wife by just appearing at his house, so he phoned her in the middle of the afternoon.

"Hallo, dear, how are you getting on?"

There was a slight pause before his wife's excited voice came down the line:

"Oh, Andrew, it's lovely to hear from you again. Do you think you will have enough leave to come and visit us, as you mentioned on Saturday?"

"I've actually got some home leave and would like to come and see you on Wednesday, but I must be back in London on Monday. How is Alfred doing? I suppose he's growing up fast?"

"We will have plenty of time to talk when you are here. What time do you think you will be arriving?"

"I thought I would catch a train from Victoria that should get me home at about 4:30 p.m., if that's alright with you?"

The arrival time was agreed. Andrew thought he should try and find some small gifts for his wife and young son, so he took a bus to Oxford

Street. He never liked shopping and felt he didn't have the imagination or experience to easily think of something, especially for his wife. He went into the ladies' department in one of the big stores and spoke to an attractive assistant. She persuaded Andrew to buy a pale blue floral frock that seemed to be the right size and then sent him to the children's department. He finally decided on a pair of dark blue dungarees with braces to match. He wasn't sure what size he needed, but the assistant recommended a slightly larger size that he could grow into and would also have enough room for a nappy!

On Wednesday, kitted out in his naval uniform that he had collected from the Broadway office the day before, Andrew caught the train from Victoria. He took a taxi to his house, arriving just after 4:40 p.m. His wife had heard the car draw up at the end of the driveway and ran out to meet him with Alfred in her arms. Andrew put down his naval kitbag, took off his cap and enveloped his wife in a fond embrace.

"You look quite well, Andrew," as she leant her head back and looked into his eyes.

"And you look well too, my dear."

They quickly walked hand in hand into the house just as it started to rain. Alfred was put down on the lounge floor where he showed his father that he could stand, even if he had to hold on to the sofa. He was unsure about his father as he had only seen him once since September, so he crawled to his mother and clung to her legs. Andrew's dog, Max, had come into the room and went straight up to his master making strange noises and wagging his tail so much that it looked as if it might come off.

"Alfred will get used to your being here before too long, he is a bit on the shy side anyway. Would you like some tea, Andrew, while you take your kitbag upstairs and probably change?"

"That would be very nice, dear, thank you."

Andrew went upstairs and left Max in the hall as he wasn't allowed into the bedrooms. He unpacked what little he had with him and looked in his wardrobe for some casual clothes instead of his naval uniform. He found something suitable, changed and brought his presents down to the lounge just as his wife was coming in from the kitchen.

"Here's the tea and I have found some cake that was left over from Alfred's birthday tea at the weekend."

Although they were pleased to see each other, it was difficult to know where to start the conversation: it was rather stilted and hesitant. Andrew knew he couldn't say anything about what he had really been doing for the last five months, if his wife should ask.

"Did many people turn up for Alfred's birthday?" Andrew enquired, trying to be in first with the questions.

"Well, as you might guess, there are mainly only ladies around at the moment: Brian is a flight officer in the RAF on coastal reconnaissance duty – in the Channel, I believe. My brother-in-law is away at sea, and the husbands of most of the rest of the women are also away. So, I asked just a few of my friends like Barbara and Pat; my sister came down on Saturday by train for the weekend and brought my father with her. Your mother – not surprisingly – declined the invitation as she was going to your brother's place in Norfolk. We had a special tea on Saturday afternoon, but we were indoors as it was drizzling."

"That sounds like a nice gathering for the little fellow. Oh! I nearly forgot; I bought you a small present."

"Oh, thank you very much; shall I open it now?"

She didn't wait for an answer. She untied the wrapping and held the frock against herself.

"That's really very pretty, Andrew, and it looks like the correct size; how very clever of you."

She rushed upstairs and in next to no time reappeared wearing the new dress and with a great big grin on her face.

"It's lovely; thank you so much," as she walked forward and gave Andrew a kiss on his cheek.

"I've got something for Alfred too, so please open it with him."

"Why don't I bring him over to you," she said, "and the two of you can open it together?"

Alfred was brought over to stand next to his father. At first, they started very carefully, but then Alfred started to rip the contents out.

"Steady on old chap," said Andrew a bit too sternly. Alfred started to cry and waddled over to his mother's open arms.

"Don't be too hard on him, Andrew. Let me finish opening the package; he'll calm down in a minute.

"They look really good, Andrew, and just enough room for a nappy underneath. He'll enjoy those during the summer months, won't you Alfred?" as she tried to gain the child's interest in something other than a toy.

"Sorry, I was getting carried away with the presents, so I think we should have some tea before it gets too cold. Would you like some cake, Andrew?"

"That would be very nice, thank you."

After about ten minutes of light chat and finishing his cake, Andrew was dying to ask a few questions, particularly about some of his friends.

"Have you heard anything recently about how Brian and your brother-in-law are getting on? I do realise that communication is difficult when there's a war on."

"I understand that, Andrew; after all, I hardly ever hear from you. Anyway, nothing has been heard from them for several months. As I said earlier, all I know is that Brian is in the RAF and my brother-in-law is in the Royal Navy. Now that you mention Brian, Alfred received a letter from him, last Friday I think it was, apologising for not being at his party as 'the king required his services'. He also sent a 10-bob note for a present."

"My goodness," exclaimed Andrew, "what a kind thought of Brian's, especially when he has so much else on his mind. Did he say anything else?"

"No, he didn't except that he would come and see us when he next has some leave."

Just at that moment, the phone rang; Andrew jumped out of his chair and went to answer it in the hall.

"Hello, Andrew here."

There was silence from the hall as Andrew listened to the person at the other end. He then let out a number of expletives:

"Oh my God, Doreen, that's dreadful news. Do you know how it happened?"

Andrew's wife detected there was some bad news, so she came to join Andrew in the hall carrying Alfred. Andrew cupped his hand over the receiver as he said to her:

"Brian's been killed; his plane came down off the coast of the Netherlands on Saturday. Apparently, three of his squadron were out looking for some German MTBs. His plane led the assault, but was badly hit in the starboard wing – they had to ditch in the sea.

"Sorry, Doreen, I just had to tell my wife the terrible news. Would you like us to come over and be with you or is your sister with you?"

"That's good, we quite understand, but if there's anything we can do this evening, we would be only too pleased to help and come and sit with you both.

"If it's alright with you," Andrew said after listening to Doreen for a few more moments, "I'll come over tomorrow morning at about 10 o'clock. Please remember, you can call us any time, day or night; I mean it. You and your sister should have a good brandy and try to get some sleep tonight."

"OK, Doreen, thank you for letting us know. We send our love to the two of you. 'Bye for now, dear, 'bye." Andrew put down the phone and stared into open space for a few seconds, then enveloped his wife and son in his arms. Max had got up from his bed and seemed to sense that something was not quite right. After a short while, they all stepped into the lounge.

"Poor Doreen; she lives in that huge house with just their dog. I can hardly believe what she's told us.

"Doreen said that Brian's squadron leader came to the house with the news this afternoon. He stayed for nearly an hour, going through how it happened and that only two of the three planes returned safely to base; there were no survivors from the one shot down."

A silence came over the room; even Alfred seemed to detect a serious air and just sat on his haunches looking up at his mother.

"I think we need a drink," Andrew suggested, as he moved over to the cocktail cabinet, where he poured two large gin and tonics.

"If you've got that letter from Brian that he sent to Alfred, I think we should put it on the mantelpiece with his birthday cards; it will help us to remember him and how badly we will miss him."

The letter was retrieved from the envelope on the side table and duly put in pride of place with the cards. Andrew handed a glass to his wife, who was wiping away tears from her eyes.

"To absent friends and our memories of Brian," said Andrew, with a bit of a croaky voice, as they touched glasses.

The rest of the evening was very sombre and Alfred was put to bed early, so they could reflect on their friends who were away at war, hoping they all would return home safely.

Early the following morning, Andrew took his black Labrador, Max, for a long walk. He didn't want to think too much about his visit to see Doreen, but he did put some thoughts in his mind of one or two important things he wanted to say to her, if the occasion arose. He thought he would take the letter sent to Alfred with him, but only show it to Doreen if she expressed an interest in seeing it.

Andrew drove up the drive of Doreen's house in his gleaming Bugatti and parked it in between her car and another one. The weather was warm, but clouds were gathering to the south west that suggested rain later; he hoped he would get back home before the weather broke.

He rang the bell outside and Doreen came to the door. She opened her arms to Andrew, he tried to give her a smile as they embraced.

"Do come in, Andrew; it really is good to see you. Thank you for giving up some of your short leave to come and see me," she said as she took his hand and led him through the hall into the lounge.

"You remember my sister, Gladys, don't you, even if you don't see her very often?"

"Of course," said Andrew with his appealing smile as he walked over to where she was standing. They kissed each other on the cheeks as he took her hands.

"It's been a while since we met, but this is a very different situation," he said, as he took Gladys' and Doreen's hands and brought them to his chest.

"I am most terribly sorry to have heard about your tragic loss; I'm sure you can't really believe it has happened."

They all sat down and Doreen went over the visit from Brian's squadron leader, how young he was and what an awful thing he had to do: visiting homes and delivering the bad news to comparative strangers. After talking for some time about Brian and with Andrew recounting some of the funny times they had had together over the years, the atmosphere improved. There were no more tears, but a few smiles and occasional laughter.

"Gosh, is that the time?" said Doreen, "how rude of me not to offer you a drink."

Each gave Doreen their order and she went to the dining room to pour them out. When she returned with them on a tray, Andrew and Gladys were talking about what Doreen might do next.

"Are you sorting my life out for me?" said Doreen, with a smile, as she returned to the lounge. "I will certainly need some help, but not for a few weeks yet."

She handed out the drinks. They all stood up and, as they touched glasses, Andrew gave a toast: "To Brian and our memories of many happy times together."

This was too much for Doreen, so she excused herself, went through the hall and upstairs.

"Oh, dear, poor Doreen. Shall I go and see if she's alright, Andrew?"

"No, I don't think so, but if she doesn't come down again in the next few minutes, then yes."

Some minutes passed, then there were sounds of Doreen coming down the stairs. Gladys and Andrew smiled at each other and then at Doreen as she entered the lounge. They continued with their drinks and started to talk about the events in Norway and the Low Countries and how many other people might be losing their loved ones.

Eventually, Andrew thought it was time to leave. Doreen wanted him to stay for some lunch, but he gave an excuse that his wife had made something special for his short time at home which Doreen well understood. They said their goodbyes and Doreen thanked him for coming over and helping her to lift her spirits. On the front step, she waved as she saw his car disappearing from the driveway. *How lucky I am to have such good friends at times like this,* she remarked to herself and went back inside to her sister.

Chapter 2
Thursday, 16th May 1940

The rest of the week seemed to fly by: Andrew took his wife and young son out to lunch on Friday. They couldn't get away from the loss of Brian, so Andrew phoned Doreen in the evening to find out how she was. Her sister had gone back home, but Brian's parents were going to come down at the weekend for a few days; by all accounts, they get on very well together.

The weather was fine and quite warm on Saturday so Andrew was allowed to go to the Red Lion before lunch to catch up with what's going on in the area. He hadn't been there since last year, towards the end of July: the last time he saw Anne and the time he met Chloe. He noticed the car park was quite empty as he swung in and parked his 'Bug' next to an Austin 7. As he entered the bar, it all seemed so different from the days before the outbreak of war: there was a new barman and they weren't serving meals – only filled bread rolls and crisps. The atmosphere was very dreary and those in the bars were of the older generation.

"So, how's business?" Andrew asked the barman as he took a good swig of his bitter.

"Very slack and it's even quieter during the week time."

"I'm sorry to hear that. Anyway, you might be able to help me: there used to be a waitress called Anne that worked here until last July; has she left?"

"The name does ring a bell," said the barman, "but I think she left just before war was declared to train as a nurse. I've no idea where she is now," he said rather bad temperedly.

Andrew wasn't surprised that she had gone to train as a nurse, but was disappointed he wasn't going to be able to see her. He still had her address and phone number, so he thought he would see if she was at home. He finished his pint and left for Anne's flat above the shops in Redhill.

He parked around the back of the shops where he had parked before and went up to the first floor. He knocked on the door and waited in excited expectation of seeing her again. After a few minutes, the door was opened by an elderly man.

"Oh, I'm so sorry to trouble you," said Andrew, "but I wondered if a young lady called Anne still lived here?"

"No, I'm very sorry, but she left here last October. She has become a nurse. She's with the troops and the British Expeditionary Forces in Europe, I believe. I'm now the new tenant of this flat."

"I know this is a bit of a cheek, but you don't happen to have an address for contacting her, do you?"

"Just come in a moment and I'll give you her contact details."

Andrew went inside, closed the door and stood in the lounge-diner while the old man went into the bedroom. He reappeared after a few moments with a piece of paper.

"Here you are," he said, as he passed the paper to Andrew.

"I'm John," said the man, "and what is your name, just in case she contacts me, which she has done on a couple of occasions?"

"My name's Williams, Andrew Williams, and I used to see her at the Red Lion pub where she worked as a waitress. I came back to her flat once and that's why I came here, hoping that she might have still been here."

Andrew studied the information on the paper and saw an address in Midhurst and a phone number; he thought it was probably where her parents lived.

"I very much appreciate your help, John; I will try to contact her when I'm next on leave."

With this, Andrew thanked John again, left the flat and went down the stairs to his car, wondering when he might have the chance to call the Midhurst number.

Andrew got home and went straight into the kitchen where his wife was preparing their lunch.

"So, Andrew, did you see anybody you knew?"

"No, I didn't. There was only a handful of people there and nearly all were about twice my age. The barman was rather unfriendly and they don't do lunches anymore. The outbreak of war has obviously had a big effect on trade; it's very sad. I don't know if other pubs are experiencing a similar downturn, but they probably are."

"Oh well; could you lay the table in the dining room, as we'll be eating in fifteen minutes?

"The main problem is that the introduction of rationing has prevented people from getting items that used to be readily available up until last Christmas. I have had to save up my coupons to provide us with a good meal today, on the off chance of your coming home at any time. As you will have noticed, we grow more vegetables than we used to. I even asked the gardener to build a run so we could have some chickens and get fresh eggs. It's not been easy, but I hear it will get worse before things improve. We import so many items from the USA and Canada, but the cargo ships are being sunk by the Nazi U-boats. Sorry to paint a bleak picture, but that's the way things are, irrespective of how much money one might have. We were able to go to the restaurant yesterday, but we could afford it; many people can't, so we are lucky."

Andrew took in what his wife was saying; he already knew that petrol was rationed and that his wife had to use the bus instead of her car to go to the shops.

They had an enjoyable lunch and Andrew managed to find a bottle of wine to go with the main course.

"I don't know if you will agree, Andrew, but I think we ought to go to church tomorrow? I have been a couple of times in the last few months and it's still the same vicar that baptized Alfred."

"That's a very good idea, my dear, particularly since Brian's tragic death. If it's a nice day, we could consider walking there, unless you've got some fuel in your car?"

"Don't worry, Andrew, there's enough petrol in those five-gallon cans in the garage to help us for some months yet."

After lunch, they cleared everything away. It was sunny and warm so they decided to sit in the garden. Alfred tottered around from one deckchair to another, but otherwise crawled on the freshly cut lawn. It was a quiet, relatively peaceful afternoon, but there were some distant thunderstorms at about 5 o'clock when they were thinking of getting Alfred's tea before his bath.

They had a quiet time together in the evening and Andrew played some of their favourite records on the gramophone, but neither said much about what might happen next in mainland Europe.

On Sunday, they arrived at church in good time for the 11 o'clock Matins service. The congregation was unusually large and there were quite a number of servicemen in uniform with their wives or sweethearts. The sermon was particularly apt and focussed on those who had died or were injured during the various campaigns of the Expeditionary Forces, and those who mourned the loss of their loved ones. They had thought Doreen might have attended the service, but maybe she thought it was too close to Brian's death for her to contemplate answering questions about how she was getting on. At the end of the service, the vicar greeted everyone as they left the church and he showed particular interest in Alfred.

"So, you're on some leave are you, Andrew?" the vicar enquired. "Are you home for very long?"

"Just till tomorrow, I'm sad to say."

"No doubt you are enjoying your time with your young son? He seems to be developing into a fine young chap."

Andrew thanked the vicar for his compliments and also for his words and thoughts in his sermon for those lost in recent battles. They exchanged greetings with some of the people they knew, but Andrew avoided talking about what he had been doing since the outbreak of war; he did, however, say he was in the Royal Navy.

When they got home, they had a pre-lunch drink toasting all those in the armed forces that were trying to defend their way of life. After lunch, Andrew did various small jobs in the garden and then took time to play with Alfred now that he was beginning to get used to his father being around in his life.

"So, Andrew, how long will it be before we see you at home again?" his wife asked after they had finished their afternoon tea.

"I'm sorry to tell you that I have no idea. The situation for the British Expeditionary Force is looking increasingly dire, unless there is a miracle in our favour. I will return to the Royal Navy, but it very much depends on what Mr Churchill has to say in the next few days."

"I see," said his wife, "so you could be away for some time?"

"As I said, where I go and what I do may very well depend on what Mr Churchill has to say. Perhaps it might be a good idea, therefore, to hear the 6 o'clock news tonight to find out if there have been any further developments over the last couple of days."

Andrew got his wife and himself a drink just before 6 o'clock. He turned on the radiogram and tuned in to the BBC's Home Service. They listened in silence as the newsreader mentioned the BEF and how they were fighting bravely with the French against the Nazi war machine near the Ardennes.

"Andrew, why doesn't the BBC give more details about these conflicts just on the other side of the Channel?"

"Apparently, now that Mr Churchill is holding the reins at Number 10, the BBC have been told to be very non-specific because, if they mentioned what is really happening to our boys, it might give helpful propaganda to the Germans and lower the morale of all those people back home. That's also why we don't get a weather forecast anymore, as it might help the German warplanes over our islands and coastal areas."

The mood in the Williams' house was very subdued for the remainder of the evening, even if Andrew was not going back to London until

Monday afternoon. After he had taken Max for a walk early in the morning, he played and laughed with Alfred during the rest of the time. After lunch, he prepared for his departure. He looked very smart in his naval uniform as he took his kitbag down to the hallway; Alfred was carried to say goodbye to his father and gave him a big smile. Max got up and wagged his tail hoping for another walk with his master, but was going to be very disappointed.

"Please do keep in contact with Brian's wife; there will probably be a proper funeral for all the airmen lost in that sortie," Andrew insisted and his wife nodded with tears in her eyes. She kissed him on the cheek and told him to keep safe.

The taxi arrived to take him to the station, but his wife could not go and wave him off as she was very superstitious: goodbyes could mean they wouldn't see each other ever again. He arrived at Victoria and decided to walk to the Service's flat as it was such a nice day. On his arrival, he was told by one of his flatmates that he should call Charles as soon as he got in. Before he phoned, he decided to change from his uniform into his casual gear, by which time it was well after 6 o'clock.

"Hello Charles, this is Andrew here; I believe you are expecting my call?"

"Yes, I am. Did you have an enjoyable leave?"

Andrew said that he did, but he was very saddened by the news of his great friend, Brian, being shot down and killed when on a recce near the Dutch coast. Charles commiserated with Andrew and told him that he had heard the news, but wasn't aware that the plane that was shot down contained a particular friend of his.

"Anyway Andrew, could you come to my office in St James tomorrow at 10 o'clock, as we have some important things to discuss?"

"No problem, Charles, I'll be there."

The following morning, Andrew was up bright and early. After a good night's sleep, he'd had a light breakfast and headed for St James. He knocked on the brass doorknocker and was let in to the reception area by a middle-aged woman with a very fierce look on her face.

"Good morning, my name is Williams, Mr Compton-Browne is expecting me."

"Yes, he is, Mr Williams. Would you go up to the second floor, but firstly please sign the visitors' book."

"That's a new procedure," remarked Andrew as he entered his name.

"There used to be a lady called Helen that worked here when I visited last week, is she still around?"

"No, she's been promoted. She is now secretary to the head of the Secret Intelligence Service, the SIS, and works in the Broadway office."

Andrew didn't want to pursue the conversation any further so he smiled endearingly and went quickly up the stairs two at a time. He knocked on Charles' door and went straight into his office.

"Hello Andrew, I'm very pleased to see you, but I am also very sorry to hear about your good friend Brian. I'm hoping to hear from his Squadron Leader in the next day or two. I'll call you when I hear more details."

"Thank you, Charles, I would like to know exactly what happened, but I do realise that it might be classified information."

Charles then turned to his boss, the head of SIS, more usually called 'C':

"You remember Andrew don't you, C? You met him just before his first assignment towards the end of last October; you've also read his report following his and George's sabotaging of the train carrying munitions in April."

"Of course," said C, "we are very fortunate to have Andrew as a key agent within the SIS. Welcome back and congratulations on the success of the mission."

"Thank you, sir. I think we had quite a lot of luck on our side."

"Please sit down, Andrew," said C. "Would you like some refreshments? We have some tea and some rather plain biscuits. Unfortunately, there's a war on and we all are subject to rationing," he said with a smile.

"Tea would be very welcome, sir," Andrew replied as he sat down next to Charles' desk.

"I'll come straight to the point, Andrew, so as not to waste precious time. As you will probably understand, with Mr Churchill at the helm, there is a different message coming from Number 10 and the War Cabinet, most of which is not being reported in the newspapers or put out on the wireless for obvious reasons. The Germans have swept through Holland, Belgium and Northern France and the bulk of our Expeditionary Force is being pushed back towards the sea. Lord Halifax wants us to negotiate with Hitler via Mussolini as the French seem to be preparing to throw in the towel. Churchill, as you might expect, has no intention of capitulating. Instead, he has agreed with Lord Gort, the BEF commander in France, to evacuate as many troops as possible back to England. Vice Admiral Ramsay has been given the task of planning the evacuation – to be known as Operation Dynamo – from his HQ inside the Cliffs of Dover."

C paused to drink his tea and then continued:

"There are hundreds of thousands of British, French, Belgian and some Polish troops that will soon be stranded on the French beaches and be at the mercy of the German forces. The prospect of getting many of our lads, as well as those foreign chaps, back to England alive is very worrying. I am being kept in the loop of the evacuation plan and, although the Royal Navy will be expected to try and bring the bulk of the troops back, Ramsay is seriously considering putting a request out to everyone with vessels – whatever their size – to be made available as they would be able to get up to the beach and ferry men back to the Royal Navy's ships waiting out in deeper waters or even back to England. We are therefore preparing to assist and we want you to be involved, together with other agents in the SIS that are not participating in other areas of the war. There is a man called Clive, who has a large motor launch down in Newhaven, and you are to get ready for when Ramsay's plans are announced to the War Cabinet and to me. As you are a fluent French speaker, you will be essential in helping any French and Belgian troops to understand the plan. Do you think you will be up for it?"

"Yes sir, I am very happy to help in whatever way I can. Isn't it likely that the Germans will want to take as many prisoners as possible or even kill those on the beaches while they're waiting to be picked up?"

"You are quite right and that's the big risk in this whole exercise. Support will be needed from the RAF and the whole operation will take many days to complete. Success is not guaranteed. All I can say is that we don't really have any alternative, if we are to continue fighting for our freedom."

"I assume, sir," said Andrew, "that you will get Charles to contact me when the go-ahead has finally been given by Vice Admiral Ramsay?"

"Absolutely," replied Charles. "Bear in mind, Andrew, this operation will definitely go ahead, it's just a matter of when and waiting for favourable weather conditions."

"Quite so; good point," said C.

The meeting then drew to a close. Andrew was thanked for his agreement to being included and was told that he should expect to be contacted before the end of the week.

Chapter 3
Friday, 24th May 1940

Andrew was phoned by Charles on Thursday and told to be at his office the following morning at 9 o'clock. As on his previous visit, he was welcomed by the grumpy middle-aged receptionist and again told to sign in before going up to Charles' office. He knocked and entered the office and was greeted by Charles and C, almost in unison; he was told to take a seat.

"What we are going to tell you, Andrew, is in the strictest confidence," explained C, "as the operation has only just been confirmed in detail by the Cabinet. You are not even to talk to anyone, not even your Service flatmates; is that clear?"

"Entirely clear, sir."

"As we said earlier in the week, we need you to go down to Newhaven and find this man named Clive," continued C. "He is not in the SIS, but is someone known to Charles and he can be trusted. Charles has already told him that one of our people will be going down to meet him this Saturday around midday, but he doesn't know your name. His motor launch is called *Annabelle* and it is being requisitioned by the Royal Navy – together with many other small craft around the south and east of England – in preparation for the evacuation of our Expeditionary Forces. You will have to use your initiative to find both Clive and his boat, but it is usually moored near the Hope Inn. Any of the bar staff will know Clive and they should be able to tell you where his boat is moored."

"Excuse me for interrupting, sir, but I assume I will be needing my French passport and papers for this mission?"

"No, Andrew, you won't and you'll use your own name, not your agent name, and you'll not need any passport. You will, however, be acting as an SIS person so you will keep your ears and eyes open for any snippets of information that might come from any of the lads that you take onto Clive's boat. If all goes well, we can assume that you and Clive will make a number of trips to the Dunkirk beaches. You will have ample opportunity to pick up what could be invaluable facts about the situation inland from the French coast and the whereabouts of the Nazi forces. It will be a very tiring and full-on mission that could last many days, but you'll have to watch out for the Luftwaffe and also mines that have been laid all along the French coast by the enemy. Do you have any questions?"

"What sort of weather is forecasted for the next week and do I need to take any provisions?"

"You'll need to take change of clothes, of course. The latest forecast I have received suggests calmer seas than are usual for this time of year with the wind blowing from an easterly direction with some low cloud. But, as you know, the weather can change quite rapidly, particularly in coastal areas, so we live in hope. There are as many as 350,000 troops in the vicinity of Dunkirk; Churchill's estimate is to successfully bring back about 30,000 troops, but we will need very many more if we are to defend our nation from possible invasion. We wish you and Clive, plus all others involved, the best of luck."

"Thank you, sir, we will do our level best. I don't suppose it's possible to have some money, so I can buy my railway ticket and buy Clive a beer? Possibly some French francs in case we have to go into Dunkirk itself for some reason?"

"Sorry, Andrew," said Charles, "we had forgotten to mention it to you. Miss Grim, as we jokingly refer to the receptionist downstairs, has sterling and francs ready for you. Just sign the order sheet and she'll give you the envelope. They all laughed at the woman's nickname.

"Her real name is Miss Jones, said Charles with a laugh."

Andrew stood up, shook hands with C and Charles and went downstairs. He signed for the envelope and left St James to return to his flat, chuckling to himself about Miss Jones' nickname. During the afternoon, he went to Victoria Station to find out the times of trains to Newhaven for Saturday and to buy his ticket. He had a snack and a pint in a nearby pub and returned to his flat late in the afternoon to put his clothes together for his next mission. He decided to have an early night and get a good night's sleep, in order to be at his best for the next few days when he might not get much rest at all.

Andrew caught a train that would arrive at Newhaven Town Station at about 12:15 p.m. He was excited about the new mission and knew it could be a very risky venture. The train arrived a few minutes late but, as it was a fine day, he decided to walk to the Hope Inn that was only just over a mile away at the end of the West Quay. He went into the Saloon bar and spoke to the man behind the bar:

"Good afternoon. Could you tell me where I can find a chap called Clive; he apparently has a motor launch moored near here?"

"Yes, I saw him earlier and he is a regular in here."

The man came from behind the bar and took Andrew outside. He pointed north towards the area where some yachts were moored.

"He should be on board at present and you will see his boat quite easily, anchored away from the quay, up past Sleepers Hole where the military craft are moored. The boat's name is *Annabelle*. If you walk along till you are in line with his boat, he should hear you if you call out his name."

"Thanks very much. My name's Andrew Williams, by the way," as Andrew shook the barman's hand.

"And mine's John," said the barman, as he gave Andrew a very firm handshake and a broad smile.

Andrew walked back along the pathway that he had walked down only a few minutes earlier. He saw Clive's boat and when he was opposite her, he shouted out his name. After a few moments, just before Andrew was going to shout a second time, a head appeared.

"I'll only be a few minutes," he shouted back, "go back to the pub; I'll meet you there."

Andrew decided to stay and watch for a short while as Clive disappeared down the hatch. After a few moments, he reappeared. Clive walked to the bow of the boat, tugged on the anchor rope to check that it was secure and walked round to where the dinghy was attached on the aft rail. He dragged the dinghy alongside the boat and clambered into it. He unhitched the rope and started to row towards the quayside. Andrew walked in line with the dinghy until it reached some steps and a pole.

"Here," shouted Clive, "catch this rope when I throw it and hold the dinghy steady while I get out onto the steps."

Andrew put down his kitbag and just managed to catch the rope as it came flying through the air towards him. He held the line firm and Clive came out of the dinghy onto the steps. He took the rope from Andrew and secured the dinghy, but left quite a bit of slack.

"The tide's in at present," said Clive, "but it will start going out in about an hour. The water goes down quite a long way at low tide, so I don't want to find the dinghy hanging from the post when we return," he said with a smile.

"I'm Clive," as he put out his hand to Andrew. They shook hands and looked into each other's eyes, trying to fathom each other out. Clive was a well-built man, probably in his late thirties, and taller than Andrew by about four inches. His curly hair was slightly bleached from being in the sun; he was muscular and wore a navy-blue shirt and shorts.

"I assume you are the chap Charles has said will be coming with me?"

"That's right. My name's Andrew Williams. I'm pleased to meet you, Clive."

They walked down the pathway and into the saloon bar. Clive asked Andrew what he would like to drink.

"A pint of bitter please, Clive."

"Make that two pints please, John."

They took their drinks to a table overlooking the water and sat down facing each other.

31

"Cheers, Andrew. So, what do you know about this exercise that we are obliged to take part in? I'm aware that many small fishing and leisure boats have been requisitioned by the Royal Navy to take part in a rescue mission to bring back our lads from the French coast, but I know no more details."

"All I know, Clive, is that you and I must prepare to go to Dunkirk. As you say, hundreds of other small craft will be involved over the next week or so from all around the south and south east of England to ferry men from the beaches to waiting Navy ships that will be further out in the Channel. It's a very risky mission as the Luftwaffe will be strafing the waiting men on the beaches and the boats collecting the men; they will also be subject to artillery fire from behind the dunes."

"Do you know when we should leave? Do we rendezvous with other vessels before heading for Dunkirk?"

"According to my information – and I need to have it confirmed on Sunday – is that we should leave Newhaven during tomorrow night and cross to the French coast. I'm assuming you have been authorised by Charles to take whatever fuel you need and will have been sent extra coupons?"

"Yes, they arrived this morning and I've already filled her tanks plus the ten 5-gallon cans that are already stowed on the boat."

"That's great news. What we now need is provisions, not only for us, but more especially for the lads we shall be picking up."

"I've made arrangements with the local shops for as much as they will allow me to take. The local baker is making bread and rolls especially for me and he will open his shop for me tomorrow at midday; we'll take all that we can on board. When I spoke to Charles the other day, he gave me a rough idea of what we would be doing."

"I can see you've spent your time very wisely," said Andrew with a chuckle, "so there's not much more for us to do except wait."

"You might be right, Andrew, but we don't have any dry clothes for these chaps to change into, nor do we have any extra life jackets.

"I don't think clothes should be a problem; they'll just be happy to be picked up and ferried back to England.

"Do you know if any other vessels are going from this harbour," enquired Andrew.

"Not that I'm aware of, but Newhaven is one of the main harbours to receive the returning ships, especially the Red Cross ships with the wounded. Even before this mission, BEF wounded have been brought here on some of the converted cross-channel steamers, such as the *HS Brighton V*, and the men are put on special trains for London. In fact, she left here yesterday and may well be back in harbour some time tomorrow.

"Finish your pint, Andrew, and I'll get another. They've got cheese sandwiches at the bar so I'll get one each."

Clive jumped up from the table, ordered the beer and sandwiches and, after a few minutes, returned to the table.

"I forgot to ask you, Andrew: how good a sailor are you? Do you know your way around a boat like mine?"

"I have done quite a lot of sailing over the years, but I've never crossed the Channel. Hopefully, I've got good sea legs," Andrew said with a grin. "I've been wondering, Clive, how many men could we get on your boat: twenty, thirty?"

"It's hard to tell. If it's a rough sea, there could be a chance of capsizing if we have thirty or more, as over half might have to be on deck. It would certainly be best if we took only the able bodied and left the bigger boats to take the wounded."

The barman brought their sandwiches so they fell silent for some minutes while they tucked in. *The bread's a bit dry*, thought Andrew, *but it's probably better than what the poor blighters are getting in France.*

"Let's finish up here, Andrew, and I'll show you around my boat; you might then get a better idea of the numbers we could take. If you've got any comments to make, please do say."

With no more conversation of any consequence, Clive paid John and they left for the dinghy. Clive got in first. Andrew held the rope, unhitched it and stepped from the lower step into the dinghy. Clive rowed to his boat, climbed up the ladder and held the dinghy steady as Andrew stepped over the rail and up onto the boat. Clive then hitched the dinghy rope to the rail.

"Welcome aboard, Andrew, this will be our home for the next week or so."

They had boarded the boat at the aft end where there was a flat section with a trap door to a compartment below. Turning away from this area, there were two seats: one on the starboard side with the wheel and all the controls in front of it, the other on the port side with a flat area in front for charts. A doorway was between the seats with a steep gangway going down into the saloon. Clive went down first, pointed out the small galley to his left and the 'heads' with a small shower behind a door on the starboard side of the boat.

"As you see, there is cushioned seating on each side of the saloon with storage areas under both that is accessed by sliding doors. A small table is stored under the cushions over there," as Clive pointed to his left.

"The main bunks are through this doorway where two people can sleep quite comfortably – weather permitting of course. Put your kitbag on this one, Andrew," as he pointed to the bunk on the left, "as I usually sleep on the right."

Andrew looked around and thought the sleeping area was quite small.

"I'm surprised this area isn't larger, but I suppose there is another storage area behind that panelling that is accessed from above?" as Andrew pointed beyond the bunks.

"That's right," replied Clive. "I store ropes, a few fenders and any other useful items in that area. Sometimes the anchor is in there, but more often than not it's on the deck."

They walked back through the saloon, up the gangway and straight on into the covered wheelhouse that had windows on three sides with a wiper on the large front window.

"As you can see, this is where all the action takes place. All the instruments are in front of the wheel plus a gyroscopic compass. The ignition key and starter are to the left and the switches for the outside lights on the right."

Chapter 4
Saturday, 25th May 1940

They spent what was left of the afternoon and early evening making a list of all they would need for their trip across the Channel. Additionally, they put the charts out on the table in the saloon and plotted their heading for Dunkirk. Andrew checked all the engine components whilst Clive looked for some extra life jackets.

At about 7:15 p.m., Clive told Andrew that they ought to take the boat out for half an hour to check that everything was in order. They started the engine, raised the anchor, brought in the fenders and set off towards the sea. Initially, Clive kept to the harbour's speed limit, but once out in the Channel, he took it to 70% throttle. He looked at all the dials and seemed very happy with what he saw. He asked Andrew for the heading to Dunkirk and set the boat in the correct direction.

"I need to tell you, Andrew, that the compass doesn't show the correct reading, but will take us 5 deg. to port. We need to bear that in mind when we set off tomorrow night."

Clive then handed control over to Andrew, so they swapped seats. After a short while, Clive said he was going down into the saloon to check something on the chart. Andrew enjoyed being in charge and felt very comfortable at the helm. His experience as a private pilot of light aircraft had taught him the invaluable routine of watching out for any craft in the vicinity: he looked to port, moved his head to see ahead of him, looked down at the instruments to see that there were no unexpected readings, looked up to the sky for any aircraft, turned his head to starboard. He repeated this procedure every minute or two.

"Can you slow the boat down to 10 knots, Andrew, and prepare to go about?" Clive had quietly come up part of the gangway and was observing how Andrew was dealing with the situation. He was pleasantly satisfied.

"Andrew, I think we should head back to the harbour as it seems to be getting dark a bit earlier than usual with this heavy cloud."

Andrew switched on the appropriate lights and followed the compass on a reciprocal heading, allowing for the compass' bias. Only a few lights were on in the harbour, but he easily saw the red port and green starboard buoys' lights at the entrance to the harbour.

"It's nearly 8:30 p.m., Andrew, so we must be at our anchor point by 9 o'clock. Except for any emergencies, the harbour master will close the port with a bare minimum of lights. We don't want to give help to any enemy aircraft that might want to disturb our night time, do we?" he said with a laugh. "Even if there are anti-aircraft batteries at the ready."

"It's a lot better down here on the coast," Andrew remarked. "We've got loads of barrage balloons over London to spoil the view."

Andrew found the buoy that Clive had used to tie up his boat to; he noticed how much the tide had gone out. Clive tied up, dropped the anchor, checked that all the hatches were battened down, locked the entrance to the saloon and made for the dinghy.

"We'll go ashore and have a light meal, Andrew, then return later to sleep aboard the boat."

Andrew didn't need to answer. They moored the dinghy at the steps as before and headed for the pub. There was a larger number of people in the bars than expected and noisy conversation between everyone. They had missed the 9 o'clock news on the wireless, but it appeared that, whatever had been said or inferred by the newsreader, it had generated much speculation about what might happen next in France.

Clive took up conversation with some of the locals and introduced Andrew to them. It appeared that quite a number were preparing to meet the hospital ship when it returned with another boatload of BEF wounded early the following morning: many of them would help to carry the worst of the wounded that would be on stretchers to the waiting train.

The pub food that was available was all locally made by some of the locals' wives and was as wholesome as it could be. There was an upright piano at one end of the bar area and some chap started to play a few of the popular tunes to try and cheer people up, but nobody really took much notice. After about twenty minutes, Andrew went and asked the man if he could play for a short while. Andrew stood at the piano and started to play and sing a few German army marching songs, at the same time occasionally mimicking Hitler with the Nazi salute and goose-stepping in front of the piano. Even though most people didn't understand the words, they all fell about laughing. When Andrew thought he had sung enough, they all shouted for more, but he declined.

"When did you learn all those songs?" asked Clive. "Charles didn't tell me you spoke German. That was absolutely hilarious. I think everyone wants to buy you a drink now and perhaps you could do a rerun a bit later?"

Andrew accepted a drink from one chap, but didn't answer Clive's suggestion about a rerun. The noise in the bar was ear-splitting and most of them were trying to remember Andrew's gestures with a modicum of success, at the same time falling over each other with laughter in the process. The barman smiled at the scene and gestured to Andrew that he wanted a word in his ear.

"This is the best evening we've had in here since the declaration of war. I know you are with Clive, but will you be coming back after your mission to Dunkirk?"

"I'm not sure how long we'll be away, John, and it all depends on whether we survive or not. Anyway, it's been a great evening. It's so nice to see some smiling faces, especially with all that's happening to the BEF in France and the number of wounded men coming back here."

John said no more as he was called away to serve more drinks. Andrew pushed through the throng of people back to Clive.

"What time are you planning to return to the boat?"

"John usually calls for last orders at 11 o'clock so we'll go when he closes up shop. Mind you, if people are going to want to carry on drinking, he might just stay open a half hour longer. Some of the local policemen are in here as well and will no doubt turn a blind eye to drinking after time. As you will have noticed, all the windows have blackout, just like anywhere else in England. On the odd occasion, some people do fall into the harbour on their way back to town, but they usually get fished out," he said with a laugh.

"By the way, Clive, I shall need to phone Charles tomorrow morning to find out if there are any last-minute changes to the plans. I believe I noticed a call box up in town towards the station, unless there's one a bit nearer?"

"The one near the station is the best one to use as the telephone people make sure it's always in working order."

The general buzz of conversation continued till well after 11 o'clock. Many people, who could see Andrew, pointed at him and started laughing as they did the Nazi salute with their left hand and the other hand above their mouth where a moustache might be, forgetting that they had a pint in their hand and spilling it over someone's trousers. Clive nudged Andrew just as John called last orders and suggested they left for his boat before the main body of people were thrown out of the pub. After they were on board *Annabelle*, they checked that everything was in order and decided to settle down for a good night's rest.

Just before 7 o'clock the following morning, they were woken by the sound of a ship's horn not far out to sea. Clive rushed out of the cabin first and onto the deck followed by Andrew who would have been there sooner had he not knocked his head badly on the hatch above the gangway coming out from the saloon. *Stupid idiot, Williams, just look what you're doing in future*, he mumbled to himself as he rubbed the top of his head.

"Are you OK, Andrew? I heard an almighty bang and saw you tumbling back into the saloon."

"Of course I'm alright," said Andrew in a very disgruntled tone. "I just didn't look where I was bloody going, that's all."

They both stood on the aft deck and looked out to sea and saw a ship steaming slowly towards the harbour. Many people had gathered on the east quayside and were shouting and waving enthusiastically to those waving on the ship. Andrew turned around to face the town centre and noticed steam coming from a train that had presumably arrived from London during the night. It was now making its way slowly towards the Harbour Hotel station.

"I believe these chaps have been brought back from Dieppe," said Clive. They'll be helped to the railway carriages where nurses and doctors will be waiting to attend to them. The train then goes to Redhill station which has become the nerve centre for transferring people to hospitals in London, Kent, Hampshire, the West Country and elsewhere. Let's get dressed and see if there's anything we can do to help."

They both dived into the saloon and changed into some casual clothes. Clive was the first out onto the aft deck, but Andrew was not far behind – this time making sure he didn't hit his head. They climbed down to the dinghy and loosed the rope that attached it to the boat. Clive rowed to the steps, Andrew climbed out and made the dinghy fast to the post. It was high tide so they only had two steps to climb up to the towpath.

By this time, the hospital ship was alongside the East Quay next to the London & Paris Hotel. Some boatmen on board threw the ropes to men waiting on the quay and they secured the ship to the capstans. Clive and Andrew came around the top of the harbour towards the men who were now putting the walkways in place for people to get on and off the ship. Nobody was to move onto the walkways until the captain or a senior officer waved them aboard.

Clive knew many of the men that had come to help transfer the injured to the waiting train: they'd been in the pub the night before and gave a wink and a smile at Andrew as they gave a Nazi salute.

"Could you do with any extra hands?" Clive enquired.

"We can always do with more able-bodied volunteers," said one of the men. "Don't I know you? Aren't you Clive, and don't you own *Annabelle*?"

Clive looked at the man carefully and suddenly it dawned on him. He slapped the man on the back.

"Of course, how stupid of me; you're Paul and you live in Alfriston, not far from an old pub called The Star, if I'm not mistaken?"

They greeted each other with a firm handshake and Clive introduced Andrew to him.

"Would you believe it, Andrew? I was at school with this chap and I haven't seen him for at least a couple of years."

At that moment, an officer waved the waiting men on board; many of them were carrying stretchers that they had collected from the train and in the station's waiting room. They were ushered down to the saloon on the lower deck where they saw some of the injured sitting on seats at the side of the ship.

"The ones who are really badly injured and require stretchers are in the cabins at the fore and aft of the boat. I suggest some of you help the ones in here off the ship first and those with stretchers follow me," said one of the junior officers. "They've had a really bad time. One of the other hospital ships, the *HS Brighton V*, was heavily bombed by the Luftwaffe whilst taking on injured men in Dieppe harbour. The ship was painted white with large red crosses on the port and starboard sides, but the Nazis didn't seem to respect the Geneva Convention, or they chose to ignore it. There were a few survivors that we picked up, but they're in the front cabins with doctors and nurses attending to them."

"Let's get some of these chaps out onto the quay, lads, and then come back with a stretcher later," said Clive to Andrew and Paul.

They, and a dozen or so others, spent the best part of an hour carrying or assisting the walking wounded to the quay, through the Customs House and to the train.

"I've found a stretcher, Clive," said Andrew, "so Paul and I will go and fetch some of the men from the cabins."

"OK, Andrew, I'll come and help, once I've got this chap to the train."

They went to the forward cabins and found the first five or so empty. They went on further to where some of the men were moaning or sobbing, some others were blind and were calling for their mothers.

Andrew looked in and saw two men on the lower bunks being attended to by a doctor and two nurses.

"Which of these chaps should we take to the train, Doctor?" said Andrew, as the nurses were busily dressing and bandaging one man's leg that finished just above the knee.

One of the nurses immediately turned around as Andrew spoke and looked at him in his eyes with disbelief.

"My goodness me, I could recognise that voice anywhere. Do you remember me? I'm Anne who used to work as a waitress at The Red Lion, not far from your home."

"How could I possibly forget you! I went to your flat only about a week ago hoping to find you there. I was given a Midhurst phone number by the chap now living in your flat; I called it last week only to find that it was your parents' home number."

"Nurse, could I please ask you to continue your work with this patient; he's not in good shape and needs to be stretchered out to the train as soon as possible."

"Sorry, Doctor Matthews, I got a bit carried away with seeing someone I haven't seen since before the war: last July as it happens."

The nurses and the doctor took ten more minutes to finish attending to the patient's wounds to his leg and his head. Andrew watched Anne very intently and saw how adept she was. He could only think of the time she and he had lain naked on her bed after she had made supper at her flat.

Andrew was suddenly brought back to the present: "Right, gentlemen, bring over the stretcher and we'll lift this chap very carefully onto it," the doctor said, as he gestured to Andrew and Paul. Getting through the saloon was easy enough, but going up the staircase and down the gangway to the quay was tricky. Once they were close to the train, two other men took the stretcher into a compartment that had been converted into something like a hospital ward and an operating theatre.

After a few minutes, the stretcher reappeared from the carriage, so they could repeat the exercise with the next patient. They went aboard and into the same cabin as before. Andrew hoped to see Anne again, but she wasn't there, just the other nurse talking quietly to the last patient in the cabin in a reassuring manner. He was very disappointed.

"Come on, Andrew," shouted Paul, "let's get this chap to the train."

As they passed the other cabins on their way to the stairs, Andrew had a quick glance inside to see if he could see Anne: she wasn't to be seen.

After about an hour and a half, they had taken ten more wounded men to the train. Andrew found Clive as he was returning to the ship.

"It's after 10 o'clock, Clive, and I need to call Charles to get the latest about the evacuation. Have you got any loose change I can borrow?"

Clive dug his hand into his pocket, pulled out some coins and handed them to Andrew.

"I'll have to leave for some minutes as I have to make this phone call," he explained to Paul, and walked briskly towards the Town station. When he got to the kiosk, it was in use. He gesticulated rather angrily to the woman inside that he was waiting to use the phone, but she turned her back on him and continued her conversation. After some minutes, the woman came out of the kiosk. She was in tears and explained that her badly wounded brother had been taken to the train, so she'd called their mother with the news. Andrew said he was very sorry and apologised for his impatience. He went inside, put some money in the machine and dialled Charles' direct number. He could her the phone ringing. After a few moments, Charles answered; Andrew pressed button 'A' and they were connected.

"Hello Charles, this is Andrew."

"Andrew, good to hear from you. I've been expecting your call. Is everything alright? You and Clive getting on OK?"

Andrew explained that he and Clive were fine and that they had been helping to take wounded soldiers off the hospital ship to the train.

"Just in case I run out of money, can you call me back, please?" asked Andrew. He gave Charles the phone number and put down the handset. After a short while, the phone rang.

"Thanks, Charles. What's the situation with the evacuation?"

Charles explained that the War Cabinet had given the go-ahead. It will be known as 'Operation Dynamo', just as C had said at their meeting. It will officially start at 6 o'clock tomorrow morning – Monday. Huge numbers of owners of small boats had responded to the call for help by the Admiralty.

"We are planning to leave tonight and will be near Dunkirk shortly after 6 o'clock," said Andrew. "We hope to pick up about thirty men from the shore. If there are no bigger ships around, we will ferry them back to Dover rather than Newhaven. By the time we return to Dunkirk, the bigger ships will have arrived so we'll transfer men to those ships, unless one arrives earlier."

"That sounds fine. You must be aware, Andrew, that the port of Dunkirk has been heavily bombed and only the East Mole can be used. The battleships and cruisers will be anchored further out to sea. You can expect a great deal of bombing and strafing by the Luftwaffe at the men on the beach and at the boats. As we have already said to you, the Germans have laid magnetic mines along the French Coast; you must exercise great caution."

"I understand, Charles. Shame we haven't got an anti-aircraft gun on the boat, instead of a few pistols!" Andrew said jokingly.

They talked for a few more minutes. Charles wished them good luck and God speed.

Chapter 5

Sunday, 26th May 1940

The helpers continued throughout the morning to take the wounded off the ship to the train. Clive excused himself as he had to go to the baker's shop to pick up the bread for the trip that night. When he arrived at the shop just after midday, the baker had everything ready and waiting.

"I've got enough here for a small army," the baker joked. "I've managed to scrounge enough ingredients from people in town to make some cakes. It's fair to say that the lads will probably not have eaten very much – if anything at all – for many days, so they will be quite weak."

"Brian, you will be seen as an angel to the men, but I'm not sure how I can keep all this stuff fresh?"

"I've boxed them all up for ease of storage and put damp tea towels in the boxes so they don't dry out. There's enough here for quite a few trips, but if you hand it out sparingly it will last for many more trips."

"Thanks a lot, Brian. There's quite a lot here so do you have a barrow or a trolley to take it all to my boat?"

"What time are you leaving, Clive?"

"Around midnight."

"So why don't you let me keep it all here till 8 o'clock, say. You come back with your friend, who can then help you with getting it to your boat?"

"Are you sure, Brian?"

"I'm absolutely certain. It's the least I can do for these poor lads; there's a war on, after all."

Clive agreed; thanked Brian profusely and said he'd be back just after 8 o'clock. He returned to the hospital ship to find Paul carrying a stretcher with someone other than Andrew.

"Where's Andrew?"

"He's chatting to the nurse he met earlier on in one of the cabins. Apparently, the ship is leaving here early tomorrow morning and it's going to Dunkirk this time rather than Dieppe."

All the wounded were off the ship by 3:30 p.m. and the vast majority were put on the train that was due to leave at 4:15 p.m. Clive had seen Andrew quite a few times taking stretchers to the train, but not spoken to him since going to the baker's shop.

"Andrew," Clive shouted from the quay, as he saw him on the ship's foredeck, "can we have a chat, please?"

Andrew turned from talking to the nurse and walked quickly to the nearest gangway and on to the quay.

"I've been to the baker, and he's keeping all that he's made for us at his shop. He has kindly agreed to reopen at 8 o'clock, so we can collect everything and take it all back to our boat. I don't think there's much more we can do here and the train leaves in about twenty minutes time."

"OK, understood, Clive. I would, however, like to have a final few words with the nurse I was talking to before we go to do anything else; I'll be less than ten minutes."

Before getting an answer or any comment from Clive, Andrew turned and ran back onto the ship. Clive smiled to himself as he watched Andrew reach the nurse. He touched her on the arm; she turned to him and they looked intensely at each other as they spoke. Clive could clearly see that there was something very special between them. He went back towards the station where he found Paul talking to one of the stretcher bearers about some of the very badly wounded men. He stopped when Clive arrived.

"The train is ready to leave," said Paul. "I think the men will be pleased to be on English soil and on their way back to wherever they are to receive further treatment. They've been through so much for such a long time."

Clive nodded in agreement. The engine whistled a couple of times and slowly started on its way with great clouds of smoke billowing from its funnel. Everyone waved a fond farewell, but only a few soldiers could be seen at the windows as the train passed by.

Paul said goodbye to Clive and told him he ought to get back to Alfriston. As he shook his hand, he wished him and Andrew well for their trip to Dunkirk. Clive looked for Andrew before he headed back to the boat and noticed he was walking quickly down the west quay; he had a big grin on his face that seemed to go from ear to ear. Once they were back on Clive's boat, they moved items around in their cabin to give space for the baker's provisions.

"Wouldn't it be better if we put the grub in the forward hold, Clive, in case we need to put the less able-bodied men in our cabin?"

"I had considered that, but I'm concerned that if there's a rough sea, water could easily get in: it's not very watertight. Also, it will be easier for us to hand out the food to them if it's in our cabin."

"Point taken, skipper," said Andrew with a wink.

They spent the rest of the late afternoon catching some sleep as they knew they weren't going to get much during the night, or maybe even over the next few days.

Andrew woke first just after 7 o'clock. He slipped out of the cabin and went up onto the deck and looked out to sea. He thought he could hear distant gunfire and wondered what those poor men were having to put up with on the beaches. He must have been lost in his thinking as he didn't hear Clive come up behind him.

"Have you been up here long, Andrew?"

He looked at his watch and then turned to Clive.

"Maybe fifteen minutes. Can you hear the distant gunfire or is it just my imagination? Those lads must be going through hell."

Clive nodded, thinking it was probably Andrew's imagination.

"We ought to get some food at the pub before we set off, Andrew, so I'm going to have a quick wash and clear my eyes. Let's be ready in ten minutes."

They each went about their chores with Andrew using the small sink in the galley; they met on deck ten minutes later. They tied up the dinghy as usual and, as it was a little after 8 o'clock, Clive suddenly remembered that they were to be at Brian's shop to collect the food for the soldiers, so they walked hurriedly into town.

"Good to see you, Clive, everything is ready for you. I've managed to get three barrows so I'll give you a hand; we'll probably need two trips."

They went into the back of the shop, loaded up and went out into the street. Brian locked up and they went to the dinghy. They handed the boxes to Clive who was now in the dinghy and there was just enough room to put all of them in. Clive rowed to the boat and at the same time Andrew and Brian went back to the shop for the next load. When they returned to the steps, Clive was already tying up the dinghy, having put all the boxes on the aft deck.

"I think that's the last of the boxes, Clive. Do you think you've got enough?"

"It will have to do, we haven't much room for many more, what with the space we'll need for all the men and any kit they might have. Thanks for your help and generosity, Brian, they'll be really pleased with some good wholesome nourishment."

Clive set off for the boat once again; Brian and Andrew took the empty barrows back to the shop. As Andrew shook Brian firmly by the hand, he asked him if Clive had paid him to which he replied that everything had been settled. He wished them a safe and successful trip. Andrew met Clive as he was tying up the dinghy and they walked together down to the pub.

It was after 9 o'clock and the pub was crowded. Everyone was talking about the wounded men that now were on their way to hospital somewhere inland. Many recognised Andrew and smiled, but there were no suggestions of a repeat performance of the evening before. Clive bought two pints and he asked if there was any food.

"You'll have to be quick, Clive," said John. "There's not much choice, I'm sorry to tell you; the gannets have been here before you! I've got two portions of warm chicken pie with a few veg and some cherry pie to follow."

"That sounds absolutely marvellous, doesn't it, Andrew?"

Andrew nodded in agreement and smiled as Clive paid for the pints and the food. They found a table by the window and sat in silence for about five minutes looking out towards the harbour. Having seen the wounded men coming off the hospital ship, the realisation of what they might be going through in the next few days came over them: what will it really be like when they get to the beach, how will they decide which soldiers to take, will they be attacked by the Luftwaffe, will they survive the ordeal?

"I've been meaning to ask you, Andrew, how do you know that pretty young nurse on the hospital ship?"

"It's a long story, Clive. She used to work as a waitress at a pub near where I live. One evening, she invited me back to her flat for supper. We enjoyed a very intimate couple of hours together; that's all. She isn't someone one easily forgets."

"I suspected as much," said Clive.

The barman unexpectedly brought them back to reality as he came up to their table with the first course.

"Here we are, chaps," as he put the plates down.

"You've got a bit more, as there was no point in keeping back a half portion, especially at this time of the evening."

He took knives and forks out of his top pocket and went back for the salt and pepper.

"This looks great, John; can you get us two more pints, please, I'm paying this time?" asked Andrew, as John returned to the table.

They tucked into their food and beer; after about ten minutes, John brought the cherry pie.

"That was just what we needed, John, and the cherry pie looks almost too good to eat!"

They finished everything, stood up and said their goodbyes to everyone.

"What time is it, Andrew?" asked Clive, as they went out into the still night air.

"Not sure, but it must be well after 10:15 p.m."

They walked carefully up the road, got into the dinghy and Clive rowed to the boat.

"We'll get a few hours shuteye before we set off for Dunkirk at about 2 o'clock," said Clive.

Chapter 6
Monday, 27th May 1940

They had lain out on the seats in the saloon under blankets, as all the food was stored in the forward cabin. Andrew woke first and went up the gangway to the aft deck. His watch told him it was just after 1:30 a.m. There was about a little more than a half moon that was occasionally visible as the clouds went slowly by. The sea in the harbour was calm, but Andrew knew it would be quite different out in the Channel. He turned from gazing out to sea to see Clive coming onto the aft deck.

"The weather seems favourable at the moment," Andrew remarked. Did you manage to get a forecast from the harbour master yesterday?"

"Yes, I did. As you know, meteorology is not a precise science, but he did think we might be quite lucky until Friday; he wouldn't predict what it might be like beyond that. He did say that for today and tomorrow, the wind will continue to mostly blow from an easterly direction, the sea will be relatively calm and there will be quite a lot of low cloud. He had been briefing me and the navigator of the hospital ship. He gave me a copy of a chart showing a large part of the Channel around Dunkirk. Apparently, a copy has been given to every voluntary and requisitioned boat captain participating in the evacuation, as well as all the naval vessels. He also reminded us of the German mines that have been laid along the French coast."

"Apart from mines in the Channel, the Luftwaffe strafing the beach and the machine guns behind the dunes, we have nothing to worry about, do we?" Andrew said with a wry smile.

"I think it's time to prepare for our departure," Clive remarked, trying to be serious. As they turned and went down to the saloon, Clive mentioned that the harbour master had given permission for them to depart as soon as they could after 2 o'clock and that they should try to be punctual.

They set about their individual pre-departure tasks as quickly as they could. Clive was at his seat with the engine ticking over, Andrew had brought in the fenders, attached the dinghy to the buoy and was ready to draw in the anchor once Clive gave the word.

"Let's be on our way," shouted Clive.

"Aye, aye, Captain," Andrew replied, as he hauled up the anchor, stowing it and the rope neatly on the forward deck. He walked back to the wheelhouse and sat in the seat next to Clive. He took out his torch, examined the charts and glanced at the compass. The engine purred sweetly as they entered the sea beyond the port. Clive had turned on a minimum of lights plus a forward search light.

"It's a bit choppy, but she will ride the waves well at 8 knots," Clive said.

Every now and then, their path was lit by the moon breaking through the clouds, so Clive turned off the search light and navigated by the compass that had a small light over it. At 3 o'clock, Clive asked Andrew to fill in the logbook the way that he had told him when they had gone out the previous day – he should repeat the exercise every hour on the hour. He returned to his seat about seven minutes later. As they were getting near the middle of the Channel, they both stared hard at the horizon, occasionally seeing flashes of light and, a little later, hearing distant gun fire. Andrew carried out his routine of looking to port and then to starboard; his eyesight was much sharper than Clive's.

"Clive, look, there to the left," he said, as he pointed half behind himself.

"I can see some craft and they seem to be going in the same direction as us."

Clive took up his binoculars and looked in the direction that Andrew was pointing.

"You're right, Andrew. There are a few small boats and one or two larger vessels. At least we're not alone, should we get into difficulties. I wonder which ports they've come from?"

They motored on towards their destination. It was just beginning to be a little less dark so they could see the outline of the French coast ahead of them, even though the moon was behind the cloud.

"Do we have a radio frequency to contact some of the larger ships?" enquired Andrew.

"Yes, I was given one at yesterday's meeting; it's written on the bottom of the chart they gave me. We are only supposed to use it in a dire emergency, in case the Nazis pick it up and listen in."

They fell silent for a while longer. Daylight was getting brighter. They could clearly see the coastline, there were masses of antlike creatures on the sand.

"There seem to be thousands and thousands of men waiting to be picked up," remarked Clive. "Once the light is a bit brighter, they are certain to be at the mercy of the Luftwaffe, but the low cloud might restrict them from flying for the time being."

Andrew looked at his watch: it was coming up to 6 o'clock and they were less than two miles from the beach. The boat slowed as Clive throttled back to 5 knots.

"Andrew, I want you to go onto the foredeck and look out for mines; shout to me if I need to change course and use your arm to signify which direction I should take. It looks as though the harbour is out of action and is ablaze so we'll head for the East Mole, which seems to be intact."

As they gently motored along getting nearer to the coast, Andrew stared at the sea about thirty yards in front of the boat's path. After a few minutes, he saw something that resembled a mine. He shouted to Clive and quickly stuck his arm out to his left. Clive responded immediately, taking a sharp turn to port. It would have thrown Andrew overboard had he not been anticipating the change in direction and if he hadn't been holding on to the rail. He carefully watched the mine go by and saw that it was only a few feet from the boat's starboard side. He breathed a sigh of relief and took no time in turning his attention once again back to the sea in front of him.

"The tide is taking us away from the Mole," shouted Clive over the top of the wheelhouse. I'll have to increase our speed to compensate and steer a slightly different heading into the waves."

The wind wasn't blowing too strongly, but as the outgoing tide was catching the boat broadside, she was rocking and rolling. Andrew stayed on the bow deck for a further ten minutes and then carefully returned to the wheelhouse and his seat. He looked at Clive and saw that he was working hard at the wheel.

"Instead of going to the Mole, why don't we head for the beach? With the tide going out, it will be shallow enough for the lads to get aboard," remarked Andrew.

"I agree and it will mean we'll be going into the waves rather than across them."

After a little while longer, they could identify long lines of soldiers on the beach very clearly and they were looking out at the few approaching boats. A destroyer had anchored just a mile from the shore and there was a ferry nearing the Mole.

"Looks as though we've got plenty of company, Andrew. I suggest we pick some men up from the beach and take them to the destroyer."

Nothing further was said as they got closer to the beach; Clive had throttled back and gently took the boat's prow into the sand. Men started to push forward towards the boat and just as Clive thought that too many would try to climb aboard, a loud order came from the sergeant telling them to wait and get in line. Andrew helped the soldiers onto the foredeck while Clive tried to keep the boat steady with the motor. The men were directed down into the saloon and Clive told them to take seats or squat on the floor once all the seats were taken. They somehow managed to get twenty-two men into the saloon with whatever weapons and packs they had, plus a further twelve on the forward and aft decks.

"No more, sergeant," Andrew shouted, "or we might capsize. We'll be back again as soon as we can get these lads onto the destroyer."

Clive put the boat into reverse and was pushed out to sea by some of those hoping to get on the next trip. The boat went about and Clive had to use more engine power with the extra load on board – even with the tide going out. It was a smoother ride with the boat lower in the water, but the engine did seem to struggle; *at least the tide was in their favour,* Clive mumbled to himself. Andrew gave some sandwiches to the men and then returned to the foredeck to look out for mines. It took nearly an hour to reach the ship and after putting down the fenders, they went alongside. Rope ladders had been hung down from the ship's deck. Andrew helped the men onto the ladders. When all the men were on board, Andrew scaled the ladder to find one of the officers.

"This is a list of the names of the thirty-four men that we've passed to you," said Andrew, as he handed the lieutenant a piece of paper. "I've also written their regiment and indicated which men might require some medical treatment."

"That's excellent, thank you."

Andrew saluted the officer and said he was now off to fetch another group. He boarded the boat, took up the fenders and sped off at speed. A few hundred metres from the beach, there was a fearful noise of airplanes. Andrew looked up to see there were many gaps in the clouds and obviously the Luftwaffe were using this opportunity to attack the men on the beaches with their Stuka dive-bombers. They came down almost vertically making a piercing, siren-like noise. As they pulled out of the dive, Andrew and Clive saw them release their bombs on to the waiting soldiers on the beach. Some soldiers tried to shoot down the planes with their rifles, but it was, of course, hopeless. Bodies were thrown into the air and a few tried in vain to run from the bombs before they hit the sand. The two of them stood mesmerised at this wilful destruction of defenceless men.

"We can't just stand here, Clive, let's get a move on and take more men to safety," Andrew yelled.

Over the next nine hours, they fetched another 190 men from the beach and brought them to the ship; they had used up only two of their ten cans of fuel in the process. For some of that time, the Stukas strafed the beaches on at least three more occasions until the cloud cover came again and restricted their flying.

"I think we should motor to the Mole and tie up on this, the west side of it. We ought to give the engine a bit of a rest for an hour, check the oil level and so on. After all, we've been lucky: the bombers have left us alone, but as there are many more vessels arriving, the Luftwaffe will probably pay more attention to the boats than the beaches," Andrew suggested.

They motored to the west side of the Mole very easily as the tide had turned and was going in. A paddle steamer ferry was on the far side and people were busily assisting wounded men on to the ship. Small boats were appearing in increasing numbers along the shoreline, but with the tide nearly in, the soldiers had to wade to the boats with the water up to their chest. Andrew saw a few falling down into the sea as the waves broke, but were quickly dragged up onto their feet by those nearby. It was a desperate sight; even though the men were so keen to get away from France, their cheerfulness and discipline was quite amazing.

Andrew drew himself away from watching the escaping soldiers and tied the boat to one of the Mole's large metal rings, after Clive had remonstrated with him to pay attention to what he should really be doing. The boat faced the incoming tide and it rocked up and down as each wave broke against its bow.

Andrew climbed onto the aft deck, opened the hatch and started to examine the engine, once the hot fumes had dissipated. They both were exhausted – mentally and physically – but essential jobs had to be completed. Clive went down to the saloon and he saw there were still a few sandwiches and cake left over. He remembered that Andrew had said he would only give them half a sandwich as they were being taken to the destroyer, where more food and drink would be waiting for them.

After nearly an hour, Andrew shouted to Clive, who was now in the wheelhouse:

"I've checked everything and all looks OK. I've changed the plugs and the oil filter. There's quite a lot of water in the bottom of the engine compartment so we ought to work the bilge pump when we next run the engine."

There was now a huge amount of activity near the Mole and in the waters near the beach. Many more boats had joined in the evacuation. One of the hospital ships had already returned to Newhaven, the paddle steamer had left for Dover, the destroyer had taken as many men as it could and was on the point of leaving its position.

Andrew went up to Clive and explained that as they weren't going to pick up more soldiers for an hour or so, he would walk along the Mole and talk to some of the men, in particular one of the senior officers, if he could find one.

"Are you sure that's wise?" asked Clive. "There are so many men and you will be going against the flow. As you can see, another paddle steamer is ready to be tied to the Mole and men will be pushing and shoving to get on it?"

"I'll be fine, Clive. In any case, I need to get information about what the state of play is further inland, especially what the French battalions are doing. Charles asked me to find out all that I could whilst here."

"Then you must do it. I will be leaving for the beach in one hour from now. If you're not back by then, I will ask a sergeant for a volunteer to come and help me." Clive and Andrew then synchronised their watches: it was 6 o'clock.

"In that case, I'll take my papers and passport from my cabin and conceal them in my jacket, so at least I will have some form of identity."

Clive allowed Andrew to pass him and go below from the forward deck. In not many minutes, he reappeared on the aft deck with his kitbag. He had darkened his hair with some cream and had put on a false, black moustache. Clive thought Andrew was ready for business. He shook Clive's hand, said *bonne chance* and clambered onto the Mole without looking back at him. Clive saw him put on a beret and noticed he walked in the middle of the lines of men against the flow. He then lost sight of him.

Andrew was jostled and sworn at by some as he barged his way forward. He decided to say nothing to anyone, but just smiled and nodded his head as he looked a few in the eye. He was now in 'agent mode'. Against Charles' instructions, he had brought his French passport, papers and money, as well as his British ones onto the boat. His British documents and money were in a small false area at the bottom of his kitbag; his French ones were in a zipped pocket of his jacket. He was now Artur Selmer; he felt very confident in that role. He had no intention of returning to the boat, certainly not for the next day or two – should he survive.

Chapter 7
Monday, 27th May 1940

Artur eventually reached the end of the Mole where there were even more soldiers pressing forward, desperate to catch the next steamer. He was looking around to get his bearings when there was a cry from some of the men that the Stukas were coming again through the gaps in the clouds. Without any hesitation, everyone fell to the ground and, even those with helmets on, covered their heads with their hands. The whining noise got closer. Artur turned his head slightly towards the sound and saw bombs being dropped by the howling Stukas as they came out of their dive, less than one hundred feet above the sea. To Artur's alarm, not only did some of the bombs explode just beyond the end of the Mole, but two also hit its side, not far from the bow of the paddle steamer.

Oh, my goodness, thought Artur, *I hope some of the debris from the wall hasn't hit Clive and his boat.*

The noise of the explosions and the cries of the men was terrible. The seven Stukas that had been involved in the sortie flew away, but German soldiers were still spraying the beaches with machine gun fire from behind the dunes. Artur carefully sat up, straightened his beret and stared at the steamer. It appeared to have escaped any major damage, but he thought the bow must surely have been hit by some rocks flying off the Mole. He couldn't see Clive's boat, probably because there were so many men obscuring his view as well as it being on the other side.

Artur stayed low for a few more moments as he unzipped his inside pocket; he took out his papers. Before he had left his London flat, he had found a copy of a rough map of Dunkirk. One of the soldiers sitting near to him had told him that French and British battalions were holding off the advancing German units: the British were positioned on the coastal side of the Bergues – Fernes Canal; the French along the canal west of Bergues, past Spycker down to the coast beyond Mardyck. It was obvious to him that he should make for the French troops.

He looked at his watch and, to his amazement, it was 7:15 p.m. He knew Clive would have left on the hour, so long as he hadn't had any problems with his boat, or was hit by debris from the Mole. He was now on his own. He walked inland past many bombed houses that were still smouldering from recent raids. He had to watch his step and not trip into a bomb crater in the road. He passed many abandoned military vehicles of varying types: some still burning, others in a mangled, misshapen mess.

He saw a house some 400 metres ahead of him that seemed miraculously to have missed the bombardment. He drew level with the downstairs window and peered inside past the two pieces of wood that were set diagonally across it. Even with the cloud cover, it was still light enough for him to see a woman sitting in a chair. She turned her head, almost instinctively it seemed, and saw Artur just as he was trying to move away. *This is my only chance*, he said to himself. He quickly looked around to see if anyone was likely to notice what he was going to do next. He knocked on the door.

"Who's there?" said the woman. "What do you want?"

She sounded strong and likely to be afraid of nothing. Her accent was not Parisian, probably from Normandy, but educated.

"My name is Artur, I'm a correspondent for *Le Figaro* in Paris. I'm here to report on the situation of the French battalions inland from Dunkirk. I was wondering if I might take shelter in your house for a while," he said in his best French.

Artur could just detect some movement inside the house as the woman walked towards the door in what would probably be the hallway. He heard a key being turned in the lock. The door was partially opened, but being held by a chain to the doorframe. The woman's face peered out into the road, her keen eyes searching for the man whose voice had spoken appealingly to her. She had a rifle in her hand. Artur could see that she would use it if she needed to, whether he seemed to be French or not.

"Why aren't you with the French forces and speaking to the officers, if you want information?" the woman said.

"I haven't been in Dunkirk more than a few hours," Artur explained. "I am on my way to the Bergues Canal, but as it's getting late in the day, I was hoping to get some shelter for the night."

Artur knew he was probably chancing his arm, but the woman looked as though she might sympathise with his predicament. Even though she was showing some spirit, she had a kindly, motherly look about her.

"Is there anyone else around?" the woman asked. "I can't see much from here, except straight in front of me. Come nearer to me, so I can take a better look at you, but don't try any funny business or I'll shoot you."

Artur slowly walked closer to the door. He took off his beret and smiled at the woman, but kept his eyes on her rifle. Just as he thought she was going to unlatch the door, there was the terrible whining sound of the Stukas making another attack at the men on the beaches. Artur instinctively threw himself to the ground and a little closer to the door. The woman stood motionless, but cursed the Luftwaffe for ruining her town. Artur heard her unlatch the door.

"You had better come quickly in doors, young man, before they strafe your body with bullets or blow you up with one of their bombs."

Artur looked up and saw the door was now wide open. She beckoned him to enter by waving her rifle. He got up, brushed any dust or dirt from his trousers and walked the few yards to her door. She smiled at him and he could see that she was a very attractive woman, probably in her late fifties.

"Now let me tell you," she said quite firmly, "I am only taking pity on you because I have a son in the French army and he's supposedly near the Bergues Canal, near where you will be heading."

Artur went through the front door into the hall and loosed his kitbag from his shoulder. The woman had a quick look outside before returning to close the door. She locked it and placed her rifle in the umbrella stand that was next to a tall cupboard with a large mirror in its centre. She turned and faced Artur, looked him up and down and gave him another smile.

"My name is Claudette Dupuis. Apart from Artur, by what name are you called, monsieur?"

"I am Artur Selmer, Madame Dupuis. I can show you my papers if you wish to confirm what I'm saying?"

"That won't be necessary, Artur; please follow me into my sitting room."

The room was very well furnished with pictures around the walls and a writing desk behind the door they had just entered, on which there were some family photos.

"Please take a seat over there," said Claudette, as she pointed to the upholstered chair to the side of the fireplace.

"I don't have much drink in the house, monsieur, but I do have some wine from a bottle I opened at lunchtime. Would you like a glass?

"I should enjoy that very much. You may call me Artur, if you wish?"

"And you may call me Claudette," she replied with a smile.

"Please excuse me while I go to the kitchen to fetch the drinks. Have a look around if you wish, Artur."

She walked quickly out of the room and Artur stood up as she left – he thought it was the polite thing to do, especially under the circumstances. He saw a picture of a young man on the desk, he took a closer look. He also saw a picture of a couple: one was definitely Claudette, the other probably her husband. He wandered around the room and quickly realised that the family was quite well off.

Claudette returned with two very elegant wine glasses, a bottle of wine and some olives, all on a silver tray. Just as she placed the tray on a low table, there was the whining sound of the Stuka bombers making another attack, presumably over the beach. As the bombs exploded, the house shook and the glasses on the tray made a tinkling sound as they knocked against each other. Artur stood up, they looked at each other and then out of the window.

"That seemed rather too close for comfort, don't you think, Artur, but no damage done to us, I hope."

She poured out the wine, they touched glasses, toasted each other and hoped for a swift end to the war.

"I expect you saw the photo on the desk of my son, Claud, in army uniform, Artur? He is a *sous-lieutenant*. He and his unit were at the Bergues Canal when I last heard, but communications are very infrequent and not very reliable."

Claudette looked at her clock on the mantelpiece and saw it was after 8:30 p.m.

"My goodness, look at the time. I ought to get you something to eat, Artur. Please come into the kitchen with the tray of drinks, I'll make an omelette. I don't expect you will want to try and find somewhere to sleep tonight, so you had better stay here. You can use the room on the first floor."

"That's extremely kind of you, Claudette, as I've been on the move for most of today and I do need to write some notes up before sending them off to my editor."

They went to the back of the house and into a large kitchen with a wooden table in the centre, surrounded by four chairs.

"Do sit down, Artur, and I'll get down to some cooking."

Claudette fussed around getting all she needed, occasionally stopping to take a sip of wine. There was not much conversation at this time except when she asked Artur if he liked potato as well as cheese in his omelette, to which he said he did.

As soon as Claudette had cooked the two omelettes, she handed Artur his, plus some bread, and she sat down at the opposite end of the table. Artur thought it was one of the best omelettes he'd had in a long time.

"So, Artur, if you're hoping to go to the French Army at the Bergues Canal tomorrow, do you know how to get there, because I do have a local map?"

"That would be very helpful, but I won't really need it till tomorrow. By the way, what's the name of your son's commanding officer, it might help me to locate his whereabouts?"

Claudette mentioned a name and Artur committed it to memory. A short while after the end of the meal, Artur said:

"If it's all the same with you, Claudette, I would be pleased to retire to my room. I have had a hard day today, keeping out of trouble, and tomorrow will probably be worse, if I'm going to be coming from behind the French lines. Also, I need to write up my article before I forget some of the important details."

Claudette agreed and she said she'd find the local map for Artur to plan his route for the following morning. She went out of the kitchen and Artur heard her searching in a drawer of the cupboard in the hall. He got up from the table and cleared away the supper items on to the draining board. Claudette returned after five minutes with the map in her hand and smiled at Artur, who was now at the sink.

"Please don't worry about the washing up, Artur; I'll do it after you have retired to your room. Please follow me; I'll show you to your room."

They went into the hall, where he picked up his kitbag and beret, and followed her upstairs. She led him into a room at the back of the house, placing the map on the bed. The curtains were already drawn and there was a dim light coming from the bedside table lamp.

"I hope you'll be comfortable in here and there's a bathroom on the right-hand side of the landing. My room is on the next floor."

"I'm very grateful to you, Claudette. What time do you want me downstairs in the morning?" Artur asked, as he placed his kitbag and beret on the bed.

"I think we should have our *petit déjeuner* at 7 o'clock, so you can be on your way about an hour later. By the way, you might like to borrow my husband's bicycle, as it will save you time getting to the French battalions at the canal. I will fetch the bike from the shed tomorrow morning."

"That's extremely kind of you, Claudette. It will make a lot of difference, but I shall have to look out for all the holes in the road and the debris lying around; I wouldn't want your husband's bike to get damaged." It was the first time that Claudette had mentioned her husband and Artur wondered where he might be.

"I assume your husband is not fighting in the war, Claudette, so he is presumably elsewhere?" enquired Artur, although he wasn't sure if he should have been so inquisitive.

"We have a house near Bordeaux and he is there. I came up to our house in Dunkirk when my son joined the army, so I could be nearer to him. Anyway, enough of that, I'm sure you want to get some sleep. I wish you a good night, Artur, and I'll see you in the morning. Let's hope we don't get disturbed with any more bombing or heavy gunfire in the night."

"Goodnight, Claudette, and thank you again."

Claudette went out of his room and Artur heard her going downstairs after she had closed his door.

Chapter 8

Tuesday, 28th May 1940

Artur woke early, turned on his bedside light and studied the map that Claudette had given him. It wasn't too far to the Bergues Canal, but he knew it should be easier going by bike rather than on foot. He took some paper and a pencil from his satchel and jotted down a few notes of what had happened during the last two days. He looked at his watch and decided it was time to use the bathroom. On returning to his room, he put on the same clothes and attached his moustache that had been on the bedside table during the night. He drew back one of the curtains just as the German artillery were firing their first burst of gun fire at the poor soles on the beaches. The flashes came first followed not long after by a thunderous noise. *They must be quite near to here,* thought Artur. He closed the curtain again, looked at his watch and saw it was 6:50 a.m. He straightened the bed and put his things back into his kitbag. He looked all around to make sure he had left nothing behind, went out of his room and downstairs to the kitchen.

"Did you sleep well, Artur? You weren't disturbed by the guns going off in the night?"

"No, I heard nothing. I slept like two logs," he said. Claudette smiled at his simile, but Artur realised he shouldn't have translated his version of the English colloquialism directly into French.

"I have a little bread, some jam and a cup of coffee. Will that be sufficient, Artur?" He replied that it would be. They chatted about various things over breakfast. Artur looked at his watch and felt it was time he made himself ready to go. Claudette noticed and she got up from the table.

"I think you feel you should be on way, don't you, Artur? I'll go and get the bicycle for you while you finish getting ready."

Claudette went out of the back door to the shed. She unlocked the shed door and disappeared into it. A few moments later, she reappeared, wheeling the bike towards the side of the house. By now, Artur was up from the table and had walked into the hall. He opened the front door and waited for Claudette to appear.

"Sorry, it's not in very good condition, Artur, but I'm sure you will manage." He saw her feel the tyres and try the brake.

Artur went out of the house and took hold of the bike. The weather was very cloudy, but no rain. Probably no Stuka bombers for a while, so he thought he should be able to make good headway. There was gun fire from the east and faint, distant noises of gunfire from further inland – *probably German tanks*, Artur thought. He had his satchel under his jacket and he slung his kitbag over his shoulder. He put on his beret. He thought he really did look the part! When Claudette was looking down the road towards the sea, he ensured his moustache was attached securely.

"I wish you all the best, Artur. Give my love to Claud if you find him. If you want to come back tonight, please do so. I won't be going anywhere."

"You're very kind, Claudette. I might just do that, but it depends what occurs when I get to the canal."

Artur cycled off up the road ahead of him. The map was in his pocket, but he had remembered enough of the route for the moment. He wondered how far the French and British forces had been pushed back towards Bergues by the German panzer divisions. The sound of gunfire, mortars and exploding shells was almost continuous, as well as numerous bright flashes. There were many Dunkirk residents hurriedly walking away in a broad file from their town with as many of their possessions as they could carry. They headed inland, to what reception they knew not. When they reached the German lines, they would probably be taken prisoner; those in good health would more than likely be taken to work in armament factories in Germany, so he had heard.

After some fifteen minutes, Artur noticed – about a kilometre ahead – large numbers of soldiers marching towards him. He immediately recognised them as being French. He stood to one side to let them pass and waited for a truck that would probably have a senior officer on board. As it came into view, he held on to his bike and waved the truck down. By some good fortune, the driver stopped – probably under the orders of the officer. The officer in the back looked at Artur.

"How can I help you?" said the officer. "I strongly suggest you don't venture too far, unless you want to join the refugees that are fleeing from Dunkirk, or be captured by the advancing German forces."

"As it happens, I'm a reporter for *Le Figaro* and I'm from Paris. I'm here to report on the situation of the BEF and the support being given to the evacuation from the Dunkirk beaches."

"If you don't already know it, there are British and French battalions on the retreat. They will set up a new and final front line to allow the evacuation of the troops from Dunkirk, to protect them from the German panzers."

"You are therefore suggesting, sir, that I should not go any further?"

"It would certainly be my recommendation," replied the officer.

"Perhaps you could tell me if there is a *Sous-Lieutenant* Claud Dupuis in one of the battalions?" asked Artur, and he repeated the name of Claud's commanding officer.

"Of course, I know the commanding officer and I recognise the name Dupuis. He has served with great distinction and courage. I'm sorry I can't stop any longer as we are on a tight schedule and we must catch up with my men. Try asking the officer in charge of the group after next; Dupuis might be with that officer."

They saluted each other and smiled. Artur just managed to thank the officer for his information as the truck moved off. He looked up the road from where the soldiers had come, but as there was a bend in the road some 300 metres away, he saw no other soldiers. He got on his bike and rode carefully – avoiding the holes and debris – to the corner just as the head of the next group of men appeared in the distance. He stood in front of a group of bombed out houses as they passed and stayed a full four minutes before the next group came by him. He waited until the truck with the more senior officers was about to be alongside before waving the driver down, just as he had done before. Once again, the officer in the second truck instructed the driver to stop.

"How can I help you, *monsieur*? I can't stay long, we are on a tight schedule and a very important mission," the officer explained, as he stood up in the back of the truck and faced Artur. He asked the officer the same questions and got similar answers, except he didn't know of Dupuis' whereabouts. Artur felt a bit deflated, so he asked who he should speak to, to find Dupuis.

"I suppose you could wait for the final group of men to come through and ask the army commander who will be in the last truck. There will be six more groups after mine. Sorry, must go now." The officer saluted, sat down and ordered the driver to proceed without further delay.

Artur waited a long time for what he thought must be the last group to arrive. He felt a little less confident about speaking to the commanding officer. Once again, he stood by his bike and waved the truck down. The officer next to the one that looked like the CO, ordered the driver to stop and Artur asked the same questions. The CO jumped to his feet and shouted to Artur that his was the name he had asked about and that he knew Dupuis and his feats of valour. He ordered a junior officer to take Artur's bike inside his truck and the CO beckoned Artur to jump up and sit next to him in the back. This Artur did, not believing his luck. The junior officer then ordered the driver to proceed with all due haste. The truck leapt forward and both the CO and Artur fell into their seats. Artur thought it amusing, but the CO reprimanded the driver for not taking better care.

"So, what do you need to know from us?" the CO asked. "You're not going to report everything I say to you in your newspaper, are you?"

"No, sir, of course not, but I would like to understand the latest situation. How long will your battalions be able to hold out against the Germans? Will France surrender to the Nazi regime, and, if so, when? Will many of the French and British men trying to hold back the German advance get away with the other evacuees?"

"*Mon Dieu,* monsieur! So many questions and some of my answers will definitely be confidential and not be for general consumption. I suggest you drive with us until we reach the place that we are to encamp and make our final stand. I will then give you some time and a few answers. As for *Sous-Lieutenant* Dupuis: I have it on good authority that, I'm sorry to say, he was taken prisoner, together with his platoon. The Germans are due to take him and his men for questioning somewhere in eastern France. I am expecting to be told the name of the place by the end of today. He has exercised his duties with great courage and was due for promotion in the next few days. Why do you ask particularly about him?"

"I stayed at his mother's – Madame Dupuis' – house last night. When I told her that I was going to find the French Army near Bergues, she said her son was most likely there; would I find out how he was. But if I return to her place tonight, I won't be able to tell her that he's been captured by the Germans."

"Quite so," the CO replied.

"By the way, I'm Colonel Michel Joubert – the name of the officer you were asking for – and we are driving behind the majority of my regiment. I say majority because a few hundred were killed in action over the last few weeks. What do I call you, monsieur?"

"Artur Selmer, sir, and I come from Paris."

"But your accent suggests that you come from this area or around Lille?"

"It's a long story, sir, but you are correct."

They chatted easily for the next thirty minutes until the truck stopped. The driver quickly left the truck and opened the colonel's door. The soldier beside the driver got out and opened the door for Artur. The colonel gestured to Artur for him to follow, together with a number of other officers. They walked to a large house that had been requisitioned by the army in case of a possible retreat. They were at the far western end of Dunkirk and there were fields to the west and the north of their position. Men were brought together in groups and ordered to start digging themselves in: a sort of large quarter circle with a radius of approximately 600 metres. The large artillery that had been towed at the back of each group was positioned pointing away from the house and over where the trenches would be. Artur followed the colonel into the house. One of the junior officers brought his bike and leant it against the wall in the hall. Artur by now had lost the colonel, but just at that moment, a junior officer came up and told him to follow him into the colonel's room that would be his headquarters.

"Ah! There you are, Monsieur Selmer. For one moment I thought you had been told to help dig trenches!"

The colonel laughed out loud, but the other officers just smiled politely. They'd heard him in this frame of mind before, but it was mainly to conceal his fear of the inevitable.

"Bring a chair for Selmer, Lieutenant, and get him a glass of red wine."

The lieutenant did as he was ordered. He went over to the glass fronted cabinet, selected six wine glasses, placed them on the smaller table by the window and took a bottle of red wine out of the case that stood on a chair next to the cabinet. He duly poured wine into each glass and they all waited until the colonel raised his glass.

"*Vive la république, vive la France,*" they all said in unison, including Artur, who, by this time was standing. The lieutenant retrieved a second bottle, opened it and placed it on the colonel's desk. After a while, more of the senior officers walked in to the colonel's office and poured themselves some wine.

"Right, gentlemen," said the colonel with a great deal of authority in his tone, "we now need to get down to some serious business. Lieutenant, please lay out the maps on that large table in the centre of the room and everyone gather round. We have to devise a plan that will keep the Nazi war machine from the centre of Dunkirk until at least Friday, 31st May.

By that time, we are led to believe that most of the men on the beaches will have been evacuated. Please remember, about one third of them will be Frenchmen."

They all started to discuss the plans for the next few days and how they could defend their positions. Artur decided not to take notes, but to listen very carefully to the decisions taken and to memorise them. He would write up some notes later.

The colonel had earlier introduced Artur to all the officers in the room and they were well aware that he could listen to the discussions. He would be told of any items that were not to be reported in his newspaper, but Artur knew he would report every single word to Charles in London.

The discussions went on for over two hours, by which time it was after 1:30 p.m. Each of the senior officers had orders. The colonel suggested they should adjourn for a well-earned lunch – albeit a bit on the late side – and asked some of the junior officers to join them. Instructions to the junior offers would be given after lunch. Artur was told to accompany the colonel to the large room on the other side of the hall, where lunch would be available.

The food was laid out on a large table for everyone to help themselves; they then sat at smaller tables that held six or eight men. When Artur saw the spread, he couldn't really believe the French were at war. The lunch lasted for over an hour and Artur moved about to several tables, listening to what they had to say about the plans of the defence of their position: how vulnerable they might be from the German Panzer Corps; would the British Expeditionary Force be able to hold their positions to the east and north of Dunkirk; could they realistically hold out till Friday or perhaps Saturday?

At the end of lunch, everyone stood up as the colonel excused himself. He retired to his office and he asked Artur to join him. Coffee was brought to them once they were seated at the colonel's desk. He asked Artur if he had any comments about the plans that had been agreed. He said, very politely, that as he wasn't an officer – let alone a soldier – he couldn't possibly make any comment, constructive or otherwise. They did discuss what the German hierarchy might have in mind next, whether or not France would surrender, would Hitler invade England and many other items of mutual interest.

"I hope you will excuse me, but I do really believe I should leave you and go back to Madame Dupuis' house and write up my article for my paper. I'm sure you have many things to discuss with your officers about how you will defend your position against the Germans."

The commander nodded in agreement. They both stood up, saluted, shook hands and smiled at each other.

"Thank you, colonel, for allowing me to listen to all your discussions and for an excellent lunch. I wish you and your men well for the next days of your operation. It is a very difficult task ahead of you, but I'm sure you will put in all the effort and skill required to do your very best."

Artur collected his kitbag and beret and went out to the hall for his bike. They shook hands once again and Artur wheeled his bike out of the house and rode away towards Dunkirk. He felt very satisfied with his day's work. However, he couldn't understand how the French officers could be so laid back and casual, bearing in mind the terrible situation they were in.

Chapter 9

Tuesday, 28th May 1940

Artur had a relatively easy journey back to Madame Dupuis' house, even though the gunfire and Stuka bombers pounded the beaches several times. Every time there was another raid, he thought about Clive and the condition of his boat.

Madame Dupuis welcomed Artur's safe return with typical French enthusiasm: throwing her arms around him and showering him with many kisses on his cheeks. She took the bike around to the shed at the back of the house and ran to the front door just as Artur was placing his belongings next to the hall cabinet, at the same time making sure his moustache was still fixed properly.

"I was very worried for you, Artur, as there were a couple of bomb attacks that would have been very close to the port."

"Thank you for your concern, Claudette, but, by chance, I wasn't near the port, but near Bergues."

"Yes, of course. How silly of me. Did you see some of the people you were hoping to see? Did you find out anything about my precious Claud?"

Artur knew she would ask about Claud soon after his arrival, so he had created a story that was close enough to the truth.

"Yes, I heard good reports about Claud. He had distinguished himself with much courage and leadership with his platoon. He is to be recommended for promotion and a decoration very soon. I didn't meet him, but his Commanding Officer spoke very highly of him."

"That is good to hear. So, where is he now? Has he been injured?"

"He's not injured," Artur replied, "but his platoon has been incorporated with another battalion for the time being. I'm sorry to interrupt, Claudette, but if you don't mind, after all today's activities, I would very much like to freshen up. Perhaps after that we could have a glass of wine, particularly after giving you such good news about Claud?"

"That's a good idea; I'll fetch a bottle of red and two glasses while you take your things up to your room and do what you have to do upstairs."

He did as he had suggested and after fifteen minutes they met again in the lounge. Artur was asked to open the bottle of wine, and he poured an ample amount into each glass. They touched glasses and Claudette looked into Artur's eyes.

"I am so pleased that you received good reports of Claud. I will try to get the good news through to his father. I will continue to worry about him, of course, but at least he's doing his bit against the Nazis and to the best of his ability. Changing the subject, I don't want you to go, but when do you have to leave?"

"I have to write up my notes from today's meetings. I will leave for Paris tomorrow at about 7:30 a.m."

"How are you going to get there, Artur? It won't be an easy journey for you,"

"I'll find a way, madame. I won't be going directly back to Paris, but heading for Amiens first."

Artur knew full well that he wasn't going anywhere near Paris or Amiens, but he wasn't going to tell Claudette that.

"I shall be fine, Claudette, please don't worry on my behalf," as he touched her gently on the arm and smiled at her. "I shall probably walk to the commander's new HQ and try to persuade someone to give me a lift."

"I'm just so sorry to see you go, Artur. You have helped me greatly during your short stay. You have found out about Claud, and that has allowed me to relax a lot about his situation."

Artur thought he could sense a touch of fondness for him. He wondered if she wanted it to develop any further before he left the following day. Claudette went and sat on the sofa and patted the seat next to her as she looked at him with her large dark eyes. He obliged and placed his glass on the table next to hers. He turned to her, but just as she was about to run her hand through his hair, he gently took hold of it. She looked a little surprised and rather disappointed.

"I'm so sorry," Artur said, looking deeply into her eyes. "Are you sure it would be wise for us to go further with our relationship? After all, you do have a husband, even if he is down in Bordeaux? Nothing would give me greater pleasure than to take such an attractive lady to her room, but not tonight."

"You are a very attractive man, Artur. Living on my own in a war zone is no easy task. I get very few pleasures, especially when all about me is being bombed. Most of my neighbours and friends from around here have already packed up and moved further inland, in the hope of escaping the Nazi war machine, or they have already perished in the bombing of the town."

"I really do understand what you are saying, but I'm not prepared to go any further with you. You have been so very kind to me: you've leant me your husband's bike, you've fed me and so on. I do strongly suggest that you seriously consider joining the people leaving Dunkirk and finding a way to be with your husband, now that you know more about your son's whereabouts."

Artur was really struggling with his innermost feelings. He knew he could take her to her bed. She didn't know it, but he was in disguise: he had a false moustache and his hair was a bit too greasy with the dark colouring agent he had applied. He was an agent and must remain one. He must not let his emotions get the better of him, however much he wanted her and she him.

He placed her hand back on the sofa, took up his glass and looked into her eyes.

"I'm very sorry, Claudette, but I have had a very stressful day getting information for my newspaper article. I really need to go to my room and write up my notes whilst everything is still fresh in my mind," he said very meekly, but still smiling.

"I suppose you are right, Artur. Of course, you must do your job and I must get something to eat for you to come down to," as she kissed him on the cheek and rose to her feet.

Wow! That was a close shave, Artur thought to himself. *For once in my life, I have exercised some self-control!*

Artur finished his wine and went upstairs to his room. He sat and wrote some notes in his note book and, after a period of time, there was a call from downstairs that supper was ready. He put his notebook in his kitbag, checked that his moustache looked acceptable and wandered down to the kitchen. Claudette was singing quietly to herself as she finished setting the table. She gave him a smile as she ushered Artur to his seat.

"I brought the wine to the table, so please help us to some more. I'm sorry that I don't have an exciting meal for you, but I have only been catering for myself recently. Also, as you might well understand, there's not much good food around at present."

"Please don't concern yourself, Claudette. You have been very generous towards me and given me shelter."

They tucked in to their meal and every now and then Claudette looked at Artur. She was hoping he might change his mind about being with her in the night. She knew, however, in her heart of hearts, that he was right. At the end of the meal, Claudette cleared the table and made them a cup of coffee.

"Black for me, Claudette, and no sugar."

They took their coffees through to the lounge and Artur sat in the single chair that he'd used when he first arrived. Conversation flowed quite freely for well over an hour, at which point Artur said he ought to get a good rest before the following day's exploits. They stood up and Claudette came over to him and embraced him. She whispered some sweet words in his ear and kissed him on his cheeks.

"Thank you for everything, Claudette. I'm sorry to be leaving tomorrow, but I must be out of Dunkirk and away to the commander's HQ. As I said yesterday, I would like to leave by 7:30 a.m., please, if that's alright?"

Claudette, very reluctantly, dropped her arms and wished him a good night's rest. He turned, leaving her standing and watching him go into the hall. She heard him go upstairs and close his bedroom door. There was an emptiness in her heart that she hadn't experienced for a number of years. She stayed standing still for some moments then shook her head and shoulders. She needed to pull herself together, as she too would have difficult times ahead. She walked into the kitchen, washed up the dishes and went up to her room. Just before she entered, she heard Artur moving about in his room, but she refrained from going to him.

Artur was up early the following morning. He had been to the bathroom and was now sorting out his things that had to be in his kitbag in a particular order. He looked in the mirror and attached his moustache very carefully. He wondered how many days more he would have to use it? At what point should he revert to his English image?

As he went down to the hallway, he was aware of Claudette busying herself in the kitchen.

"I can hear you in the hall, Artur. Please come for some coffee, and bread and jam, to help you on your way." Artur detected that she said it with some feeling of regret. He put his kitbag next to the hall cupboard, placed his beret on top of it and followed the smell of coffee into the kitchen.

"Good morning, Artur. I trust you slept well? Please sit there," as she gestured to the chair at the end of the table.

"Good morning, Claudette. Thank you. I heard you wandering around in the night, so I assume you didn't sleep very soundly?"

"I'm sorry if I disturbed you, but I had a bad dream and had to go down stairs. I needed a drink to help me sleep. I had a small brandy," she remarked with a smile.

"I nearly came in to your bedroom, looking to be consoled and comforted."

"You must have had a really bad dream. Do you remember what it was about?"

"I do, but I don't want to talk about it, in case it turns out to be true. Now, finish your coffee while it's still hot and help yourself to bread and jam."

Silence came over them. After twenty minutes, Artur rose from the table and looked at his watch.

"Sadly, Claudette, I must be on my way. Once again, I thank you most sincerely for your kindness and hospitality."

"As you know, I am so pleased you arrived when you did. You have helped to cheer me up and given me good news about Claud."

They walked into the hallway. Artur collected his kitbag and put on his beret. They put their arms around each other and said their farewells. Claudette opened the front door and walked out behind him. Just as they did, there was the noise of shelling along the beaches away from the town. Artur raised his eyes to the Heavens.

"Fortunately, it is quite cloudy so there might not be any Stukas flying for the time being. Take care, Claudette, and do seriously consider getting out of here and going to your husband in Bordeaux."

Artur turned, went out in to the road, but didn't look behind him as he walked away. He heard the door close so he changed direction slightly and went down the road he had come up two days before.

Chapter 10
Thursday, 30th May 1940

Artur walked down the road passing the bombed-out houses, carefully avoiding the potholes and debris that lay in his path. Stray dogs – probably family pets that had been left behind by families that had abandoned their homes – were wandering in amongst the ruins to the side of the road, scavenging, searching for a morsel of anything edible. They took no notice of Artur as he got nearer to the road that ran parallel to the beach.

Artur looked down at the beach. There were thousands of soldiers, mostly in well-ordered lines, snaking their way towards the numerous small boats that were waiting to take them away from a hellhole back to the comparative Heaven of England and safety.

Artur turned his attention to the Mole. He saw a hospital ship moored against its side. It was painted white from stem to stern on both sides and had a large red cross painted midships on the starboard and port sides. Injured men were being brought along the Mole on stretchers by crew members, as well as by the more able-bodied soldiers. The lines of uninjured men on the Mole gave as much room as they could to let the stretcher-bearers pass. There were two gangways linking the ship to the Mole. Doctors and nurses were on deck to receive the injured and escort them below deck to the wards. He wondered if Anne was on this one. He noticed that the ship's name was different, so probably not.

Andrew thought he just might have time to catch the ship, if he hurried. He walked smartly to the beach end of the Mole and muscled his way past the lines of soldiers. Mutterings came from some of them, as they thought he was a Frenchman:

"Come off it 'Froggie', we've been 'ere ages!"

Artur ignored all the barracking, but nodded and smiled as he steadily moved forward. He was aware that the sun had come out and he thought the Stukas would be flying again before too long. He could now clearly see the first gangway and he recognised that some were French soldiers being helped towards it. He shouted in French that he was coming to help and – by some miracle – the lines of British injured parted sufficiently for him to reach an injured Frenchman. One of them turned around and greeted Artur. Seeing that he looked like he was French, he smiled at Artur.

"You've arrived in the nick of time, monsieur, this man is very heavy and very badly injured. I couldn't find a stretcher, so I had to practically carry him all the way from the beach."

Artur and the French soldier lifted the injured man and placed his arms around their necks. They staggered a bit further along the Mole and reached the first gangway where he was carried to the deck of the ship. One of the officers receiving the men was noting their names, regiment and numbers of those that could identify themselves. He looked at Artur and seeing he was not in a soldier's uniform, but looking like a Frenchman, nor was he injured, he said:

"And how do you qualify to be on this ship?" he said in English, with a broad Yorkshire accent.

Artur had worked out what he was going to do and say, as he was making his way along the Mole.

"I came to Dunkirk in a small boat two days ago to take soldiers from the beach to the destroyers waiting further out to sea," Artur said in English. He proceeded to take off his false moustache and beret with a smile.

"Well, I'm buggered!" said the officer. "Can I see your papers please?"

Artur had taken his British papers from his kitbag before he had left his bedroom. He took them out of his jacket pocket and handed them to him.

"So why didn't you go back with your boat?" as the officer thumbed through the documents.

"I'm in the Royal Navy, as you can see, and was tasked to make a report on the defensive situation of the BEF and the French army around Dunkirk," Artur replied with what he thought would be sufficiently near the truth to convince the officer to take him on board.

The officer looked at Artur again and ushered him through, together with the injured Frenchman and his fellow comrade. The two Frenchmen were now looking rather perplexed at the man that had suddenly changed his nationality.

"Welcome aboard, Lieutenant Williams. We are pleased to be taking you back home. Once you have made sure the injured Frenchman and his friend are comfortable down in the ward, you may like to join the captain on the bridge."

Artur couldn't believe his luck. He saluted the officer and thanked him for allowing him on board. Before accompanying the Frenchmen to a lower deck, he put his moustache and beret into his kitbag. He returned his British papers to his inside jacket pocket that he then zipped up. *I'm no longer in agent mode*, he said to himself, *so I don't need to play the role of Artur Selmer for the time being.*

Just as Andrew was about to join the two Frenchmen at the entrance to the passageway to the lower deck, there was the most terrible screaming sound of Stuka bombers making yet another attack. He looked up to the sky to his right and saw half a dozen of them. Three seemed to be aiming for the destroyer that was anchored about two miles out to sea, and the other three were directing their line of attack at the Mole. The hospital ship's air raid siren went off and everybody on deck – as well as many of those on the Mole that could do so – threw themselves to the ground.

"Get yourselves down, immediately," one of the sergeants on the Mole bellowed – just as the ship's siren went off for a second time – to the men around him; he was near to the gangway, and not far from Andrew. The sound of the Stukas got louder and louder. Andrew saw the bombs being released just as they came out of their dive. Two of the bombs exploded in front of the beach end of the Mole, throwing gallons of seawater over it and the men on it. The second bomber dropped its load on the edge of the beach, less than forty feet in front of the Mole. Bodies, equipment and sand flew up in the air, accompanied by the cries of the men that had been wounded. The third bomber's load dropped near the sea-end of the Mole, only metres away from the bow of the hospital ship. Large pieces of rock fragments and splinters flew off the wall of the Mole. A few hit the ship's bow, some sailed over the wall towards the small boats, others over the ship.

Andrew quickly got to his feet and looked around him to see what damage had been done. He saw that the Frenchman had hurled himself on to the passageway floor and had cleverly pulled the injured man on top of him, so as not to hurt him more than necessary. Andrew walked purposefully to the bow and saw there were holes in the forward deck area. When he reached the rails, he leant over and saw there was damage to the woodwork above the water line. He thought it didn't look too serious, but he knew it had to be repaired before they could set out for the Channel and into rough water.

Andrew walked back to the officer that had been making note of new arrivals onto the ship; noticed he had recovered his composure and was continuing with his job.

"That was a close shave," Andrew remarked, "but there is damage to the bow sections above the waterline."

The officer handed his pad to a petty officer and told him to continue registering all those coming on board. They had to be injured men only, he told him.

"Come with me, Lieutenant, we need to report the extent of the damage to the officers on the bridge. They will give orders to the chippie and his mates, who will repair the damage as best they can before we sail."

They turned and went up to the bridge. The captain had been watching what had happened to the destroyer further out to sea.

"You probably didn't have a chance to see the attack on the destroyer," as he turned around to look at the lieutenant and Andrew.

"The destroyer shot down two of the Stukas, before they could release their bombs. The third one's load was way off target and it headed away smartish when the pilot saw what had happened to the other two. Jolly good show that was.

"Have you come to report any damage to our vessel, Lieutenant? It certainly was a close encounter?"

"Yes, sir. But I need to introduce Lieutenant Williams to you."

The captain was told what Andrew had been doing in Dunkirk and how he had helped a wounded Frenchman to his ship.

"I have allowed him to join us on our trip back to Newhaven. I hope this meets with your approval, sir?"

Andrew and the captain saluted and shook hands.

"Of course, Lieutenant. Very right and proper to help a fellow naval officer. You might like to join us on the bridge during our return journey, Lieutenant; another pair of eyes will always be very welcome," said the captain as he smiled at Andrew.

The lieutenant asked Andrew to describe the damage to the bow and the forward deck. The captain listened very intently and issued an order for the chippie and his mates to make best repairs, *post haste*, and report back when the job was completed.

"And be smart about it," said the captain via the intercom. "We need to try and be on our way in an hour at the most, before any more of those Nazi Stukas return."

The captain dismissed them and reminded Andrew he was invited back to the bridge, once the damage had been repaired. On the main deck, Andrew went to the bow and watched as the men did what repairs they could above the waterline. After about an hour, he heard from the lieutenant that there was no more room for any more wounded men: he told Andrew there were more than 450 on board. The gangways were unhitched and dragged on to the deck. The ship's hooter was sounded twice as the mooring ropes were taken off the capstans on the Mole and curled neatly on board; Andrew went up to the bridge. The captain mentioned that he had been sent word that the chippies had done their best some ten minutes earlier.

All men on the bridge were given lookout positions that covered nearly 360 degrees as they left the Mole. Many of the soldiers that were left behind, cheered and raised their helmets – no doubt wishing that there had been space for them. The ship slipped away from the end of the Mole, past one other smaller boat and headed out into the Channel. Andrew looked back and saw how many other ships and boats were roped to the Mole on both sides and the number of men that were being taken on board. Turning his attention to the beach, he saw so many lifeboats and other small craft either heading for the beach or making their way away from land with soldiers being taken to the destroyer about two miles out.to sea. He thought it all looked rather chaotic, but somehow it seemed to be working.

As he was scanning the small boats, Andrew thought about Clive and wondered if *Annabelle* was still intact. He picked up a pair of binoculars and studied the beach beyond the Mole where they had been operating two days before: none resembled Clive's. He searched further out to sea: still nothing familiar.

The officer on the starboard side of the bridge remarked that, in the far distance, towards Nieuwpoort on the Belgium coast, he could still see smoke rising from the British ships that had been torpedoed by German subs the previous day. Seeing a sinking or crippled ship with loss of life, always brought a lump to his throat – *there, but for the grace of God, go I,* he always said to himself.

The captain drew the attention of his officers:

"Keep a keen eye out for mines, gentlemen. Also, some of the small boats will be quite heavily laden with rescued men; they might not be so easy to steer when there's a swell, especially as we get close to the destroyers further out in the Channel. We might have to try and give way to them rather than the other, more usual way."

"Aye, aye, Captain," said the officer at the wheel.

After about an hour, the navigating officer stated that, as their ship was heading for Newhaven and not Dover, very few, if any, small boats should now cross their path as they were headed westward down the Channel. All the officers nodded in agreement. Andrew pointed out, however, that there might be other hospital ships coming from Dieppe or Newhaven that they should also look out for.

"After all, Andrew commented, "if they are going towards France, they will be empty and are likely to be going a bit faster than our smaller ferry."

"Point taken, Williams," replied the captain.

The chief engineer was given leave from the bridge to go to the engine room and check the status of everything below. The ship had twin diesel engines that drove two propellers and they had only been in service about two years. He returned twenty minutes later and stated that all was in order.

From time to time, nearly all the officers on the bridge looked back at the port of Dunkirk. They saw the thick clouds of smoke rising high into the sky; the jostling of the numerous small boats as they navigated their way out to sea against the empty boats going to the beach; the masses of men lining up to be evacuated; the waves of German planes strafing the beach and bombing the ships carrying out the evacuation.

They were all suddenly aware of a squadron of RAF spitfires coming towards them, on their way to Dunkirk. They saw them splitting from their formation and heading for the Luftwaffe's planes. They all had front row seats of the 'dog fights' that occurred astern of their ship. In the distance, they could see the destroyers firing salvos at the enemy aircraft.

"I suppose with relatively clear flying conditions, this activity is what we should expect to see," remarked the captain. "Let's hope we will escape without any incident, unless one of the enemy airplanes wants to take a pot shot at us."

"We've been sailing for over two hours, Captain," said the navigating officer. "By my watch, it's coming up to midday, and by my calculation, we ought to be in Newhaven by about 4 o'clock this afternoon, if we maintain our current speed of 15 knots. Perhaps even a bit earlier, as the tide will be in our favour."

"Bravo," replied the captain. "I think at this stage in our journey, I ought to go and see how everyone is coping below decks. I'm handing over to you, Number 2. Let me know immediately of any concern or any enemy activity near us – especially U-boats."

"Aye, aye, sir," the second officer replied, as he saluted the captain, who by now had left his position on the bridge. The remaining officers still kept their eyes skinned for any enemy planes or U-boats, as they continued to make good progress.

"Out of interest, Number 2," asked Andrew, "do you think it would be a good idea for someone to look at the repairs to the bow area, especially as the Channel is a little rougher now? We don't want too much water entering the lower decks."

"Good point, Lieutenant. Perhaps you would like to relieve yourself of bridge duties and do a recce."

Andrew saluted the second in command and went to find the chippie. They went to the bow of the main deck and looked over the railings.

"I did come and have a look about an hour ago, sir," the chippie remarked, "and all repairs looked to be holding, but the chaps in the engine room said that some holes were leaking. We made some additional repairs to the inside and things have improved to a certain extent. As a result, the chief engineer has instructed us to use two extra bilge pumps."

"That sounds as though you've done as much as you can for the time being. It would be wise if you carried out another inspection at 2:30 p.m. Report back to the bridge if you have any concerns," said Andrew.

"Will do, sir."

Chapter 11
Thursday, 30th May 1940

The rest of their journey to Newhaven was uneventful. Everyone thought they were the lucky ones. The officers on the bridge had been updated over the radio with the situation developing in and around Dunkirk.

To everyone's surprise – including the British government – news had been officially declared that the Belgian king and military had surrendered to the Germans after 18 days of fighting. It therefore meant that the country was now under the control of a German military government.

The hospital ship had been in communication with the Newhaven harbour master and the ship's crew were permitted to bring her alongside the East Quay, next to the Harbour Station. People that were lining the quays, waved Union flags and smiled as the ship was slowly brought into position and moored.

Andrew saluted the officers on the bridge. He thanked the captain for letting him experience the journey from Dunkirk. He wished them all 'God speed' in their future evacuation trips. He collected his kitbag from the back of the bridge and went down on deck. He thought he should stay to help some of the wounded men to the waiting train, but he was more concerned about Clive and his boat. He, therefore, walked over the swing bridge and down the path on the West Quay. He looked at the small number of boats moored near the quay, but he couldn't see Clive's *Annabelle*. He went further down the path to the Hope Inn. His watch showed it was 5 o'clock and he hoped someone would be around.

Andrew found the door to the Saloon bar open, so he went in. There was nobody around, but the door leading from the back of the bar area was open.

"John? Are you there, or is there anybody else around?" he enquired, in quite a loud voice.

A few moments later, a man appeared, but it wasn't John.

"Can I help you, sir? We are not open yet, but we will be, just as soon as those helping to take the injured soldiers to the train have finished."

"I understand," Andrew replied.

"I wondered if you know anything about a chap called Clive? I went with him on his boat to Dunkirk very early Monday morning. My name's Andrew Williams by the way."

"Mine's Bert," as he leaned forward and shook Andrew's hand.

"Clive has not been seen in Newhaven since the time he left. Reports came in yesterday that his boat was badly damaged and sank a couple of days ago, but no news of Clive, unfortunately."

"Oh, my goodness," Andrew exclaimed. "So, if he's alive, he might still be in Dunkirk?"

"As I said, nobody knows anything of Clive's whereabouts."

"Thanks, anyway, Bert. I'll see if I can catch the train back to London. I'll phone the Hope Inn tomorrow, to see if there's any further news."

Andrew walked smartly out of the pub towards the Harbour Station. He had noticed as he started to jog up the West Quay that the train was still in the station, so he thought he could be in luck. One of the doctors from the hospital ship saw Andrew as he walked along the platform.

"I suppose you want to catch this train, do you, Lieutenant? It will be leaving in four minutes," the doctor said, as he looked at his watch. Tell the ticket inspector that you have just returned from Dunkirk. He shouldn't ask you for any money, but you might have to change trains in Redhill. Have a good journey back to London, sir." They shook hands and saluted each other, as Andrew alighted the train.

The train left at 5:50 p.m. Andrew couldn't stop thinking about Clive. *He surely should be still alive,* he said to himself, *but perhaps he was on board when his boat sank.* To take his mind off Clive, and to pass the time, he decided to chat to some of the injured lads on the train. Most of the carriages had been converted into wards. The front half of about four of the carriages had become operating theatres, so he didn't venture into those, but walked further along the corridors to the other wards. He chatted and joked with many of them and they all seemed very chipper, even if they had lost a limb or were injured from shrapnel.

Before Andrew knew it, he could just about make out – over the crackly speaker system – that they were entering Redhill station. He picked up his kitbag, wished the men good luck and stood by the carriage door as the train came to a halt. Once on the platform, he walked to the station master's office and knocked on the door.

"Can you tell me if the train on this platform is going to Victoria station?"

"No, it isn't. But you could stay on it and change at Clapham Junction."

"That sounds like a good idea. Roughly how long will it be before this train leaves?"

"It very much depends on how many wounded men have to be taken off the train for other destinations. I'd say it could leave in thirty minutes."

"Thank you," replied Andrew. "Please could you tell me if there's a station buffet on one of the platforms?"

"You should find some refreshments on platform three," the station master said. Andrew thanked him and walked out of the office.

Andrew found the buffet and looked at the small number of items on the trays.

"One tea, please, and no sugar."

He didn't fancy the curled-up sandwiches or any of the biscuits – he just paid for the tea. Sadly, it was only just warm and rather strong, so he swallowed it down quickly. He thought he ought to buy a ticket to Victoria, so he went to the booking office inside the entrance to the station. He paid for a second-class fare and returned to the platform where the train was just about to leave. He changed at Clapham and arrived back at his Service's flat shortly after 8:30 p.m. No one else was in. He went to his room and settled down to complete his report.

The next morning, he phoned Charles and they arranged to meet at his office at 10:30 a.m. Charles was pleased to hear Andrew's voice and that he had returned safe and sound. Neither of them mentioned Clive, but Andrew knew he would be asking about him at the meeting.

Andrew arrived at Charles' office building in St James on time. He greeted the grumpy receptionist, signed in and knocked on Charles' door on the second floor.

"Very good to see you, old boy," said Charles very cheerfully, as Andrew closed the door behind him.

"You don't look to have suffered much since I last saw you, but no doubt you've got a few stories to tell," remarked Charles with a chuckle.

"Yes, I have, but I'm more concerned about Clive. Someone at the Hope Inn told me his boat sank at Dunkirk. Can you please tell me what has happened to him?"

"It's not good news, Andrew. His boat was hit by one of the Stuka's bombs and was blown up. He was on his way back to the beach after he had ferried some soldiers to the destroyer. There was nothing he or anyone could do. He was killed instantly and wouldn't have known much about the incident. This happened on Wednesday afternoon at about 3:30 p.m. A few small craft near to his were also hit, but there was no more loss of life, just a few serious casualties."

"That's terrible news, Charles; what rotten luck for the man. You have presumably been in touch with his next of kin?"

"Yes, I have. He was a single man with two brothers and a sister. I sent someone around from the Service to speak to his parents, who live in Wimbledon. They were devastated, as you can imagine."

There was a brief period of silence as they both contemplated the event. Charles then asked Andrew to take a seat and poured him a cup of tea.

"You should be aware, Andrew, that you and Clive made a significant contribution to the Dunkirk evacuation on the day you were with him.

Operation Dynamo is going far better than expected. Yesterday, I have been reliably informed, more than 53,000 men got away from the beaches and the Mole. With the weather forecast for this afternoon being low cloud, the Luftwaffe are unlikely to fly, so everyone is expecting over 60,000 to be evacuated today."

"That sounds amazing, Charles. The Gods certainly seem to be on our side for the moment. Here, Charles, I've prepared a report for you, and I would like to talk through my mission."

Andrew passed his report to Charles and apologised for it being in a rather rough and ready state. He said he would get it typed up properly by someone in the Service's typing pool later on. Charles was all ears as Andrew went through the details of his time with Clive and what happened to him in Dunkirk. How he met up with the French commanding officer during his regiment's retreat, and his good fortune at getting back on the hospital ship.

"Well, that's quite a story, Andrew. You did, however, go against my orders by taking your French papers etc. as well as your British ones."

"In my defence, Charles, it was just as well I did. I wouldn't have found it nearly as easy to acquaint myself with the French commander, nor with Madame Dupuis, who gave me accommodation for two nights."

"I agree, Andrew. For those reasons alone, no mention will be made of my recommendation to only have British papers in my report. But I do emphasise the importance of following orders. It's similar to the way you behaved at Ringway Airport when you had that flight in the Swordfish and you changed a stall turn into a spin without getting permission from the senior pilot. I do readily admit that some of your strengths are your initiative and your decision-making ability at times of duress. Just take care in the future."

Andrew nodded, but not really in agreement with Charles' reprimand – more a question of 'hearing what he had said' type of gesture. He also knew that Charles was obliged – as his senior – to put him in his place every now and again.

"Enough said for the time being, Andrew. As you may recall, when war was declared last September, the Belgians were invited to join the BEF, but King Leopold and his government refused. They preferred to maintain their neutrality. They – rather pompously and somewhat foolishly – felt they had prepared themselves well enough to repel an invasion by the Germans. You might remember that the German forces invaded Belgium on 10th May and, after eighteen days of fighting, the Belgian military surrendered on Tuesday. The Belgian forces were totally overwhelmed by the Nazi paratroopers and ground forces. King Leopold surrendered without his government and ministers even being consulted."

"Good Heavens! What was the British and French governments' response to that? Where does that leave Belgium in this war?"

"The governments haven't said too much yet, but our newspapers have had a field day, calling Leopold's pronouncement a treasonable act. After all, they said, he was only a constitutional monarch. He had handed over Belgium to the Germans and now the German military will run the country. The majority of the Belgian ministers have taken exile in France, but if France falls, some will no doubt have to move to London, where they will join the Dutch and Luxemburg ministers and their Royal Families. And how long can the Norwegian and allied forces in Norway hold out against the Germans, I might ask? The Nazis, of course, are hell-bent on obtaining free access to the iron ore deposits coming out of Narvik for their armament production."

"It very much sounds as though London will get very crowded, what with all these foreign dignitaries living here!" Andrew joked.

"On these cheery notes, why don't I take you for some lunch? We'll go to the Oxford and Cambridge Club. How does that suit you? We can talk further about these and other situations over a pint or two, so long as we can find a quiet area."

"A damn fine idea, Charles; thank you."

"We can't expect it to be as good a meal as it used to be, what with a war going on, but it will be good surroundings and we'll enjoy the drink."

As it wasn't raining and it was warm, they decided to walk to the O&C Club in Pall Mall. They were greeted on arrival and they went straight to the bar, once they had reserved a table in the dining room. They took their drinks to a table in the corner away from other occupied tables. Andrew detected Charles had a rather serious demeanour about him and wondered what was on his mind.

"I am fully aware that you have only just returned from France," said Charles, as they raised their tankards to each other, "but a lot has been going on in Norway over the last few weeks – let alone months. On the 1st May, King Haakon and his government left Oslo for Tromsø. So, in effect, the capital of Norway is now Tromsø, which, as you might already know, is about 100 miles north of Narvik. Southern and central Norway was lost to the Germans at the end of April, so the Allied forces focussed their attention on northern Norway and the area around Narvik in particular. The Allies recaptured Narvik on 28th May, but this was more of a smoke screen for their retreat from Norway: the commanders having already received orders to leave Norway a few days earlier."

"My goodness," exclaimed Andrew, "apart from France and Britain, Germany is in control of the whole of western Europe, except for those countries that have declared themselves neutral."

"Exactly so, Andrew, but, at present, the Norwegian cabinet and King Haakon are still in Norway. The British government – together with a British diplomat in Norway – have been trying to persuade the Norwegians to go into exile. In view of this, and as you have now returned from France, the Service want you to travel to Tromsø and assist in the discussions."

"But I don't speak Norwegian, Charles, so how can I possibly help? I'm not always the most diplomatic of people, either."

"I am well aware of all that, but I do know that Norwegians and Danes can understand each other, even when they are speaking their own language. C has said – and he's supported by the Foreign Secretary – that it's very important for the Service to give guidance and assistance. We and the British government believe this to be the right decision.

"We have arranged for you to be flown from Croydon to Wick on Sunday morning. You will be taken by car to Croydon, so you must be ready to leave your flat at 8 o'clock. You must wear the uniform of a naval lieutenant. You will use your agent name of Artur Selmer and your new passport – plus your uniform – will be ready for you to collect from my office after we've had lunch. Pack whatever other clothes you need in your kitbag. When you arrive at Wick airport, you will be met by Lieutenant Saunders, who will accompany you on the next leg of your journey: Wick to Lerwick in the Shetlands. There will be three MTBs: you will be on one and the other two will each have a lieutenant that will look similar to you. Now that Denmark and the Netherlands are controlled by the Germans, there are frequent Luftwaffe attacks on Wick and the areas around the Scapa Flow in the Orkneys. It could be a dangerous trip, but we wish to ensure that at least one of the MTBs gets to Lerwick – hence three on this part of the journey. Assuming you get through this ordeal, you – and not either of the other lieutenants – will board a County-class heavy cruiser and head with her escort to Tromsø. A meeting will have been set up by a British diplomat from Oslo for you and an RNVR captain – who speaks fluent Norwegian, by the way – to persuade the Norwegian cabinet and King Haakon on the good sense of accepting the British government's offer of exile in London."

"Phew! That's quite an assignment! But what would you have done if I hadn't returned from Dunkirk yesterday?"

"Spies have spies, Andrew! We knew you would be back before the weekend. Anyway, it is certainly a very important mission. It has the full backing of the PM and the Foreign Office. Its importance is not just helping the Norwegians to leave their country, but in return for our hospitality and safe keeping, we hope to receive from their cabinet, authority to use their very large merchant fleet in the Atlantic convoys. Anyway, as it's getting on a bit, why don't we continue over lunch."

They finished their drinks and ordered a second one. Andrew was still in a bit of a trance after what Charles, the SIS and the government, wanted him to undertake. He wasn't sure he felt very hungry either, but he knew he wasn't to show any apprehension about the mission, so he started to smile.

"What has made you smile, Andrew? Or are you just trying to put on a brave face?"

"You are obviously very good at reading people, Charles. I am trying to put on a brave face, but it's just the sort of assignment that the SIS chose me for. I know I'm up for it, but the situation – particularly from Wick to Tromsø and back to England – is totally outside my control. If the Nazis get wind of what we are planning, they will throw a lot of their strength at trying to prevent us from being successful."

Charles made no response, but continued to look at the menu. He knew what Andrew was saying was absolutely correct. The mission might fail for the reasons Andrew had mentioned. It was, however, imperative that the plans were not compromised in any way; only a very few knew of the plans' details: the ship's captain and his Number 2. All other personnel will think they were on a normal wartime mission, but they all knew they were at war.

They had their lunch and talked only a little about Andrew's new assignment, but a bit more about the Dunkirk evacuation and how successful it was turning out to be, even though Clive had been lost. After their meal, they took a taxi back to Charles' office. Andrew collected the envelope containing his new passport and some Norwegian currency, plus his new naval uniform, all of which he signed for. Charles shook his hand and wished him a safe trip. He looked forward to seeing him back in London in the fullness of time – with the Norwegian cabinet and the king. Charles had asked the taxi driver to wait and gave him instructions to take Andrew back to his Service flat.

Chapter 12
Sunday, 2nd June 1940

Andrew rose early, even though he had sorted out what he needed to take in his kitbag the day before. He had a light breakfast and was ready just before 8 o'clock.

The doorbell rang. Andrew jumped a little, put on his cap and picked up his kitbag. As he opened the door, he and the driver saluted each other as he went out to the waiting car. The driver was one of the men that took C around London – and various other places – and was very trustworthy. The secrecy of the operation had already begun. Contrary to Andrew's normal wishes, he was asked to sit in the back, placing his kitbag on the floor between his legs. He looked very smart in his new naval uniform and he felt at ease with himself. The traffic was quite light, even for a Sunday. As the car entered the front of Croydon airport, the driver was directed through a side gate to a waiting aircraft. Andrew was told by the guard that he would be flying in a de Havilland Dragon Rapide that was operated by the Royal Navy.

The driver came around and opened the door for Andrew to step out onto the tarmac. He put on his cap and glanced up at the twin-engine biplane. He shook hands with the pilot and they saluted. He thought he might have been the only passenger as he stepped onto the wooden box next to the port wing, onto the wing and into the cabin, but he was joined by two other passengers: a naval officer of similar rank to himself and a woman in civilian clothes. As they all took their seats and fastened their seat belts, they acknowledged each other's presence by nodding and smiling. The plane didn't usually have a hostess, but there was a woman in naval uniform who welcomed them on board, explained that they would be landing in Glasgow to refuel before heading for Wick. She wished them a comfortable flight and sat on the front left passenger seat.

The captain started the engines, received instructions from the control tower, taxied to the end of the runway and – without any further delay – took off smoothly. They turned onto a northerly heading. Once the plane had achieved its cruising altitude, the hostess brought around a biscuit and a half-filled glass of water to each of them. She suggested they should stay seated with their seat belts fastened, as they were expecting some turbulence about an hour into the flight.

The aircraft had four rows of two seats and Andrew sat behind the other two passengers, who were in the second row. He wondered who they were and what roles they would be playing over the next few days – if any. Maybe they wouldn't be going all the way to Wick?

When they reached the area of turbulence, it was much less uncomfortable than Andrew had expected. He cast his mind back to the time when he flew his Tiger Moth out of Croydon in 1935. He was heading for Bristol when he entered thick cloud and became very disoriented. His brain had told him to turn to the left, but his instruments wanted him to turn right. He knew he had to believe his instruments, but it was a very bumpy and scary few minutes.

Andrew was brought back to the present by the attractive naval hostess informing them that they were only fifteen minutes away from Glasgow – it wasn't yet midday. The captain landed the plane perfectly and he taxied to a parking place in front of the terminal building. The hostess told them that they would be at the airport for twenty minutes and that they should go into the terminal's lounge during the refuelling, where there would be some refreshments. Andrew picked up his cap and kitbag; he was first out of the plane and into the lounge.

As Andrew was helping himself to a large black coffee and a biscuit, he was aware of someone quite close behind him. He turned around and his eyes fixed on the dark brown eyes of a very attractive young woman, probably in her late twenties.

"Hello," she said with a lovely gentle voice.

"My name's Helena. It appears that only you and I will be travelling on to Wick, as the other naval officer has been taken to a waiting staff car."

"It will be a great pleasure to accompany you on the next leg of our journey, Helena," he said with a smile and in his usual charming manner. He detected an accent that he thought he recognised.

"My name is Artur. May I ask if you will be stopping in Wick or will you be going on elsewhere?"

Helena leant over the table, poured herself a coffee and added some sugar and milk. She turned to face Artur as she stirred her coffee and looked at him with her smiling eyes.

"I won't be stopping in Wick. How about you, Artur?"

"I will be getting a boat out of Wick," he said, in a similar, uncommunicative manner.

They moved away from the table towards the window and watched the plane being refuelled, as they sipped their coffee. No more words were exchanged. Artur finished his coffee and asked Helena if he could take her cup and saucer back to the table for her, but she declined his offer, as she hadn't quite finished. Just as Artur was at the table, an airport staff member entered the lounge and told them that they were to be ready to board in seven minutes. If they needed to avail themselves of the facilities, then they should do that now.

Artur waited for Helena to come out of the ladies before leaving the terminal lounge.

"Oh, that's kind of you to have waited for me, Artur, but I probably would have found my way to the plane on my own," she said, with a broad grin.

They walked out to the plane and Artur went up onto the wing first. He waited at the entrance to the cabin and offered to take Helena's hand and assist her into the cabin, but she declined very graciously with a smile.

Andrew waited for Helena to take her seat as he wanted to sit on the seat in the same row. He put his cap on the seat in front together with his kitbag. Before too long, the plane had taxied to the end of the runway and was in the air. They were now going in the direction of Wick. The hostess came to them with a soft drink and explained that the flight to Wick would only be about an hour and a half.

Artur could see through the window and saw that the weather was changing – it was becoming very much more cloudy. It was noticeable that the pilot had climbed to a higher flight level in order to fly above the clouds and the turbulent air, but without success. He contacted air traffic control and was granted permission to fly at a lower altitude and below the clouds for the next forty minutes. He spoke over the speaker system apologising for the uncomfortable flight and announced that they would be landing at Wick in twelve minutes.

Artur looked at Helena, but she seemed to ignore him and continued reading her book, quite unperturbed at everything. She looked up as the plane landed and then glanced at Artur, who mentioned that they had arrived at their destination.

"Where do you go from here, Artur?" Helena asked, but she was looking out of the window as she said it.

"As it happens, I'm taking a boat to Lerwick, as I mentioned earlier."

"That's very interesting, Artur, so am I!"

Artur looked incredulously at Helena and wondered what on earth she would be doing, going to the same place via the same method as he was. Charles had not made any mention of someone else going to Lerwick. He then realised that her slight accent meant something to him.

"I don't suppose, by any chance, you're Norwegian, are you?"

"That's very clever of you, Artur. As you've spotted my accent, I can tell you that I work at the Norwegian Embassy in London; I'm a First Secretary handling Commerce."

"My goodness, I had no idea you would be that senior; that's most impressive. Does that mean I must always stand up when I want to speak to you?" Artur gibed as he saluted her.

"Now you are mocking me, Artur, and that's not entirely fair."

At that moment, the plane came to halt outside the terminal. The naval hostess opened the door and Artur allowed Helena to leave the aircraft first. He followed her into the arrival hall, carrying his kitbag. A senior naval man came up to them and welcomed them to Wick.

"Madame Olsen and Lieutenant Selmer, I am Lieutenant Saunders. There has been a slight change in plan: the sea is very rough at present and as Lerwick is some 130 miles from here, the powers-that-be have decided in their wisdom that you should fly to Lerwick and not go by sea. Permission has been granted by the RAF for your plane to land at Lerwick's Sumburgh Airport that is located at the very southern end of the main island. As there is a danger of the Luftwaffe attacking your plane, the RAF will provide an escort to Sumburgh, once your plane has taken off from Wick. You may not be aware that the RAF has been given total use of Sumburgh. It is a base for the Coastal Command squadrons operating in the North Sea between Britain and Norway. I hope you will find this arrangement, which has been made only a few hours ago, to your satisfaction?"

"How could we refuse such a generous offer, Lieutenant; thank you, sir," said Artur as he saluted the naval officer.

"Your flight is due to leave Wick in fifteen minutes," the officer informed them, "so make yourselves comfortable and take refreshments while you wait. Madame Olsen, your case will remain in the hold. Unfortunately, the weather forecast is for strong winds and heavy cloud over the Shetlands, so be prepared for a bumpy ride. One consolation is that the conditions will reduce the chance of any enemy aircraft being around, but nobody is taking any chances, so you will still be escorted out of Wick by three RAF fighter planes. Once you arrive in Sumburgh, you will be taken by MTB out to one of His Majesty's ships that will be anchored to the west of the islands, about two miles out from the land."

"It seems as though we are being treated like royalty," said Artur with a grin, as he looked at Helena. She moved towards Artur and gently took hold of his hand, as she looked up into his eyes appealingly. He thought this change of attitude towards him was rather sudden, but unsurprisingly enjoyable.

"Can I count on you to look after me on the next stage of our journey, Artur? I'm not very good in rough flying conditions, and the trip on the boat might even be worse, if the sea is rough."

"Of course," he said, as he put his other hand on top of hers. "Somehow, I thought Norwegians were good sailors, but maybe this is a very different situation. I therefore understand your concerns."

Helena took away her hand, moved towards the table and poured out two coffees.

"Do you always take your coffee black, Artur?"

"Not always. I sometimes add cream, or a brandy, if there is any." Artur thanked her for pouring out his coffee. He brought a couple of chairs to the table and they sat facing each other, contemplating what might be in store for them over the next few hours.

The naval officer returned to the departure lounge and came over to them.

"Your flight is ready to leave now, so please follow me to the plane," said the lieutenant.

Artur stood up, put his kitbag over his shoulder and followed Helena out of the building. As they walked towards the plane, the wind suddenly gusted and blew Helena's hair over her face. She struggled to see and for a brief moment, she stumbled on a raised piece of tarmac. Artur noticed the difficulty she was in and immediately stepped forward to take her arm to keep her upright. She brushed her auburn hair back from her face and thanked him with a smile for coming to her aid.

"I thought for one moment, you were about to fall arse over apex, but I managed to steady you just in time," remarked Artur, as she leant against him with a great deal of relief. Artur put his arm around her, led her to the plane and followed her into the cabin, putting his hands on her hips to steady her as she went inside.

The naval hostess took Helena's hands and assisted her to her seat. Artur followed and when he was seated, asked her if she was alright, as she took out a brush from her handbag and started to repair the damage to her hair.

"Thank you for your kind attention, Artur. I thought for a moment that I was going to fall, but you were there to catch me."

No more was said as they followed the hostess' instructions to fasten their seat belts. Artur could see the pilot and could hear him speaking to the traffic controller in the tower, just as another gust of wind made the plane rock backwards and forwards, rather unnervingly. He glanced over to Helena, but she seemed to have regained her composure; he noticed that her hair was much tidier too.

The pilot taxied to the end of the runway, and as it turned, Artur saw that the wind sock was horizontal, indicating a strong crosswind from the starboard side. The engines came up to full revs and, as they started down the runway, the pilot fought with the controls to keep the plane travelling down the centre line. At the right speed, the plane lifted off the runway easily, the pilot dipped the right wing slightly and kept the plane going straight by applying some rudder. Before too long, they were away from the airport and were turning into the wind, following a northerly heading for the Shetlands.

Artur looked out of the porthole and noticed an RAF fighter plane some 300 yards from their starboard wing. He assumed there was another one on the port side and probably one would be above them in due course. These were their escorts, of course, and would be with them until they landed at Sumburgh.

Their flight was not enjoyable. The strong wind blew the plane about a lot, and – on several occasions – the plane dropped several hundred feet without warning, but the skill of the pilot brought the aircraft back to its original altitude. The headwind blew fiercely, so their time to the east of the Orkneys took rather longer than Artur had expected. Once past them, they all looked forward to hearing the pilot contacting the tower at Sumburgh, requesting permission to join downwind and eventually onto finals in preparation for landing.

"Not long now, Helena," as Artur looked at her and saw that her hands were holding firmly to the seat's armrests, but she made no response.

Artur never liked looking out of the porthole as he was coming in to land, but he couldn't help himself doing so this time. The pilot was obviously fighting with the plane's controls in the strong crosswind, because the attitude of the aircraft was almost sideways on to the direction of travel. The starboard wings were slightly down from the horizontal, to prevent the plane from being thrown upwards by the crosswind. He knew the pilot would only change the plane's attitude just before the undercarriage was about to touch the ground. Any sudden gust of wind could force the plane to the ground before the pilot was ready, thereby landing sideways with the possibility of the lower starboard wing hitting the ground. This was exactly what happened.

The hostess immediately told them to take the brace position, as there was a danger of a forced landing.

Artur braced himself and saw that Helena had bent herself almost double, with her head well below her knees. The noise from outside made Artur look out of the window again. He was in time to see the struts separating the two starboard wings snap; with the lower wing being bent backwards after its contact with the runway and the inertia of the plane's forward movement.

Somehow, the pilot managed to straighten the aircraft as he attempted to bring the plane to a standstill. There was then a terrific scraping sound as the undercarriage under the stricken wing collapsed. The propeller blades were bent backwards and two flew off. The plane was not now being controlled by the pilot and flames started to come from the starboard engine. By some miracle, the plane came to a stop on the long grass, some yards to the side of the runway. A fire engine appeared from its camouflaged building. As it reached the plane, the men began to direct their hoses at the flaming engine.

At this moment, the pilot came into the cabin and opened the door. He apologised for a noisy landing and told them all to get off the plane as quickly as possible. Helena still had her head between her knees as Artur took her arms and lifted her to her feet. Even though he had his kitbag over his shoulder, he virtually carried her to the door. The pilot took hold of her hands, guided her out onto the wing where one of the firemen helped her jump down on to the grass. She looked very shaken and another gust of wind rearranged her hair once again. Her skirt billowed up above her waist, revealing her slender long legs and her pink underwear. She quickly rearranged her dress, looked at Artur and tried to give him a smile.

Artur had now joined the others on the grass just as a vehicle arrived from the airport building. The driver ordered them to get into the vehicle and get far away from the plane in case it caught fire, or the fuel tanks exploded.

"But my suitcase is in the hold," Helena shouted. "Please could someone fetch it before I leave in the car."

The hostess ran to the side of the plane before anyone could stop her. She produced the special key to unlock the door. She had to stretch up and lean into the hold, as everything in there had moved around during the plane's awkward landing. She threw the suitcase out towards the vehicle. Just at that moment, the wind suddenly gusted more strongly than ever and the flames of the starboard engine somehow blew over the port engine. There was a huge explosion as the tanks ignited. Everyone was thrown to the ground. The door of the hold immediately swung closed, hitting the head of the hostess very hard. She fell to the ground in a heap and looked, for all intents and purposes, as though she were dead.

An ambulance had followed the vehicle across the grass so, as Artur got to his feet, he saw a nurse and a man – presumably a doctor – jump out of the ambulance and rush towards the woman.

"There's nothing we can do to assist them, so please get inside the vehicle," the driver said to Artur and Helena, as he picked up Helena's case and helped her get to her feet.

"We must get you two away from this scene and into the airport lounge before anything else happens."

"But surely we can't just leave this situation without doing something to help?" Artur exclaimed, as he looked at the poor woman on the ground.

"Please," said the driver, as he ushered them into the car, "all the airport's services are there to deal with this type of situation." They climbed into the car. He set off at speed for the airport's terminal, at the same time reminding them that they had a boat to catch.

Chapter 13

Sunday, 2nd June 1940

After they had been in the airport lounge for twenty minutes and freshened themselves up, Artur noticed that the ambulance was no longer near the smouldering plane. The firemen had put the fires out, but were standing by, just in case something else caught fire. He was about to go outside, when the driver of the car walked towards the lounge and came inside.

"Please be ready to leave here in five minutes. We will be driving to a small harbour where the MTB will be waiting for you."

"Could you tell us how the lady is; we are very concerned? It looked quite serious," said Artur, trying not to suggest the worst.

"We are reliably informed, Lieutenant, that she is in a very serious condition. We are, however, confident that, with all the skilled surgeons and nursing staff we have here for the RAF squadrons, she will get all the proper attention that she will need. That's the only thing I can say at present. As you may probably have noticed, the ambulance left about ten minutes ago and she will no doubt already be in theatre. Can you please use the facilities as we need to leave for the boat? There is a tight time schedule to this leg of your journey."

Artur looked back at Helena and beckoned her to come with him.

"Are you feeling alright after that landing experience and the fire that followed, Helena?"

"I've felt better, Artur. I can't wait to be on your country's battle cruiser and heading for Tromsø. It has been a very long day; it's already nearly 6 o'clock."

Artur took Helena's arm and carried her case out to the waiting car. The driver took Helena's suitcase and placed it on the passenger seat, having first helped his two passengers into the back seats.

"It's only a short journey to the south of the airport," said the driver. "Contact has been made with the captain of the MTB and he's awaiting your arrival just off the beach. There will be a rowing boat on the beach and a naval man will row you to the MTB. We should be there in less than ten minutes."

Neither of his passengers said anything; they just wanted to be safely on the ship that was a couple of miles out to sea.

The driver pulled off the road to the left, heading towards the beach. He pulled up, got out of the vehicle to help them onto the unmade road. He carried Helena's case and Artur took her arm to steady her as they went towards the waiting boat. The oarsman saluted them, put Helena's case in the bow of the rowing boat and helped her onto a seat at the rear. Artur went next, having thanked the vehicle driver for getting them to the boat and they saluted each other. The driver pushed the boat away from the beach and the oarsman set off for the MTB that was just over 200 yards further out to sea.

The sea was only a bit choppy, because of where they were in the sheltered inlet. Helena didn't feel too uncomfortable at the start – especially after what she had been through on the plane's last leg into Sumburgh – but she knew it could get worse going from the MTB to the ship.

The oarsman rowed for all he was worth. The bow rose and fell as it reached each wave. Artur tried to take Helena's hand and comfort her, but she insisted on holding on to the board she was sitting on with both hands. The MTB helmsman saw them coming towards him. He very slowly reversed towards the rowing boat, looking out all the time for any submerged rocks. After a few more minutes, the rowing boat was alongside the MTB and was being held fast by two burly sailors. Another sailor told Helena and Artur to make their way to the side. Helena was literally hauled into the MTB as though she weighed nothing, whereas

Artur was expected to fend for himself, once he'd handed over Helena's case and his kitbag. They thanked the oarsman for getting them to the MTB safely, as he turned and headed back to the shore.

The MTB seemed to make light work of the early waves, but it was thrown about quite viciously as it got further out to sea. As they got closer to the ship, Artur could see that the men on the deck had hung a ladder from the railing on the starboard side that almost reached down to the sea. The ladder seemed to stick out from the ship's side and Artur noticed it had a rigid bar near the top and the bottom on each side that kept it away from the ship, thus making it easier to ascend.

"We are preparing to go alongside in a few minutes," said the MTB helmsman. "You can see the ladder and you will have to climb it to get on board. Just take great care and don't look down as you climb up it."

Helena stood up and even with the movement of the MTB, she managed to finish tucking her dress inside her underwear. She looked at Artur and winked with a broad smile.

"I don't want everybody to see my jewels," she said in a loud voice that everyone heard.

"I would like Artur to go first so I can see how it's done. He will then be on deck to help me with the last few steps."

They all agreed. Artur slung his kitbag over his head and shoulder, grasped the ladder and climbed up very confidently. Everyone was watching, both in the MTB and from over the ship's railings. He reached the top where he was helped over the rails and onto the deck. It was now Helena's turn. She asked one of the sailors to bring her case up, once she was on board. All on the MTB thought she was a plucky, fearless young lady and that she should have no problems. Just over halfway, however, she lost her footing as one of her feet slipped down to the next rung. Everyone held their breath. She hung on tightly and regained her composure, with Artur shouting instructions from the ship's railing. She looked up at Artur and smiled as she started to ascend the ladder again. She was only some fifteen feet from the railing and the sailors' outstretched hands, when a strong gust of wind took her skirt up above her waist. She let out peals of laughter and with one hand free from the ladder, brought her dress down below her knees. She clambered up the last few steps into the arms of the waiting sailors, giggling all the way. They all cheered as she was gently put down on the deck.

The ship's captain had been standing by and he congratulated Helena on arriving on board, albeit by a rather unusual and difficult route. Her suitcase duly arrived and one of the junior officers was instructed to take Miss Olsen and Lieutenant Selmer to their quarters without further delay, as they needed to be on their way, as soon as the anchors had been raised. He told them that his ship would join the rest of the fleet off the eastern side of the Faroes and proceed towards Tromsø. All being well, they could expect to be north west of the islands off the coast of Narvik in three days and arrive in Tromsø early on 6th June.

"Just before you go to your cabins," the captain said, "I am inviting you to join me and some of my officers for an informal supper. One of my officers will escort you to my quarters in half an hour."

Helena and Artur's cabins were next to each other. They thanked the officer for escorting them and disappeared into their respective cabins to quickly prepare themselves for supper. Artur was aware that the ship was on her way: he could feel it gently rolling as her speed increased. Almost before he knew it, there was a knock on his door. He looked at his watch and saw that half an hour had nearly passed. He drew up his trousers, slipped the braces over his shoulders, quickly fastened his flies and opened the door. To his surprise, he was face to face with Helena, looking radiant and smiling.

"Can I come in, Artur?" she asked. Just at that moment, the ship gave a lurch to starboard and she half-fell into his open arms.

"It seems as though you already have," said Artur with a smile, as he helped her to a more stable standing position by gently holding on to her shoulders. He shut the door behind her and beckoned her to sit on the only chair in his cabin.

"How are you feeling after our rather interesting trip from Croydon?" Artur enquired, as he touched her on the arm and put on his tie.

"I have to say, in all honesty, that I'm very pleased to be on board this ship and heading for Tromsø, after all the excitement of today. It seems to have been a very long day too. I do hope that hostess lady is alright and that she has no lasting injuries. That incident on landing at Sumburgh was very frightening; we all could have been very badly injured." There was then a knock on the door. Artur put on his jacket and opened the door to be faced by a smartly dressed junior officer.

"If it is convenient, sir, I have come to escort you both to the captain's quarters for some light refreshments?" the officer said as he saluted them.

"We're ready to follow you, aren't we Helena?"

She smiled as she got to her feet, followed the officer out of Artur's cabin, with Artur coming along behind.

They went up two decks and then towards the stern of the ship. The officer knocked on the door and entered the large cabin.

"Ah, there you are. Please come in Miss Olsen and you, Lieutenant Selmer," the captain said. He then introduced them to seven officers, as well as a vice admiral. They were then offered drinks and told to help themselves to the spread on the table, after which all the officers took what they needed. Conversation was easy and quite light-hearted for the next thirty-five minutes.

"Please may I have quiet for a few moments," said the captain. "Please raise your glasses to the king, King George." Everyone toasted His Royal Highness.

"I would like to welcome our newly arrived guests on our ship: Miss Helena Olsen and Lieutenant Selmer," whereupon they all raised their glasses to the two of them. "We hope you have an uneventful journey to Tromsø. I'm sure I don't have to remind you, however, and this especially goes for everyone in this room, that we are definitely on a war footing here in the North Sea. We soon will be joining the rest of the fleet and their priority is to escort us to our destination and back to England. If the weather improves, we will certainly be of interest to the Luftwaffe and probably to the Nazi submarines. We will be on full alert for the next three days, although we will not be at battle stations, unless ordered to be so.

Miss Olsen and Lieutenant Selmer will be safer in their cabins, but I will quite understand if they want to get some air on deck from time to time. Lieutenant Selmer, you may join us on the bridge whenever you wish to. For the first few times, I advise you to be accompanied by one of my officers, until you are familiar with your way around this ship. You will usually find one in the ward room. Admiral, do you have anything else you would like to add?"

"Thank you, Captain. One thing I would like to say is this: as you know, we only have half the normal compliment on board, the rest are on shore leave in Rosyth, together with a few officers. The main reason for this is that we expect to be bringing several hundred Norwegians, and other nationals, out of Tromsø. If any of the seamen ask questions about this mission, tell them it's routine, nothing out of the ordinary. Only the captain, his Number 2, Lieutenant Selmer, Miss Olsen and I know our real purpose, it is essential that it remains confidential for as long as possible. Is that quite clear?" the admiral said very emphatically, looking at everyone.

"Lastly, if we should be under attack at any time, I highly recommend that Miss Olsen and Lieutenant Selmer return to their cabins without delay, unless the lieutenant is already on the bridge. Thank you to everyone, and God speed for a successful assignment."

Murmurings from everyone followed the admiral's words. Artur felt he should say something in acknowledgement:

"Gentlemen, I would just like to say on behalf of Miss Olsen and myself that we are very grateful to you all and the fleet for taking us to Tromsø. We hope we don't run into any difficulties, but, as the admiral rightly pointed out, we are on a war footing. It would be unwise of us not to expect some interference from the Germans. Their intelligence machine is very likely to be well aware of our mission and will be determined to thwart us, if they possibly can. Thank you again to everyone."

Conversation returned between them all, but the admiral came over to Artur and drew him and Helena away from all the others.

"Excuse me for taking you to one side, but I thought I ought to inform you of what this ship has been involved in up to recently. She ferried troops to Stavanger and Bergen following on from several months late last year of exercises in the Mediterranean Sea. Early in May, she was under orders to search for German ships that were in the area of Trondheim. We were unsuccessful, although she did encounter a near miss from a U-boat. This mission is as risky as any of the others, but the crew are battle-hardened and ready for any action, particularly with the escort ships that will accompany us. Our mission is clear and comes from the highest authority in the war cabinet.

"I need to tell you that in late May, the Norwegian and Allied forces had successfully retaken Narvik. If you are not already aware, orders then came from Whitehall for all allied troops and aircraft to be withdrawn from Norway, as the *Wehrmacht* had entered the Low Countries and France. This will end the allied campaign in Norway and virtually hand the country over to the Germans. You can imagine that when King Haakon and his cabinet receive this news in the next day or two, they will be horrified and be in disbelief. I'm telling you this as it could affect the willingness of King Haakon to accept your recommendation of moving into exile in London."

"Thank you, sir, we will definitely bear that in mind and we appreciate the update," Artur remarked as he looked at Helena, who nodded in agreement.

"If I may say so, Lieutenant, as it's getting late and you've had a long and difficult day, you both would be wise to get some well-earned sleep. There's no knowing what tomorrow will bring."

Helena and Artur agreed. They thanked the captain for his hospitality and one of the officers was assigned to accompany them back to their cabins. Artur sat on his bed and mulled over in his mind the day's events. He took his clothes and toiletries out of his kitbag and hung everything up in the small wardrobe. He sat himself at the desk and wrote up his notebook. On completing his notes, he looked at his watch and saw it was a few minutes before 11 o'clock. *Time for some much-needed shuteye,* he said to himself.

Chapter 14
Monday, 3rd June 1940

Artur awoke with a start. His watch told him it was 7:30 a.m. He tried to remember the time he and Helena were supposed to be in the officers' mess for breakfast. He was sure it was 8 o'clock, so he quickly washed, put on his uniform, went out and lightly knocked on Helena's door. There was no reply, but just at that moment an officer came towards him.

"If you are looking for Miss Olsen, sir," said the officer as he saluted Artur, "I have just returned from taking her to the mess. Please follow me so you can join her for some breakfast."

Artur followed the officer and they entered the mess on a deck two levels up from their cabins.

"Good morning, Artur," Helena said with a broad smile. "Did you have a good sleep and some nice dreams? I haven't been here very long, so there's plenty of food left for you!" she said, as she brushed past his arm to put some cereal into her bowl.

"Hello, Helena. The sleep was much needed, but no dreams of real interest or excitement, I'm sorry to say. Maybe tonight?"

They had their breakfast with only light conversation between them. Artur had looked out of the porthole in his cabin before breakfast and had noticed some of the escort ships nearby. He peered out again and he saw a lot of low cloud that would probably keep the Luftwaffe on the ground. He excused himself from Helena and asked the only officer in the mess to take him to the bridge. On his arrival, he was greeted by the captain and other officers that were searching the waters all around for any possible German subs.

"It all looks quite calm at the moment," the captain remarked, "but even with those six ships escorting us, we can't be too careful. Here, Lieutenant, have a look through these spare glasses," as he handed a large set of binoculars over to Artur. He adjusted them for his eyesight and scoured through an arc of about 270°, starting on the starboard side and searching beyond the escort ships. He had slowly surveyed the area twice and was just about to put the glasses down when he thought he saw something.

"Captain, if you look over there," and he pointed in the direction immediately to starboard, "can you see something just above the waterline? It looks remarkably like a submarine's periscope."

The captain looked and told some of the officers to take a look.

"My goodness, Lieutenant, you could be right; well spotted. I'll have a coded message sent immediately to the ships on that side. Keep watching, Lieutenant Selmer, and give me the bearing," he said to the navigating officer.

The coded message was duly sent and their replies mentioned that neither had seen the periscope. They noticed that one of the escorts turned away from the convoy in the direction of the siting. After some minutes, as they were watching, they saw the escort ship turn through 180° and two depth charges were rolled off the stern of the ship. A few moments later there were two explosions and plumes of water were sent high into the air. They continued viewing the scene, but what might have been a U-boat's periscope was no longer visible.

"Let's hope that has at the very least, frightened the blighter away from our ships," said the admiral, who had been taking a keen interest in the activity. "We must, however, remain very vigilant as we pass north west of Trondheim, still within range of the Luftwaffe, if the weather should clear."

The rest of the morning and afternoon watches went by without any sightings or incidents with Helena joining them on the bridge during the late afternoon. The captain was not always present in the officers' wardroom, but on this occasion, his Number 2 invited him and asked him to bring Artur and Helena to join him. Dinner was to be at 7:30 p.m., so they were escorted to their cabins at 6:00 p.m.

"Do join me in my cabin at 7 o'clock, if you can, Helena. I smuggled a little something into my kitbag before leaving my London flat."

"Sounds very intriguing, Artur. I look forward to it," she replied as she slipped into her cabin.

Artur was ready just before 7 o'clock and had put two small glasses on the desk. There was a gentle rap on the door and Artur went over to let Helena in. She kissed him on his cheeks and walked in.

"Very glad you could make it here before supper. You really look gorgeous, Helena, in your dress, by the way. It seems to resemble your country's flag colours. It really does suit you."

"Thank you, Artur. So, what is this pre-dinner drink all about?"

Artur poured some pale brown liquid out of the bottle into each of the glasses and handed one to Helena. They touched glasses and both said, "*Skol.*"

"I'm sure it was a surprise to you, as it was for me, when the admiral mentioned that the allies were to withdraw from Norway and leave your country in the hands of the Germans, especially as your forces and the allies were about to retake Narvik. What do you think will be the reaction of your king and his cabinet when they hear the news?"

"That's very difficult to foretell. I'm certain, however, that he will be concerned for the families of those who have been killed and injured in the defence of their country. He will see their sacrifice to be for nothing and be disappointed that London didn't consult his cabinet first before making the decision."

"I tend to agree with you, Helena. Perhaps we should continue this discussion after supper. Are you enjoying your aperitif? It is a very fine, dry sherry."

There was a knock at Artur's door.

"That must be our guide," said Artur with a smile at Helena; they finished their drink.

They left his cabin and as they entered the wardroom, everyone turned to greet them. To a man, Artur could read their minds as they looked at Helena: she was a picture of beauty and elegance.

The dinner went well and everyone was very jolly. The admiral and the captain were on either side of Helena and she seemed to easily keep them amused and interested in what she had to say. Artur was half-hearing some of her stories and was starting to think that she might not be who she claimed to be. When dinner was over, Artur excused himself and went back to his cabin, but without an escort this time, as he was beginning to know his way around the ship by now.

I'll take a chance and go into Helena's cabin, Artur said to himself; *it will be a while before she returns, I'm sure.* He went inside and turned on the light by the bunk. He looked about him and, as he suspected, everything was tidy. He didn't know what he was looking for or what he might find. He carefully opened the desk drawer where there were papers and envelopes. The top envelope was addressed to Miss Helena Olsen, but all the other four beneath had a different name on them: *Fraulein Olga Schwartz.* He carefully replaced all the envelopes exactly as they had been and closed the drawer. He turned to the wardrobe and opened the door. He put his hand into a few of the jacket pockets, but there was nothing except for one lady's handkerchief. He saw the suitcase under the bunk, put it on the bunk and opened it. There was underwear and a nightie on top of what looked like a false bottom. He undid the button and lifted the lid.

My goodness, he said to himself. *Why should she be wanting a German Luger pistol, similar to the ones used by the Wehrmacht?* He replaced everything as it was, slid the case under the bed and smoothed the bed clothes. Artur looked at his watch: it was 10:30 p.m. He stood by the door and listened – nothing! He carefully went out, closed it and went in to his own cabin. He sat on his bed and sighed with relief that he hadn't been found in her room. His mind was spinning. He knew he should send a coded message to Charles the next morning. He prepared for bed, but he slept fitfully. A slight amount of daylight came through the porthole at this latitude and this time of year. The gentle movement of the ship eventually sent him to sleep.

He was suddenly woken by a loud wrapping on his door.

"Just a moment," he said, as he gathered his thoughts and wondered who it might be. His watch told him it was 7:30 a.m. He went and opened the door. To his surprise it was the navigating officer, John.

"I'm sorry to disturb you, sir, but the captain wants you to come to the bridge as soon as possible."

"OK, John, tell him I'll be there in a couple of shakes. He won't mind if I haven't shaved, will he?"

"Not at all, sir."

"Is there a problem, John?"

"It's just that the sky has become much clearer over the last couple of hours and there is a distinct likelihood of the Luftwaffe coming to have a look at our convoy; he needs as many hands as possible on the bridge."

"I understand. Thank you, John."

Artur quickly dressed in his uniform, placed his nightclothes on the bunk and left his satchel on the desk. He looked around his cabin as he opened the door. He went straight to the bridge.

"Sorry to have disturbed you, Lieutenant, but we need everyone to be here to look out for enemy aircraft and, after yesterday's sighting of the U-boat's periscope, I think your eyesight is better than everyone else's," said the captain as they saluted each other.

"Aye, aye, sir," Artur replied. "Do you have a preferred station for me?"

"Yes, you take the starboard side. Be careful, because they might use the low sun as a shield and come at us from the east. We have had a message half an hour ago from a colonel in charge of a British and French battalion. He reported from a vantage point overlooking a German occupied airport that they are preparing bombers and fighter planes for a possible assault somewhere. They suspect it might be used against us, but they have no intelligence to confirm their thinking. We have just passed some of the southerly islands of Lofoten, which, as you know, are off the coast near Narvik."

Artur took up his position and stared towards the east as his eyes adjusted to the sunlight. He picked up the spare binoculars and started his search just above the horizon.

"Captain, will we get a message from the colonel when he sees the first aircraft take to the air?"

"He said he would if he could, but he thought he might be more concerned with defending his own position."

"But surely, sir, if he's as close as he suggests, he couldn't miss the noise of the aircraft taking off?"

"You're quite correct, Lieutenant, but he has said that any further attempts to send us a message might be jammed by the enemy."

Artur returned to his station and scoured the horizon just above the islands. Nothing yet!

"Captain, may I have leave from the bridge for about ten minutes as I would like to send a message to my boss in London? I haven't updated him yet about my arrival on your ship."

"Very well, Lieutenant, but make it snappy. Something could happen at any minute."

They saluted each other and Artur left the bridge. He went directly to the wireless and communications room. He had already written his message out; it was in code and ready to be sent. The wireless operator stood up as Artur entered the room, but he told him to stand easy. He told him he wanted a message to be sent to London. Once it had been transmitted, Artur returned to the bridge some fifteen minutes later. He immediately continued to scan the horizon with most of the officers searching the same area.

All of a sudden, the door to the bridge opened and in ran one of the wireless men with a piece of paper.

"Sir, a message has been received and it is marked for your attention: URGENT," said the man as he stood to attention in front of the captain, but ignoring the admiral who had entered the bridge a few moments earlier.

"Thank you," said the captain as he took the piece of paper and started to read the message. "You may stand at ease."

"It appears, gentlemen, that the colonel has thought it important enough for us to know that the Luftwaffe are about to take to the air. Number 2, I order you to tell everyone to go to battle stations at once. Our convoy is very likely to come under attack any time now. We don't want to be taken by surprise, but if we are ready for action, the Luftwaffe might be the one to be surprised.

"Lieutenant, I want you to stay on the bridge and look out for approaching enemy aircraft," the captain said to Artur.

"Before everyone leaves the bridge to carry out your orders, sir," Artur said, "has anyone seen Miss Olsen this morning?"

"I was the last to see her leave the officers' mess last night and that was just after midnight," one of the second lieutenants replied.

"How about this morning?" Artur asked as he looked around at everyone else.

They all shook their heads in denial.

"Sir," Artur said, directing his question at the captain, "May I suggest that the same second lieutenant goes to Miss Olsen's cabin to find out when she's coming to the bridge? After all, wherever she must be, she must hear the order to go to battle stations and she won't know where she has to go to, if anywhere."

"Good point, Lieutenant," the captain responded as he waved his hand to send the second lieutenant on his way.

Artur waited till the majority of the officers had left the bridge, leaving only the admiral, the captain, the navigating officer and the helmsmen.

"Could I have a confidential word with you before the action starts?" Artur said to the admiral and the captain, ushering them to one side and out of earshot of the others.

"This is probably a rather delicate question to ask, gentlemen, but what do you know about Miss Olsen? What do you believe to be her mission?"

"It's quite simple, Lieutenant. She's an employee at the Norwegian Embassy in London and she's coming with us to help persuade King Haakon and his government to take exile in London. Why do you ask?"

Just at that moment, a young seaman came onto the bridge, saluted and handed a message to Artur.

"Would you excuse me for a moment, I have received a reply from my boss in London?"

Artur stood to one side and looked at the text, but it was mostly in code. He wouldn't be able to decipher it till later. He put it in his pocket, turned to the two men, but they had returned to their stations. He picked up his binoculars and searched along the starboard horizon. He couldn't believe his eyes as he shouted:

"Enemy aircraft at 2 o'clock; six perhaps eight."

The captain immediately communicated with the gunnery officer on deck and then ordered Artur to join him to give him assistance, as the senior gunnery officer was on leave. Artur left straight away, but not before double checking the direction of the enemy planes.

Chapter 15

Tuesday, 4th June 1940

When Artur arrived on the main deck, there was a significant amount of activity as men went quickly to their battle stations. He went briskly to the anti-aircraft guns looking for the junior gunnery officer.

"I've been ordered to give you some assistance so how can I help?"

"Good show, Lieutenant. As you know, we left nearly half our complement at Rosyth for shore leave. A few were gunnery men, including the senior gunnery officer. Your experience will be invaluable.

"Here, put this helmet on and I've found these ear pieces. As well as deadening the sound of the guns, you will also be able to communicate with other gunnery boys, as if it were a two-way radio," as the officer showed Artur the switch.

Artur put the gear on and sat in the seat behind the guns. He wasn't going to tell the officer that he had never been anywhere near an anti-aircraft gun before, let alone fired one. After all, his papers said he was a lieutenant, but he'd not been through any training yet. He just had to use his common sense.

He thought by now the planes would be very close as he had heard the escort ships opening fire a few moments earlier. He searched the sky and one of the three men assisting him pointed skyward to a Stuka that was just about to dive towards the ship. The gun was swivelled around and Artur looked through the sight as it moved. He squeezed the trigger and a great burst of shells shot into the sky. Ships that were part of the convoy were also firing at the enemy planes. Two more Stukas started to dive towards the cruiser and four others were attacking the escort ship to Artur's starboard side. There was so much noise, even with his earphones on, but Artur concentrated on aiming at the planes heading for the cruiser. To his surprise, he hit both of them and they exploded before releasing their bombs and fell into the sea. The escort ship was not so lucky: it was hit several times in midships near the munition holds. There were huge explosions as it burst into flames. As it started to heel over, men were putting down some of the lifeboats, but the angle of the ship sent many of the men straight into the sea.

Hard to starboard, came the order over the speaker system. *Prepare to pick up men in the water.* Artur was aware of men rushing in an orderly fashion around the cruiser's deck gathering life belts. He returned to his task of searching the sky, but he saw the remaining planes were heading back to the land.

"Well done, Lieutenant; you saved our bacon by downing those two blighters," said the gunnery officer as he lifted Artur's earphones. "Looks as though that escort ship has had a bad hit. It seems to have gone quiet for the moment so let's report back to the bridge."

Artur left his post and followed the officer back to the bridge. They opened the door and saluted the officers. He noticed that Helena was there and she was watching the enemy planes leaving the area through some glasses.

"Good shooting, Lieutenant," said the captain, as he stretched out his hand to shake Artur's. "They might have inflicted some serious damage if you hadn't shot them down. There were eight of them altogether and five were shot down by our convoy and us.

"The admiral has ordered our ship and two others to pick up as many men as we can from the stricken ship," the captain said to the officers. "Number 2, go down to the main deck and help organise the men with the life rafts and the belts. It will be much easier to get men out of the water into the rafts first. Make sure the nets are hung over the side of the ship so those chaps who are able to can climb up on deck."

"Yes, sir; straightaway."

The officer left the bridge and Artur looked at Helena, as the order went out for the ship to be slowed to a crawling speed.

"I'm recommending you for a medal, Lieutenant, and it will be endorsed by the admiral," the captain said to Artur. The admiral nodded in agreement.

"That's very good of you, sir," Artur replied as he turned away from looking at Helena, "but I was only doing my duty, to the best of my ability and limited experience."

Artur thought he would direct attention away from himself at this point and looked at Helena again.

"Did you have a good sleep last night, Helena? I thought you might have been up here earlier, so as to witness the excitement!"

"I heard the call to battle stations, but as I didn't think I could provide any direct assistance, I remained in my cabin."

Artur then remembered the reply he had received from Charles and asked the captain if he could leave the bridge for a short while; his request was granted.

On reaching his cabin, he closed the door behind him and cast his eyes around. Everything seemed to be in its place, so he moved over to the small desk that had one drawer. He had placed a piece of black cotton over the front of the drawer and he noticed that it had fallen to the floor. *Someone's been in my cabin and has opened the drawer,* he said to himself. *It was fortunate that before I left, I took my code book out of there and placed it under the mattress, near the top of the bunk.* He walked to his bunk, lifted the mattress and saw it was exactly where he had left it. He sat at his desk, spread out the piece of paper containing Charles' reply and wrote down the decoded text. Before he had even finished, he had guessed what most of the answers to his questions would be:

Miss Helena Olsen is not known at the Norwegian Embassy in London STOP *nor to any of the Norwegian embassies in Europe* STOP *Fraulein Olga Schwartz is a known agent of the Abwehr* STOP *she was last working in Oslo supporting Norway's Fascist party run by Vidkun Quisling* STOP *Adolf Hitler had told King Haakon to appoint Vidkun as prime minister, but he refused* STOP *Treat 'Miss Olsen' with kid gloves. I say again, take great care* STOP *Make sure she doesn't attend your meeting with the king and his cabinet in Tromsø* STOP *Charles* END.

Artur sat back in his chair and wondered what he could say to anyone on board about Helena. He was as certain as he could be that she must have come into his cabin after he had left for the bridge earlier in the morning, just as he had been to hers the night before. He picked up the cotton thread and put it back in its place over the front of the drawer. He went to his kitbag and made sure that his pistol was still at the bottom: he was relieved to find that it was. He checked it over, made sure the magazine was still full and returned it to his kitbag.

He went back to the bridge. By this time, the life rafts had been hauled on to the ship and the men were being handed blankets to wrap around themselves. Those in the water with life jackets, were clambering into empty rafts and would be brought up on deck over the next twenty minutes or so.

"How many men have been rescued?" Artur asked the captain.

"It's hard to say, as so many have been rescued by other ships. I would say we have some fifty-five on board. I think the rescue operation went as well as can be expected, Lieutenant.

"With your permission, sir," the captain said to the admiral, "we should now go full steam ahead." The admiral nodded in agreement.

"Number 2, let's not spend any more time here. It's after midday so full steam ahead for Tromsø. There's not much more we can do for the sinking convoy ship and we have a deadline to meet."

Within a few moments, Artur felt the surge forward provided by the Parsons steam turbines that would soon take her to a cruising speed of over 27 knots. He couldn't stop thinking about Charles' reply: *has he been given the correct intelligence report and how will he be able to prevent Helena from attending the meeting in a few days' time?*

Helena had been on the bridge when Artur had returned and had been observing the rescue operation going on by the other ships in the convoy.

Now that they were underway again, she told the captain that she wished to return to her cabin, to which he agreed.

The day was passing quickly, but there was still a long way to go. Artur realised that he couldn't really say anything to any of the officers about Helena; he would have to see how things panned out, once they were moored in Tromsø.

"Would you like to join me and the admiral in my quarters for a rather late light lunch, Lieutenant?" the captain asked. "Nothing fancy, but it's been a long and somewhat exciting morning, has it not? We are no longer at battle stations, so we ought to take this opportunity in case those Luftwaffe planes return later in the day."

"I would enjoy that very much; thank you, sir."

A few of the officers went with them, leaving Number 2 with some junior officers in charge of the ship. The sea was quite rough and the cruiser was bucking and rolling as they entered the captain's cabin.

"Have you asked Miss Olsen to accompany us?" Artur asked the captain.

"I believe she appears to be more comfortable on her own in her cabin, especially after the encounter with the Stukas. She seemed to be quite upset at the downing of the ones that were aiming at our ship. She doesn't know that you were the one operating the anti-aircraft guns that did the damage."

"Shall I go and see her after we've had some food?"

"That sounds like a jolly good idea, Lieutenant. Do report back to me afterwards, if you need to."

Artur tucked in to the meal and chatted casually to some of the officers about the Luftwaffe attack.

"Can't be too careful in this part of the North Sea," remarked one of them. "The Nazis are certainly intent on taking over Norway; it will give them access to the North Atlantic, as well as the iron ore deposits across the border in Sweden."

Artur made no real response, but he knew the man was right in what he was saying. After nearly an hour, he excused himself from their company saying he would go to his cabin for a short while and to be contacted if he were needed.

He arrived at his cabin, but before going in, he put his ear to Helena's door. He didn't expect to hear anything, as he thought she would be asleep or just resting. He heard nothing, so he entered his cabin and made a point of closing the door noisily, thinking it might draw Helena's attention. He undressed down to his trousers, washed and shaved, then put on his uniform again. He went over to his desk and saw that the piece of cotton was still in place. *At least she's not delved in there again*, he said to himself.

He was just about to leave his quarters and go to find out how Helena was when there was a gentle knock on his door. He opened it and, to his surprise, he saw she was just in her night clothes. He unconsciously looked at his watch.

"Are you alright, Helena, it's only 4 o'clock in the afternoon, or have you been resting?"

"I'm so sorry to disturb you, Artur. Can I come in?" She stepped inside and closed the door without waiting for his reply.

"As I told you a day or so ago, I'm not a very good sailor, especially when the sea is rough. I thought I would try to take my mind off it by coming to see you. I heard your door close about forty minutes ago, so I knew you would be in here. Can I sit on your bunk as there's only one chair?"

"By all means, Helena. Perhaps you would like a little more of the sherry we had yesterday; I have plenty left for the two of us?"

"That would be a very nice idea, thank you."

Artur rinsed out the glasses, dried them and poured out the liquid.

"Perhaps we should pretend it's aquavit and down it in one?" said Artur with a great big smile.

They touched glasses and said, "*Skol*." Artur watched Helena swallow all the liquid. She hadn't noticed that he had only taken a small sip and had cheated her: he had obscured his glass in his hands.

"It might not be aquavit, but it is still quite strong," she said with a smile and used her long tongue to reach the rest of the liquid at the bottom of her glass. Artur moved towards Helena and put his hand out to take her glass, but she put her arm behind her back. He looked into her dark brown eyes and gave her a smile. He got very close to her when he reached around for her hand that held the glass. She fell backwards onto his bunk and pulled him onto her with her free hand. He thought he should try to resist her by rolling away to the side, but she was strong. She wrapped both arms around his neck, having left the empty glass near the pillow.

"So, Artur Selmer, I know how you've been looking at me as I boarded the plane in Croydon. Why don't you have me now? There's not much activity around the ship at the moment, we have plenty of time to have some fun."

He was tempted, but now that he knew so much more about who she really was, he thought he would tease her and resist her advances. He took hold of her wrists and pressed them against the bunk each side of her head. He was leaning against the side of the bunk and her legs were either side of his waist so that her nightdress had risen well above her knees.

"Surely, Lieutenant Selmer, you can see that I'm ready and willing for you to have me," she said, smiling and revealing her light brown hair at the join of her thighs.

Artur suddenly stood up and brought Helena up into a standing position. Her arms were now in front of her and he held her very still.

"You are hurting my arms, Artur. I thought you liked me?"

"Enough of this, Helena, I'm taking you back to your cabin, as I'm expected back on the bridge."

Artur led her out of his cabin and into hers, sat her on her bunk and departed back to his quarters. He wiped his brow with his towel, brushed his hair and left for the bridge.

"Everything 'a okay', Lieutenant? You look a little flushed?" the captain remarked.

"All is fine, thank you, Captain. I came quickly to the bridge as I had not realised the time," he lied. "Any more sightings of the enemy, sir?"

"No, everything seems suspiciously quiet, Lieutenant. I wouldn't put it past them having another go early in the morning. After all, there'll be plenty of light, even if they attacked the convoy at midnight."

"That's very true, sir. We will have to keep our eyes skinned at all times until we get to Tromsø. What news of those chaps we picked up from the stricken escort ship; have they settled in alright?"

"Good point, Lieutenant. Perhaps you should go and see how everything is down below. A couple of my officers were giving them what they needed."

Chapter 16
Tuesday, 4ᵗʰ June 1940

Artur went directly to one of the lower decks where he knew the rescued sailors would be and saluted the officers in charge.

"Is everything going alright down here, gentlemen? Have these chaps been made as comfortable as we can and got all they need?"

"All is fine, Lieutenant. At the last count, we rescued fifty-five of which ten were sent to be treated for mostly minor injuries. They've been fed and they've all been given dry clothes. They seem to have had a very lucky escape."

"Do you mind if I relay the situation back to the captain, or is he already aware?"

"He has been briefed, but by all means tell him what I have told you."

Artur saluted the officers and left for the bridge. He decided, however, that he'd go via the comms room first. As he entered, he saluted the leading seaman as everyone stood up to attention.

"Stand easy everyone. Don't let me interrupt your very important job."

He went to the young sailor that had brought the coded message to him.

"I don't suppose Miss Olsen has asked you to send a message to anyone since she arrived on our ship, has she?"

"It's funny you should say that, sir, but she has sent two messages: one yesterday and the other today."

"Do you have copies of what she sent and any of the replies?"

The sailor got up from his chair and searched through one or two pigeon holes for a few minutes.

"Here we are, sir," the sailor said, as he handed the slips of paper to Artur.

He saw the date of the top one and as it was today's date, he placed the two papers that were clipped together under the other two. He read the addressee's name and number: a junior diplomat in the Norwegian Embassy in London. She told him that all was well after a tricky flight into Sumburgh and that the plane caught fire on landing. The reply was non-committal and wished her success with persuading King Haakon to take exile in London. Artur thought it was strange that it wasn't in code – or was it?

Artur turned to the second pair of papers, dated today. He noticed it appeared to be in code as he couldn't understand any of it. It had been sent to someone in Oslo, but the name was not clear. He examined the reply and it was in a similar format. He decided he would send them all to Charles in London and ask for the Intelligence Service's assistance.

"Could I borrow these for a few minutes?" he said to the seaman.

"Of course, Lieutenant. I'll still be here till 8 o'clock."

Artur pocketed the papers, left the comms room and returned to his cabin. He entered very quietly and went over to his bunk to retrieve his code book from under the mattress. He returned to his desk and wrote a coded message to Charles asking him to have Helena's messages deciphered. Once he'd finished, he put everything back in its place together with a copy of a false message to his bank manager that wouldn't be sent. He left this one on his desk top.

He knocked as he entered the comms room, the same man stood up and they saluted each other.

"I need you to send these four messages of Miss Olsen's together with this new one which should be the leading page. Are you happy with that?" The man nodded. "Once you've done that, do not put any of them in the pigeon holes, but keep them on your person. This is very important; do you understand?"

"Yes, sir. I will send the messages myself and keep them safe in my pocket afterwards."

"Good. Thank you. When you receive a reply or each time you get a reply, bring it to me straight away, even if it's in the middle of the night. I will either be on the bridge or in my cabin or in the officers' mess. If Miss Olsen is present, you must find a way of attracting my attention without Miss Olsen noticing; that is very important."

The man nodded that he understood the instructions. Artur smiled at him, saluted and left for the bridge. He felt very satisfied that he'd covered all aspects as well as he could. He entered the bridge and he was surprised to see that Helena was already there. He greeted everyone and told the captain that the rescued sailors seemed to be in good shape, all things considered, and being well cared for. He looked at his watch and saw it was just after 6 o'clock.

"Are you going off watch soon?" Artur asked the captain.

"On the hour, as it happens, Lieutenant, and going to my quarters for some refreshments. Would you care to join me?"

"I would indeed, sir, thank you."

The captain left the bridge with his Number 2 in charge at 7 o'clock, followed by Artur and two other junior officers. He had instructed his Number 2 to contact him immediately, should there be any enemy activity. Helena stayed on the bridge and wasn't invited to join them.

The officers entered the captain's quarters and were told to help themselves to some food and drink. They sat at the larger of the two tables and talked mostly about the demise of the sunken escort ship and the loss of so many of her sailors.

"Do you think we stayed long enough at the scene of the attack, Lieutenant?" the captain asked Artur.

"We did all we could under the circumstances, sir, and it seemed that two of the other escort ships had hastened to the sinking vessel and picked up many chaps from the water."

"I'm aware of that, but I don't want to give the impression of our rather swift departure to be seen as an act of neglect for those poor men."

"One mustn't forget, sir, that our main mission is to arrive in Tromsø to pick up all those wishing to leave Norway. In any case, we did pick up fifty-five men and gave them what they needed. I don't think you have anything to fear, sir; you and your crew have done their best.

"When do you anticipate reaching Tromsø, Sir – assuming no further activity from the Germans?"

"By tomorrow evening at about 8 o'clock, all being well," replied the captain.

The other officers finished their meals and left the mess. Only Artur and the captain were still present and Artur saw an opportunity to raise the subject of Miss Olsen.

"I need to tell you, sir, that I have some concerns about Miss Olsen and why she's on this ship bound for Tromsø." The captain stared at Artur, not sure what he might be going to hear. He went through what he'd found in Helena's desk in her cabin, the communication slips in the comms room, the Luger pistol in her suitcase, the reply received from Charles and what he had told him to do.

"What on earth did you think you were doing by going into her cabin like that, Lieutenant?"

"I just seemed to have a hunch; something to do with my Service training, I suppose, sir."

"Did you really think she was a spy that has been planted by the Germans?"

"It might sound a bit smug, sir, but you can now see that my hunch was correct."

"So, your man in London has information that says she is working for Vidkun Quisling, the Norwegian Fascist party leader, who has serious links with the Nazis?"

"Exactly. Back in April, just after the German forces invaded Denmark and Norway, the Germans intended to kidnap King Haakon and his government. They had, however, secretly moved 150 kilometres east to Elverum, whereupon Hitler demanded Haakon should appoint Quisling head of a new government. The king rejected this demand and – over the next two months – Quisling's support from the Nazis waned somewhat. He still has ambitions of taking over the running of Norway, but this can only happen if he can remove Haakon. Hence Miss Olsen's involvement with Quisling and her mission to kill Haakon, the crown prince and the prime minister."

"My goodness, Lieutenant. I'm very pleased you have put me in the picture. None of this should go any further, do you agree?"

"I agree, sir, but it's your choice as to whether or not you tell the admiral."

"I think we've spent enough time discussing Miss Olsen, or whatever her real name is. I'll stay in my quarters to take some rest. I'll mull over what you've told me. Good work, Lieutenant, I'll see you later."

"Thank you, sir. I hope you get some well-earned rest. I'll go back to the bridge."

All was quiet and Artur went back from the bridge to his cabin at 10:30 p.m. There was no sight of Helena, so he assumed she must be in her cabin.

Artur awoke at 6:15 a.m. and hastily washed and dressed. He went to the bridge to find Helena there with the captain and a few officers.

"Good morning, Lieutenant. I trust you rested well?" as Artur saluted the officers.

"Indeed, I did; thank you, sir. Anything of note going on?"

"We've had another message from that colonel chappie, who's still near Narvik, saying that there's no activity on the ground at the airport. That's a relief."

"I think we might be a bit too far north for them to be interested in us now," said Number 2, to which everyone nodded in agreement.

Most of the officers on the bridge scanned the horizon and the skies for over half an hour for possible enemy ships and planes. Nothing.

"As it seems quiet, I'm going for some breakfast," said the captain. "I shall go to the ward room rather than my quarters, so I can be with some of my men. Would anyone like to join me?" as he looked around. Helena said she would, as did some of the officers. Artur stayed behind with

Number 2 and two other officers. Over an hour and half passed by before the captain and the officers returned to the bridge.

"Miss Olsen has returned to her cabin to rest as the sea has got rather rough again," the captain remarked. "She thought she might be there for some time."

Several hours passed without any further incident or sighting of the enemy.

"We are ahead of our schedule," said the navigating officer. "We have just passed the northernmost end of the Vesterålen Islands and at our current speed, we should be moored in Tromsø by 6:30 p.m. The sea might have been rough at times, but the tide will be in our favour for the rest of our time in the Norwegian Sea. We intend going around the northern end of Vanna and be coming from the NE to Tromsø."

"Good news!" said the captain. "Can't wait to get there. You had better get a message sent to our contact in Tromsø who can alert the harbour master of our estimated time of arrival."

"Aye, aye, sir," said the navigating officer, who sent his junior officer from the bridge to go to the comms room.

An air of excitement, mixed with some apprehension, came over the officers on the bridge, as they all realised that the really tricky part of their mission was not far off. During the afternoon, the ship was brought back to 20 knots, as they navigated her past Ringvassøy towards Vanna. Everyone on the bridge kept their eyes on the skies and the water, searching for any possible enemy attack. The convoy of ships was now in single file – two escorts at the front and the three remaining ones bringing up the rear – as they headed for Tromsø. The captain had instructed his Number 2 to let the ship enter the harbour at no more than 8 knots; the escorts by then will have let the cruiser go past.

A pilot tug came along side and her captain climbed up the ladder that had been lowered earlier on.

He entered the bridge and they all saluted.

"Captain, as you will no doubt be aware, do you give me permission to take over your ship and get it moored?" he said in very good English.

"You have my permission, sir. Please go ahead; we will give you whatever assistance you may require."

The Norwegian pilot took over and manoeuvred the ship to the side of the main harbour wall with ease. The ropes were thrown to the men waiting on the quayside where the ship was soon secured in position. The gangways were fastened against the ship's side and some men were waiting for instructions to disembark.

"There we are, Captain, all safe and sound. Please would you sign these papers. Do you have any injured men on board that need hospital treatment?"

"Yes, we do. Number 2, please take the pilot and a few junior officers to the sick rooms and arrange for those who need it most to be taken to hospital."

"Aye, aye, sir," he said as he went through the door, followed by the pilot boat's captain and two other officers.

"May I ask where Miss Olsen is, Lieutenant?" the captain enquired.

"I'm assuming she's still in her cabin, sir," replied Artur. But, just at that moment, he caught sight out of the corner of his eye down from the bridge, a woman being escorted rather hurriedly down the gangway to the quay by one of the junior officers. She seemed to place something in his hand and he responded with a bow of his head.

"It appears that Miss Olsen has left the ship without so much as a by or leave to you. Where do you think she might be going? In so much of a hurry too?"

Only the captain and Artur were on the bridge at this time, as all other officers were carrying out duties in other parts of the ship.

"Can I read your mind, Lieutenant? Do you want to follow Miss Olsen?"

"Not yet, sir; I would like to find the junior officer that escorted Helena to the quayside and ask him what she gave him."

"You are not a regular hand on my ship, but you are under my orders when you are. You are dismissed, Lieutenant. Do what you need to do. I'll wait to hear what you discover."

Artur thanked the captain, saluted him and left the bridge. He walked quickly to his cabin and looked around it. All seemed to be in order – even the thread was still in place. He took his kitbag and cap from the cupboard, collected his code book from under his mattress and left his quarters. He wasn't sure if, or when he would be back on the ship – maybe not till the following morning.

Before leaving the ship, he slipped into Helena's cabin. He looked in her wardrobe: no suitcase and no clothes. He went to her desk: no papers. He looked under her pillow and in her bed: no nightclothes. *She's obviously not intending to return to the ship,* he muttered to himself. *She must have a contact in Tromsø and knows where to find him.* He knew it was a long shot, but he thought he would quickly see if he could find the junior officer that took Helena down the gangway.

He went to the junior officers' recreation room and asked the few that were there if they had taken Miss Olsen off the boat – nobody knew anything. He went to the mess, asked the same question: same reply. He wasn't sure, but from the brief glimpse he got of the man on the quayside, he thought he recognised him as someone who reported to the senior navigating officer. He wasted no more time and went to the top of the gangway. He explained to the officer that the captain had given him permission to leave the ship. It was no problem, as they had met each other on several occasions during the journey from the Shetlands.

Chapter 17
Wednesday, 5th June 1940

Artur tried to get his bearings and remembered Helena had turned left down the quay, probably towards the exit from the harbour. Guards were stationed at the exit and stopped Artur; they wanted to see his papers. As he took them from his pocket and presented them to one of them, he asked slowly, in Danish, which way the lady had gone some fifteen minutes earlier. They smiled at his accent, but told him that she had walked quickly down the main street, away from the port.

"Did she ask you for any directions?" Artur enquired.

"Yes," one of them replied. "She wanted to know where the main hotel was in town. She spoke perfect Norwegian," one of them said, with an element of surprise.

Artur thanked them and proceeded up the main street. There was a hotel on the right-hand side of the street and one on the left further up the road. He entered the first one and asked the receptionist if a young woman had come in to the reception about fifteen minutes earlier, again in Danish. The receptionist smiled at his accent, but said she'd seen nobody. He thanked her and went to the next hotel. It looked a bit bigger and smarter than the first one. He asked the receptionist the same question – she'd also seen nobody. Artur began to think that Helena knew he would follow her, so she had left a false trail with the harbour guard.

Artur thought hard about where Helena might have gone. He had the name of the British diplomat that was coming to Tromsø for the meeting with King Haakon, so he asked the receptionist if he was staying at the hotel. She looked down the guest register, pointed to an entry and read out a name.

"That's him," said Artur rather excitedly. "Please call his room and tell him that Artur Selmer is in reception to meet him."

She did as he asked. After a few moments, she was speaking to someone, presumably the diplomat.

"The gentleman says he will be down in five minutes. Please take a seat over there," as she pointed to a couple of chairs near the hotel's entrance.

Artur waited for what seemed much longer than five minutes; he was getting a bit anxious. He was just about to go and speak to the receptionist again when a man appeared in the hallway from the staircase.

"Lieutenant Selmer, how nice to meet you," as the man walked over to Artur, who was now standing, and shook his hand.

"My name is Ballantyne, Harry Ballantyne. I'm the First Secretary of Commerce at the British Embassy in Oslo. It's very good to meet you. I trust your trip from the Shetlands was relatively uneventful, although I did hear about the sinking of one of your escort ships? Rotten luck that."

"Please call me Artur. Can we go somewhere to talk that is private?"

"There's a bar up the road so let's go there." Harry went over to the receptionist and told her he would be unavailable for about an hour.

They walked to the bar and Artur was pleased to see there were only two other people in there.

"What will you have, Artur? I recommend the beer, or would you like something else?"

"A beer will be fine, thank you."

Artur chose a table near the window. The two beers duly arrived and they touched glasses as they said, "*Skol.*"

"You are no doubt aware that we have this meeting with King Haakon and the Crown Prince tomorrow afternoon?" asked Harry.

"I knew it was tomorrow, but was not sure it was to be in the afternoon," replied Artur.

"Do you know where it will take place, Harry? I presume I may call you Harry?"

"As you may know, the king and his heir are wanted by the Germans, so they have been living the last few days in a cabin in the Målselvdalen Valley, not too many kilometres from the centre of Tromsø. The meeting is scheduled for 3:30 p.m. Until two days ago, I was staying in a house of a friend in Trondheim. I have the use of a car, so we can go together to the meeting –"

"I'm sorry to interrupt, Harry, but I need to tell you something of great importance that might affect our mission. A woman whose name is Miss Helena Olsen was on the plane with me from Croydon and was also on the ship to here. She claims to be employed at the Norwegian Embassy in London, but my contact in the Intelligence Service in London told me that nobody has ever heard of her. I found documents in her cabin that were addressed to a *'Fraulein Olga Schwartz'*. I also found a Luger pistol in her suitcase. My contact in London believes she is working for Vidkun Quisling, the Norwegian Fascist Party leader. You are no doubt very well aware of the Fascist Party and of Quisling's ambitions. Miss, whatever her name is, has an aim to either handing over the king and his son to the Germans and forcing them to agree to appointing Quisling as Prime Minister, or shooting them both."

"That's very interesting, Artur. I had had reports of a possible additional person at this meeting, but I did not know of the king's possible kidnap or killing. Where is this woman now?"

"That is a very good question, Harry. She left the ship before anyone else and by all accounts was heading up this road outside this bar. I suspect, however, that she deliberately gave a false trail to the harbour guard that I spoke to as she knew I would come after her."

"Well, there's not much point trying to hunt her down tonight as she could be anywhere. The king's cabin is discretely guarded by some of his loyal soldiers. I need to get a message through to them to warn them of this woman. We would look very stupid if she tried to gain access to the cabin during the night and abduct them away."

Harry looked at his watch and saw it was after 8 o'clock.

"They have a change of half the guard members at 9:00 p.m. I need to contact the commander and tell him about Miss Olsen's possible intentions so that the guards can be put on full alert and kept on their toes, particularly during the night. My main concern is that Miss Olsen will definitely have contacts in Tromsø that will be supporters of Quisling. They might chance their arms and make a surprise attack during the night. Let's quickly finish our beers and go back to my room to make the call."

Artur was happy with Harry's urgent response and followed him out of the bar and up to his room in the hotel. He asked the hotel's switchboard for a number and waited to be connected.

"Hello, Commander, this is Ballantyne speaking," he said in Norwegian that Artur understood.

Harry then spoke seriously to the commander about the possible arrival of Helena and some of Quisling's supporters, but he didn't quite understand everything Harry was saying as he spoke very quickly. After about seven minutes, Harry came off the phone and explained to Artur what he had arranged with the commander – they both were satisfied.

"Shall we go and get something to eat while the restaurant is still open?" Harry asked, as he stood in the middle of his room.

They went to the restaurant that was on the first floor. They talked generally about the situation in Europe, and Norway in particular. They finished by 10 o'clock and Artur said he ought to report back to the ship, rather than stay at the hotel.

"What are we to do about Miss Olsen?" Harry asked.

"When I get to the ship, I'll find the junior officer that escorted her to the quayside. I'm certain to get help from the captain and the navigating officer, if my hunch is right. I'll stay on the ship overnight and return to your hotel reception at 11 o'clock tomorrow morning. Does that sound alright with you?"

"That's fine, Artur. Have a good sleep as we'll need all our wits about us tomorrow, I'm sure."

Artur thanked Harry for the meal and set off back to ship. He went straight to the bridge and he thought he was really lucky to find the captain there on his own, especially at this time of the night. He explained about how he didn't find Helena, his meeting up with Harry Ballantyne at the hotel and what they had told the guards' commander to look out for.

"Good work, Lieutenant. I hope nothing happens at the cabin during the night. It might be a thought for you and Harry that you move the king and his son sometime in the morning to a new location. You would have to consult Haakon before doing it, of course."

"That's a good idea, sir. The thought had crossed my mind for something similar. I'll talk it through with Harry in the morning. Anyway, I'm going to get some sleep, if you'll excuse me. Tomorrow might be another exciting and challenging day."

"That's certainly one way of putting it, Lieutenant. Get some good sleep; see you in the morning in the wardroom, maybe."

Artur returned to his cabin and once in bed, was out like a light.

Chapter 18
Thursday, 6th June 1940

Artur woke very suddenly: he had been dreaming that he had been shot in the arm by Helena as he was sheltering the king behind him. He looked at his arm and found there was a red bruise where he thought he had been shot. *It must have been squeezed against the side of the bunk. I hope this is not a bad portent of this afternoon,* he said to himself.

His watch told him it was 6:30 a.m., so he got up, dressed in casual clothes and checked his pistol. He wiped it carefully with his towel and spoke to it softly as he did so. It was one of his superstitions with inanimate objects, particularly when he might be wanting them to do a job for him. He returned it to his kitbag, together with a few of his clothes, even though he was fairly certain to be sleeping on ship that night.

As he exited his cabin, he thought he would go into Helena's one more time before going to the mess. The door was unlocked, he went to the cupboard in case he might have missed something, but it was quite empty. He opened the drawer of the desk and put his hand right to the back. He felt something and pulled it out. *That's very careless of you, Helena, leaving a Nazi armband behind,* he mumbled to himself. He pushed it down to the bottom of his kitbag and under his pistol. He searched inside the bedding of the bunk, under the mattress and under the bunk. Nothing else was to be found. He was 100% certain she wouldn't be coming back to the ship again.

Artur went to the officers' mess and had a moderate breakfast. He hoped to see the navigating officer, but he wasn't there, nor was the captain. He waited till 9 o'clock and went to the bridge. Neither of the two that he wanted to speak to were there either. Just as he was about to leave the bridge, the junior officer who he thought had escorted Helena to the quayside came in.

"Excuse me, officer," as Artur saluted him, "did I happen to see you with Miss Olsen on the quayside late yesterday afternoon?"

The officer looked around him rather nervously, looked at Artur and denied knowing anything about being with Miss Olsen.

"You do realise, officer, that if I find you have lied to me, I could have you court martialled. It would be my advice that you reconsider your reply to my question. I say again: did you escort Miss Olsen from the ship yesterday almost immediately after we had docked?"

He was just about to answer when the captain, his Number 2 and the navigating officer came to the bridge. The captain came over to Artur and asked him if he had had a good rest.

"Excuse me, sir, but before I update you, I need to tell you that I believe this officer escorted Miss Olsen from your ship, but he is not prepared to agree with me."

"Stand to attention, Second Lieutenant Hood, as I speak to you," the captain said, with a great deal of authority. "Tell me, and the others here, exactly what happened between you and Miss Olsen yesterday after we had docked. You understand the consequences if you are found not to be telling the truth, don't you?"

"Yes, sir, I understand."

The officer explained that Miss Olsen had singled him out to help her escape from the ship as soon as it was docked.

"She had made up some story that I had slept with her two nights ago and that if I didn't do as she asked, she would report me to you, the captain, Sir. It was blackmail, of the worst kind. I felt I had no option but to carry out her wishes. When I had taken her to the quay, she gave me a five-pound note and walked hastily away to the harbour exit. That is the honest truth, sir. I swear to God." The officer took the five-pound note out of his trouser pocket and gave it to the captain.

"Stand easy, Lieutenant. Now answer this: did you sleep with her as she alleges?"

"I might have liked to, sir, but I didn't," he said with a cheeky smile on his face; the others grinned too.

"One last question, Lieutenant: what else did Miss Olsen say to you while she was in your company up until the time she walked away from the gangway?"

"It wasn't so much what she said, it was more her behaviour. She seemed very anxious and rather nervous. She looked a number of times into her handbag, she stopped before leaving the ship to look in her suitcase. I asked her if she was alright, but she replied that she was just double checking that she had brought everything from her cabin."

Artur opened his kitbag and brought out the Nazi armband, waving it about his head as everyone looked at him.

"She just happened to leave this in her desk drawer. She probably thought she might have left this behind and needed to see if she was right by searching her bag and case."

"We are now quite clear where her allegiances lie," said the captain. "To think that we've given free travel and hospitality to Miss Olsen all the way from Croydon airport to here."

Other officers had come to the bridge during the discussions and were quietly asking questions of the others about what had been going on. Artur waved his hand in the air to get everyone's attention:

"What many of you don't know, as I've only told the captain, is that I found four letters in Miss Olsen's desk addressed to *Fraulein Olga Schwartz*. My contact in London has confirmed that the Fraulein and Miss Olsen are one and the same person. She is working for Mr Quisling, the Norwegian Fascist Party leader and has been instructed by him to abduct King Haakon and the Crown Prince, or kill them, so that Quisling can appoint himself prime minister of Norway. What some of you are not aware of is that your ship's mission is to take King Haakon, the Crown Prince and the Norwegian cabinet back to London. What you also might not know is that a British diplomat from Oslo and I have a meeting

145

scheduled for this afternoon to persuade the king and his heir to leave Norway and return with us to London."

"All this information, gentlemen, MUST go no further than you men on the bridge," said the captain. "Is that clearly understood? The crew, and other officers not on the bridge, think we are on a humanitarian mission to take several hundred people away from Norway back to England. This we will be doing, but the king and his heir are our primary concern, under orders from the British government."

"Yes, sir," they all said in unison.

"Lieutenant, I believe you should be free to successfully complete your assignment," the captain said to Artur. "Watch out for that *Fraulein* missy! Please report back later today with an update."

"Thank you, sir," Artur said, as he shook each of the officers' hands and saluted the captain. He winked at Lieutenant Hood as he left for the gangway.

Artur left the ship, walking purposefully away from the port entrance and towards the hotel where Harry Ballantyne was staying. He saw it was already after 11 o'clock. He was late and they needed to put together plans for the meeting, as well as the arguments that will help the king see that the only real option was to leave for London.

Artur went to the receptionist and asked her to tell Mr Ballantyne that he had arrived for their meeting. After a few moments, she said that Mr Ballantyne was in his room awaiting his arrival. He took the lift, but didn't need to knock as Harry was waiting for him at his open door.

"So sorry I'm late, Harry."

"No problem; good to see you again, Artur. Please come in," as Harry ushered Artur into his room and closed the door.

"I have to tell you that I went to see the king this morning and asked him if we could bring the meeting forward to 2 o'clock, to which he agreed. The reason I did it – although I didn't give the king my reason – is that if this Miss Olsen woman knows about the original time of our meeting, she is very likely to arrive soon after we would have started, and probably not on her own either.

"In addition, I spoke to the commander of those guarding their Royal Highnesses. He has found two local men that look reasonably like the royal men and we have agreed to change the meeting place. The two locals will be dressed similarly to the king and Prince Olav and they will remain in the original cabin, whereas the two royals will be moved to a new cabin further up the valley."

"That's very clever, Harry. So, the chances of Miss Olsen and her men getting at King Haakon and the prince have lessened considerably, unless someone has informed her of your change of plan."

"Exactly, Artur, but we have no way of knowing that until the time comes. I have arranged for a car to arrive here by midday, so you go in that one for Prince Olav and I'll go in mine for the king."

"Are you sure you won't be seen by Miss Olsen and her men as we move to the new location?"

"We'll have to take that risk, Artur, but remember, the commander and his troops will still be focussing on the original cabin. Once we have the two royals in the new lodge, we will return one of the cars to the original cabin."

"Have you put together your points for persuading King Haakon to leave his country, Harry?"

"You may not be aware, Artur, that the British, French and Polish armies, with the considerable support of the Norwegians, had virtually won the battle of Narvik: the Germans being on the point of surrender. However, the generals and commanders involved were told by London in late May to evacuate Norway. The Norwegian government and their commanders were not told until a couple of days ago, to their bitterness and complete disbelief. The reason given by London and Paris was that as the westward advance of the Germans into the Benelux countries and France was going at such a pace, the forces in the Norwegian campaign were needed to assist the BEF, or even defend Britain from a possible German invasion."

"I was aware of the forces' withdrawal, but not the details. So, we might be given a rather hostile reception when we meet King Haakon?"

"The king is a very confident and calm man, who has already turned down the German demands in April 1940. He has been greatly admired for his stance, but he is 67 years old and not in the best of health. To persuade their Royal Highnesses to leave will be against the king's better judgement and his preferred solution. He will, however, understand our argument and see that it really is the only sensible way forward."

"So, you have worked out how to persuade them?" Artur asked. "Once they have agreed, when will we take them all on board our ship?"

"He will need to tell the cabinet of his decision and this will be in the form of a letter signed by the king. I will be authorised to deliver the letter to the cabinet's hideout which is in a large house in the centre of Tromsø. You will stay with King Haakon and Olav until I return with their signed reply of the agreement. It is really just a formality as all the cabinet members are known to be right behind whatever the king decides to do for the best of his country and his people."

"If the military are at the original cabin, who will be protecting the one further up the valley?"

"Look, Artur, the commander knows what we are doing, so he will allocate sufficient troops near both cabins," Harry said rather impatiently.

"What intelligence do we have about Miss Olsen's whereabouts and do we have any idea what she is going to do? She's not likely to run at the cabin singlehanded and fire shots at the people inside, is she?" Artur stated. "We are, after all, in a state of war, with the Germans hard on our heels. We have to allow for the unexpected at all times. Hitler's henchmen have their desires on taking over Norway, so if they can get Helena and some of Quisling's supporters to spoil our party, they will certainly do it today, and at a time when we least expect it, don't you think?"

"I do agree with you, Artur, but what do you suggest we do in addition to what we already have planned?" said Harry rather fiercely.

"I reckon we go as soon as possible. We don't ask the king about what he wants to do, but tell him, firmly, that to leave for Britain is the only way out of the situation. Have you got a pistol, Harry? We ought to smuggle them out of their hideaway and bring them back here."

"I don't have a gun of any sort, Artur, but I think your idea is the best. It's long after midday so let's get moving."

Artur took out his pistol from his kitbag and put it into his right-hand jacket pocket. They left the hotel and went to where Harry's car was parked.

"Give me the keys, Harry, and I'll drive. We'll leave the other car here just in case it's needed later, we don't need to take it to the cabins."

Artur took his pistol out of his pocket, cocked it and placed it on the seat between his legs, once he was in the car. They drove towards the valley and Artur told Harry to look out for anything suspicious. Harry just remembered in time to tell Artur to take a road to the right after about ten minutes of driving out of the town. They travelled for a further twenty minutes and the road became a lot narrower.

"How far now, Harry?"

"About another ten minutes. There's the original cabin to our right. I can just make out the commander in the light wooded area to the right of the cabin."

"I'm going to stop and have a word with him," said Artur, as he brought the car to a halt and ran in a crouched position away from the back of the cabin. The commander saw him coming and walked in a crouched fashion towards him, looking left and right as he came forward.

"We've changed our plan," Artur said. "We're going to take the king and the prince by car back to the hotel in town. We need you and your men to cover the car as we return from the cabin up there," Artur said, as he pointed up the road. "We expect Miss Olsen and some of Quisling's men to see us and to try and stop us, probably by firing at the car. You must at all costs do whatever you need to do to give us safe passage. Is that understood?"

"Yes, sir," said the commander, as he saluted Artur.

"This mission has to be successful and Their Royal Highnesses need to be protected."

"I understand, sir. We will do whatever is required."

Artur ran back to the car and continued driving up the road. He turned the car around in front of the cabin and told Harry to go inside to tell the king of the plan. He then followed a few moments later inside, once he had carefully surveyed the nearby area. He heard Harry ask the king and the prince to follow him and Artur to the car.

"Your Highnesses," said Artur. "It's of the utmost importance, and for your safety, that we leave here without further delay as there is a distinct possibility you might be abducted or even killed by some of Quisling's men and a German woman, who is working for Quisling with Hitler's agreement."

The king and the prince looked at each other, spoke a few words and nodded in agreement. They had some suitcases that they said they wanted to take with them, so Harry carried them to the car and placed them in the boot. Artur told the two men to take the back seats. The prince was to be in the well in front of the rear seat and the king on the back seat, both of them covered with the blankets that Harry gave them.

"I'm very sorry for any discomfort, your Highnesses, but we can't be too careful," Artur said in Danish rather slowly, as he closed the car doors."

They set off at some speed, but Artur found he had to slow every now and again, as the road was rather rutted. As they arrived at the original cabin, Artur was aware of movement in the light wooded area to his right. *The commander and his men are on the other side of the road*, he muttered to himself. *Those over there must be Quisling's lot.* He told Harry to get down in the passenger seat's well and to wind down the window in case he needed to open fire. He kept moving his head from the road in front and over to his right, trying to take in the situation.

Just as he returned looking at the road ahead, there was gunfire. He saw six men running from behind the trees to the right, firing over the top of the car. He heard gunfire coming from the commander's troops on the left; the car was almost caught in the middle.

Artur turned the steering wheel so that the car had its rear facing Quisling's men. He saw some of them fall as they were hit by the commander's snipers. He then noticed a woman – dressed in a khaki uniform – running towards the car followed by the last two remaining men. Artur got out of the car, hid in front of the bonnet, raised his pistol and held it until Helena was only about twenty paces from the car. She was brandishing a gun – probably the one he found in her cabin – but was not firing it. Artur felt she would have thought the king was in the cabin, not the car, and that her preferred solution was to take him alive.

Artur took in a deep breath, held it and fired two shots at Helena. She fell and didn't appear to move. He saw the two men throw themselves to the ground when they saw Helena fall. He thought one of them had a semi-automatic submachine gun, like a *Schmeisser*: a very powerful and accurate rifle. They were about thirty yards apart from each other and nearly forty yards from the cabin. They were partly obscured by the long grass. One of the men fired at the cabin.

Artur waited a few moments in case any more men came out from the trees. There was more firing from the commander's men that had moved further up from the cabin and the man nearer to Artur was hit. That just left the one with the submachine gun. There was a boulder not far from Artur that would bring him about twenty yards nearer to the last of the enemy. He ran as fast as he could in a crouched position, weaving left and right, hoping not to be hit. Gunfire came in short bursts, but he was not struck. He reached the boulder and got his breath back. The man with the semi-automatic knew he was on his own. Artur thought the man wouldn't chance going for the cabin, but would probably try and make a run for it back to the wooded area as he was heavily outnumbered. This he did, turning every now and again to fire rounds at Artur, but he only hit the boulder. As Artur got up to run after him, a splinter of rock thumped against his leg. He looked down, quickly pulled up his trouser leg and saw blood. He had to go on regardless. Just before the man entered the woods, Artur stopped, knelt on one knee, took aim and fired his remaining rounds. The man went down. By this time, two of the commander's men had crossed the road and were now close to the man that had fallen near to the car.

Artur put his pistol in his pocket and went back to Helena. He felt her pulse: nothing. He looked at her and thought she had been brave, but a bit foolish. He closed her eye lids and stood up.

"Well done, Lieutenant. I think you can safely drive back to the hotel now," the commander said, as he arrived at the scene.

"Together, we seem to have got the job done," Artur commented, "but I don't think we've seen the end of Quisling's men seeking out the king. I strongly believe there were one or two more men in the woods that didn't join in the battle. They will doubtless report back to their seniors and explain what had happened. They'll have another attempt later, I'm sure."

"Don't worry about them; me and my men will be around until the king is on your ship. Meanwhile, I will deal with all the bodies, Lieutenant. What do you want me to do with the woman?"

"Get someone to take a photo of her and tell the editor of the national newspapers to write an article describing how close Norway came to losing their king and crown prince. Mr Ballantyne will assist you, but you must not mention my name."

Artur looked at the car and saw the king looking out from the opened back door. It looked as though he was smiling. He said something to Artur, but he didn't quite hear what he said. He went to the car and asked the king to hand him one of the blankets. He returned to Helena and placed the blanket over her. He went back to the car and noticed that Harry hadn't moved during the whole exchange.

"I'm not a military man, Artur. I have to admit that I was terrified we might lose the king."

"Don't worry, Harry. Everything so far seems to have worked out OK. I have told the commander to contact you to submit a report for the national papers, but not to mention my name."

"I will do that with a great deal of pleasure, Artur. Thank you."

Artur drove away, as he waved at the commander and his men. The king and the prince were asked to remain hidden in the back until they were at the hotel.

Chapter 19

Thursday, 6ᵗʰ June 1940

Artur parked the car in front of the hotel's main entrance. The king and the prince were now sitting on the back seat. Harry jumped out and opened the rear door. As they all walked into the hotel lobby, the receptionist immediately recognised the king and jumped into a standing position.

"Your Royal Highnesses, welcome to our hotel."

"Please give the king and the prince two of your very best rooms," Artur said. "They have had a rather exciting time and will want to freshen up. If anyone comes here asking if the king is in the hotel, contact Mr Ballantyne in his room immediately."

Harry came in with three suitcases. He took the room keys from the receptionist, who ushered the men to the lift. On the way up to the top floor, Artur asked if they would be ready for a meeting – that should have been at the cabin – by 5 o'clock, as he looked at his watch. They agreed to meet in the king's room at the time suggested; they all would have enough time to prepare. Harry and Artur returned to Harry's room on the second floor and immediately got to work on their case for the king's departure from Norway.

"There's blood running down your sock and onto the floor, Artur. Don't you think it should be attended to? I've got some plasters in the bathroom." Without waiting for a reply, Harry fetched them, together with a damp towel. Artur took off his shoe and sock and attended to the wound.

"It looks like a deep cut, Artur. Should I call a doctor?"

"No, Harry. I'll be fine, thank you." Artur dabbed the wound with the damp part of the towel and attached a few of the plasters.

"There we are, all better now," Artur replied, knowing the injury was quite bad.

They talked through the points that they would be discussing with the king and the prince. They reckoned that the incident at the lodge – with men trying to kill them all or kidnap their highnesses – might work in their favour, or at least they hoped so.

"It's nearly 5 o'clock, Harry," said Artur, as he carefully put his blooded sock on and his shoe. He picked up the few papers that they had scribbled notes on and left Harry's room for the lift. They knocked on the king's door.

"Come in," said the recognisable voice of the king, in Norwegian. "The door's unlocked."

"Forgive me for saying so, your Highness," said Artur, as they went into the king's room, "but I think we would be happier if you kept your door locked, especially when you are in the room."

The king didn't reply, but pointed to two chairs near to a table. They sat down once the king and the prince had taken their seats. The king opened the meeting and Artur was a bit surprised at his attitude towards England. He did, however, thank them for organising the rescue operation from the hut and for bringing them safely to the hotel. He expressed in no uncertain terms, his complete surprise and dismay at the allied forces withdrawal from Norway, especially without having spoken to him and his cabinet first.

"I understand your position, your Highness, but the British and French governments were looking at the bigger picture. With the rapid advance of the Nazi forces through the Benelux countries and their forcing the BEF to evacuate through Dunkirk, they saw no other option."

"But we and the allies were so close to defeating the Germans in Narvik. Withdrawing at this stage means the men we lost was for nothing."

"Once again, I understand how you feel, sir, but the German forces would have overpowered the allied forces in Norway before too long. We are now more concerned with you and the prince," Harry remarked. "As you probably realise, it is very likely that France will capitulate and this leaves Britain on its own to face the Nazi war machine. Most of the other countries' governments and royal households have decided to accept the British government's offer of exile in London. I would strongly recommend that you follow suit."

Discussions went on for a further three quarters of an hour, after which the king raised his right hand to halt any further talking. He asked Harry and Artur to leave his room and come back at 7 o'clock, at which point they will give them their decision.

Harry and Artur went down to the restaurant on the first floor and bought some refreshments, which they took to a table in the corner.

"How's your leg, Artur? Shouldn't you have it looked at? The wound might contain some stone fragments that will turn it sceptic?"

"Harry, I thank you for your concern, but it isn't throbbing and it's stopped bleeding," he lied. "What concerns me more is getting their Royal Highnesses back to the ship, assuming they make the decision to go into exile. Presumably you know where the cabinet members are located?"

"They are in a house not far from here, Artur. We should be able to get a message back to the ship by 8:30 p.m. at the very latest, with any luck."

"What will you do, Harry, once we're all on board? Are you expecting to leave for London with the rest of us?"

"My instructions are to see the royal pair safely to England, so I will accompany you all."

They talked for some while and Artur looked at his watch.

"It's coming up to zero hour, Harry. We had better go to the king's room and hear his decision."

They took the lift to the top floor and knocked on the king's room's door. They heard someone come to the door and unlock it.

"It looks as though they've taken our suggestion seriously," Artur said to Harry in a whisper and with a smile.

They went in and the door was locked behind them. All except the king sat around the table. He thanked Artur and Harry once again for helping them to safety and from Quisling's men. He wasted no time in coming to the point of the meeting. He told them that it was with great sadness that he felt his cabinet and his son should leave Norway and go into exile in England. He, on the other hand, would remain in his country, build up a resistance group and work with his countrymen to fight against the German invasion. Harry spoke very courteously, but firmly to the king as he paced slowly around the room:

"In no way am I here to change your mind, Your Highness, if that's your final decision. I would graciously point out to you, however, that the British Government – via the embassy in Oslo – has received a message from Crown Princess Märtha, who, as you know, has been staying with her relatives in Sweden since early April. She expressly implores you and the Crown Prince to take up the offer of exile in London. The offer not only comes from Mr Churchill and his cabinet, but also from your relative, King George. She says that for you to remain behind and fight with your countrymen would, in her eyes, and in her words, be very foolish. The managing of a resistance movement can be done just as well, if not more effectively, from London."

"Well, what do you think, Olav?" said the king. "Is the princess being persuasive enough for us to agree to leave our beloved country and let it be ravaged by the German war machine?"

"I believe she has put forward a strong enough argument in favour of our going to England."

The king shrugged his shoulders and sat down. He felt resigned to leaving the country he loved. He took out his pen and wrote two separate notes on the paper in front of him.

"Mr Ballantyne, please arrange for this letter to be taken to the house where the cabinet ministers are staying as soon as possible. I have asked them to agree to our decision and told them to be ready to board the ship, that is moored in the harbour, at 10:30 a.m. tomorrow. This second letter is for Lieutenant Selmer to take to the captain of the ship, requesting his permission to allow us on board and for him and his crew to take us to England. He should also send a message to Mr Churchill thanking him for offering us exile in London, and we are very pleased to accept his hospitality."

"It will be a pleasure to carry out your wishes, your Highness," Harry said, with a great deal of relief.

Harry and Artur got to their feet and told the king that the letters would be dispatched without delay. Harry told them that, even though the decision had been a very difficult one, they had come to the right conclusion.

Harry told Artur that he hoped to be back in his room shortly after 8 o'clock, at which time they should have a drink and something light to eat. He would order it all after he returns from presenting the letter to the cabinet and returning with their acceptance of the king's decision.

Harry left the hotel for the cabinet's house and Artur walked briskly off to the harbour entrance. He showed his papers and was allowed to proceed to the ship. He went straight to the bridge and was pleased to find only the captain and his Number 2 present. He saluted and handed over the letter. He waited for a response.

"That's good work, Lieutenant. I'm sure it wasn't an easy exercise? Do you think the king needs a written reply or will your word be sufficient?"

"If you are happy for me to tell the king that all will be ready for their arrival at around 10:30 a.m. tomorrow and that you and the crew will be honoured to take them to England, that will be fine by him."

"Then please do so, Lieutenant. Once again, well done."

"Thank you, sir. I will write my report on today's events and present it to you sometime during tomorrow morning, if that's alright with you?"

Artur thought he should go through a short summary of what happened at the cabins and how he really had had no choice but to shoot Miss Olsen. He then left the bridge and went to his cabin. He picked up the small bottle of dry sherry and put it into his pocket. *I think some of this nectar will be just the ticket for this evening,* he muttered to himself. *What a pity it isn't aquavit and that it's ice cold.*

When Artur reached the hotel reception, he asked if Mr Ballantyne had returned.

"Not yet, Lieutenant. He did ring and leave a message for you."

She passed the piece of paper over and Artur read that Harry would be back by 9 o'clock. He noticed it would be about another half an hour before he was expected. He found the receptionist very attractive, so he thought he would spend the time talking to her. She said she was a local girl and that her elder brother was in the army, stationed in Trondheim. She lived with her mother, her father having died a few years ago. She didn't have a boyfriend, as most of the men of her age had joined the army to defend their country from being overrun by the Germans.

"What time do you go off duty, Hansine? They surely don't expect you to work all night?"

"It has been difficult for the management to find staff during these troublesome times, so I have to work longer hours. In any case, we are not exactly busy at present."

Hansine's English was very good, as it is with most Scandinavians, so Artur thought there was no point in speaking Danish to her.

"Don't you take a break at any time or are you here throughout the night?"

"I'm allowed to stop for an hour at 10 o'clock, as that's usually the quietest time. I go to the kitchen to find some refreshments and chat to the few staff that are still around."

Just at that moment, Harry came through the main door and walked up to Artur, who was leaning on the reception counter, staring into Hansine's eyes.

"I have the signed response from the cabinet ministers, so I shall need to go straight up to the king's room," he told Artur. He turned to Hansine and asked her to phone the king to tell him that they were on their way up to speak to him. Hansine did as she was asked and she told them to go straight up. Artur felt disappointed not being able to speak to Hansine for longer, but he knew he had a very important job to do. They took the lift and knocked on the door.

"Just a minute," said the king, as he unlocked the door. He ushered them inside and locked the door behind them. Harry gave the cabinet's letter to the king, who read it quickly and smiled.

"Ever since they gave me the absolute right to make decisions concerning my country, I expected nothing more than their full agreement to leave Norway and go into exile in London. And what news from you, Lieutenant?"

Artur repeated exactly what the captain had said and hoped the king wouldn't need a formal message.

The king smiled at Olav and shook Harry and Artur's hands.

"Everything now seems to be arranged. If you wouldn't mind, gentlemen, I'm in need of some rest after today's excitement. If there's nothing else to discuss, I thank you once again for all that you've done for me and Prince Olav today. I would be obliged if you would leave us. We look forward to seeing you again in the morning just before 10:30 a.m., if that's still to be the arrangement?"

"That will be perfect timing, Your Highness. We hope you have a good rest tonight," Harry replied.

They all shook hands, leaving the king and the prince in the king's room.

"Are you going to stay the night at the hotel, Artur, or should you get back to your ship?" Harry enquired as they went down the stairs to his room.

"If you don't mind, Harry, I ought to get back to my cabin and write up my report while everything is fresh in my mind. I had brought some sherry to share with you, but perhaps I'll keep it until we have set sail tomorrow. By the way, did you say earlier that you have arranged for a bus to take the Norwegian cabinet to the harbour tomorrow?"

"Yes, that's all arranged. They know they will be collected from their house at 10 o'clock."

"Excellent. Good night, Harry. I'll come here at 10:15 a.m. I just need to collect my kitbag from your room."

Artur went down to reception and gave a big smile and a wink to Hansine, as he said 'good night'. He thought he noticed in the dim light that she blushed just a little, but he had run out of time to pursue her acquaintance any further.

Chapter 20
Friday, 7ᵗʰ June 1940

Artur had spent an hour writing some notes on the events so far before he took to his bunk. He was well pleased with himself for his commitment, instead of going straight to bed on his arrival back on board the ship. Before turning in, he had another look at his wound as it was beginning to throb again. He thought it ought to have some attention from the ship's medic in the morning.

He rose at 6:30 a.m. feeling very satisfied with the previous day's accomplishments. He quickly completed his ablutions and went to the officers' mess for some refreshments.

"Did you manage to tuck the king up safely in bed before you got back to the ship last night, Lieutenant?" said the ship's Number 2, with a smile on his face, looking around and ensuring nobody else heard what he had said.

"No, I left that pleasant task to the Crown Prince. I hope nobody paid them a visit in the night, especially from any of Quisling's mob," Artur replied, in a more serious tone.

"So, what's the next step?" the ship's Number 2 asked, rather surprisingly, Artur thought.

"I'll need to speak to the captain first, if you'll pardon my saying, sir."

"I quite understand, Lieutenant."

Artur finished his food, excused himself for leaving the officers, saluted and left the mess. Before going to the bridge, he thought it best to have his wound looked at by the ship's doctor.

"Hello, doc," he said, in a very informal manner, as he went into his surgery. "A tiny bit of stone has scratched my ankle during yesterday's skirmishes in Tromsø. I'm sure it's alright, but the captain thought you ought to take a look at it," Artur said, trying to play the whole thing down.

Artur sat down, took off his shoe and sock for the doctor to examine the wound.

"That's quite nasty," he said as he put Artur's leg on another chair so he could get a better look at it. He went to a cupboard above the sink and took out some cotton wool and a bottle of iodine. He carefully examined the two-inch long cut.

"Look at this, Lieutenant," as he showed Artur the minute stone particles to him on the cotton wool. "If you had come to me a day or two later, the wound would have become very sceptic. You could have been completely unable to exercise your duties for a number of weeks."

The doctor finished cleaning the wound, dabbed on the iodine, placed a lint gauze over the leg and wound a bandage around his ankle.

"How's does that feel?" as Artur stood up.

"Very much better already, doc. Thank you very much indeed."

"Hopefully, I've been able to get all the pieces out of the wound. Just remember to come back to me in two days to have another look and change the dressing. In the meantime, if it should start throbbing or it swells up, come and see me straightaway."

"Will do, doc. Thanks again."

He shook the doctor's hand, trying not to limp as he left his surgery. He went straight to the bridge. He wasn't sure if the captain would be there, but he hoped he would be.

"Good morning, sir," as Artur saluted the captain.

"Good to see you, Lieutenant. You are aware, are you not, that we plan to leave Tromsø harbour by 2 o'clock this afternoon, just as the tide is turning? You have made their highnesses aware of our departure time too, I trust?"

"Not yet, sir, but they will be ready to leave the hotel by 10:30 a.m. this morning. We will be bringing them directly to the port by car. The cabinet members will be coming by bus at about the same time. I assume their highnesses cabins have been prepared for their arrival?"

"Don't fret, Lieutenant, everything is ready. The cabinet members will have to squeeze into one of the seamen's quarters that can accommodate twelve men. As you will recall, we will also be taking a few hundred Norwegian and other nationalities as well. It could be a tight fit, but they are already on board sorting themselves out."

"I wasn't aware we had to take all those extra people, sir. A good humanitarian gesture by the Royal Navy, I would say," he said, with a wry smile.

"You may also not be aware that the British and allied forces have been evacuated from Narvik over the last two weeks. That operation is due to be completed by Saturday at the latest. Our tour of duty in Norway will very soon be over for the time being, leaving the country to be overrun by the Nazis.

"There is an RNVR captain here in Tromsø. He speaks fluent Norwegian and he is well-known to the king. He has told me that he will be meeting the king this morning to discuss certain things with him: most particularly the last remaining amounts of Norwegian gold reserves that we've been asked to take to England."

"My goodness, sir. Is it really necessary for it to leave Norway or is his highness worried it might fall into the Germans' hands?"

"That's precisely the case, Lieutenant. Most of it left Tromsø for England nearly two weeks ago, apparently having been brought here via a very circuitous route from Oslo, hotly pursued by the Germans. Three Royal Navy cruisers rescued the gold under extremely arduous conditions. They were attacked here in this port and by the Luftwaffe as they travelled south along the Norwegian coast. Thankfully they escaped any serious damage, arriving safely at a number of different English ports. The remainder will go with the king, once it is transferred from a bank in Tromsø. I expect the naval officer to come to my ship very soon to tell me when the bullion will be delivered here. He has arranged for all the paperwork and we will have it craned on board. Nobody, other than the admiral, myself and you, is aware of what the load contains. The officer will ensure everything is signed by me and he will return all documents to the king."

"Do you think Quisling or any of his supporters will know what is to happen with the last of Norway's gold?"

"We must assume that it is highly likely. Because of what it is, and the fact that the Germans were already thwarted last month, we will be on full alert at the time of its embarkation. About ten of the king's loyal army guards – plus those men that defended the cabins, will be involved. An armoured vehicle carrying the gold will be accompanied by the king's guards. The other men will be discretely situated on the quay in case of any trouble. We have put together a plan that is as full-proof as possible, but we cannot be too careful. We are planning for the king and his group to already be on board before the gold arrives."

At that moment, one of the junior officers came onto the bridge and told the captain that the RNVR captain was on the quayside and was requesting permission to come on board.

"Show him to my quarters, Lieutenant. I will be there in two minutes."

The officer saluted and left the bridge.

"Do you want me to join you, Captain, or shall I go to my cabin?"

"If it's alright with you, I'll deal with this matter on my own. Should I need your help, I'll ask someone to fetch you."

"Fine by me, sir. Before you leave, I have prepared my report of yesterday's events." The captain took the papers. They both saluted and left the bridge.

Artur had plenty to think about in his cabin, so he went through his notes for Charles covering the last few days. His mind drifted to Helena and how close he had come to being drawn into her web of attraction. He wondered why she was part of the *Abwehr* or was she just someone that Quisling trusted and perhaps paid her for her services?

Artur looked at his watch; he was surprised to see it was after 9 o'clock. He thought he should leave the ship and wander around the town. He contacted the ship's Number 2 and asked him to tell the captain that he'd left the ship. He strolled past the hotel and into the bar that he and Harry had been in the day before. He ordered a beer in his best Danish and sat at a table near the window. He sipped his drink and thought through the alternatives of what might happen during the rest of the day. He looked out to the road. He was suddenly aware of four trucks driving past towards the port with about four soldiers in each. *Two must be going to the bank for the gold, the other two to the quay to protect the loading operation,* he said to himself. After some minutes, another two vehicles went past in the same direction, but going more quickly than the previous four. He downed his drink, thanked the barman and went into the street. The road went around to the left so he was too late to see any of the trucks. He ran across the road and could just make out in the distance two vehicles waiting at the port's entrance barrier. He reckoned they contained the men that defended the cabins the previous day, but he couldn't be sure.

He decided to go to Harry's hotel and tell him what he thought was going on. He went to reception and the same attractive lady was on duty.

"Please could you tell me if Mr Ballantyne is in his room?" he said slowly in his best Danish with a smile.

"I'm afraid he isn't, sir. He said he would be back by 10 o'clock; he didn't say where he went."

"By any chance, is the king in his rooms?"

"No, sir, all three went out together."

"As it happens, they weren't expecting me till 10:15 a.m. I'll come back later. Thank you."

He went outside and decided to walk back to the port to see what was going on – he had nearly three quarters of an hour to kill. He passed a road to his left and he just caught a glimpse, about a quarter of a mile away, of two trucks waiting to turn in through what appeared to be a metal gate. *Probably the entrance to the side of the bank where the bullion is to be collected from,* he mumbled to himself. He stopped to watch what he thought must be a security guard talking to the driver and looking at his papers. After a few minutes, the vehicles were ushered through the gates.

The guard closed them and seemed to walk through a side gate to follow the trucks.

Artur walked on to the port gate – he spoke to the guard:

"Hello," he said, as he showed his papers. "Have any trucks come through here in the last ten minutes?"

"Yes, sir," replied the guard, "Two trucks have been given permission to enter the port. They asked to be allowed to park opposite the large British ship further up the quay, but behind equipment and near the crane."

So, what is going on here? Artur asked himself. *Where have the other two trucks gone to?*

Arthur was not happy with the situation. He thought some of Quisling's men must be around somewhere. They will either try to steal the bullion or abduct the king and his heir, or both. He knew he had to alert the captain with the latest information. He went on board and straight to the captain's quarters: he wasn't there. He went to the bridge: he wasn't there either. He decided to look in the officers' mess, at least he could ask his whereabouts if he were not there.

"Excuse me," he said, to the ship's Number 2. Do you know where I can find the captain as I need to talk to him urgently?" Artur asked, as he looked around the mess.

"He went with the RNVR captain somewhere on the ship, but that was about twenty minutes ago. Could I be of any assistance, Lieutenant?"

Artur was just about to brief him of his concerns when the captain entered the mess, alone. He went up to him, whispering in his ear. He needed to tell him about his concern with the activity of all the trucks in Tromsø and on the quay.

"Shall we go to my quarters, Lieutenant; it's difficult to hear above all the chat in here; it would be more private too."

They arrived in the captain's quarters after some five minutes.

"So, Lieutenant, tell me what's on your mind."

Artur went through everything that happened from the time he left the ship up to when he returned to the quay. He also gave his theory about the other two trucks.

"I'm not surprised you have arrived at that conclusion, Lieutenant, especially with your experience of the Service. The RNVR captain told me that he would be amazed if Quisling's men didn't try to steal the gold. We all shall have to be extremely vigilant over the next few hours."

"Sir, I am pleased to have had a chance to tell you what I think, but you will have to excuse me; I must now return to Mr Ballantyne's hotel as we are due to bring the king to your ship," as he looked at his watch.

"You are excused, Lieutenant. Do take special care." He thought Artur seemed to be rather on edge and not as self-assured as usual.

They saluted each other. Artur decided to go to his cabin first to fetch his pistol – just in case.

He arrived at the hotel, having run most of the way: it was just after 10:15 a.m. The receptionist told him that Mr Ballantyne was in the king's rooms and that he was to go up as soon as he arrived. She said she would tell them that he was on his way. As he knocked on the door, he heard it being unlocked. He entered, bowed to the king and the crown prince and shook Harry's hand. Without any preliminaries, he told them all about the trucks and his theory concerning the two that probably contained some of Quisling's men.

"It doesn't surprise me in the slightest," remarked the king. "They've been trying to get their hands on it all for a number of weeks. They are very likely going to try to steal it as it is being loaded onto the ship. I suggest we go straight away to the port so that we're aboard before the action starts."

They all agreed. Artur picked up two of the king's cases, Harry took the third one. They arranged to meet in the lobby as Harry needed to go to his room before leaving the hotel. After a few minutes, Harry arrived and they all thanked the receptionist for her help. Once outside, they put the luggage in the car's boot. The king and the prince sat in the back. Artur told Harry that he would drive.

"Should we go to the bank first or direct to the harbour entrance?" Harry asked.

"Straight to the port, please," said the voice of the king from the back.

Artur had a sneaking suspicion that they might be apprehended before too long by the men in the other two trucks. Before he set off, he took out his pistol, cocked it and placed it on the seat between his legs. He glanced in the mirror and told the king and the crown prince to keep their heads down. He told Harry to keep his eyes skinned. He drove them up the road at a steady speed.

Chapter 21
Friday, 7th June 1940

Artur drove up to the barrier just as the guard was coming out of the pill box. He noticed that he was a different man from the one he had spoken to only an hour earlier, but had seen him the day before.

"Can I see your papers," asked the guard, as he saluted and looked into the back of the car.

"Don't you recognise me from yesterday?" said Artur in a rather abrupt manner, knowing full well that he wouldn't. He showed him his papers, but he didn't let the guard take them from him.

"Sir, I need to check your name against the register and the names of the others in the car."

"Come on, I know you have a job to do, but I need to get these men on board that ship by 11 o'clock and it's nearly that time now," replied Artur as he pointed to the ship further down the quay.

Just at that moment, Artur saw two trucks in the rear-view mirror, travelling fast towards them. He put the car in gear and drove as fast as he could at the barrier. He warned his passengers to get their heads down as the wooden fragments flew over the windscreen, and not into it. He drove very quickly towards the gangway. He noticed to his left that men were coming out from behind the base of the crane, running and firing at the trucks that were pursuing the car. The leading truck's front tyres were hit and the driver lost control as it veered to the left and then the right. The truck flew into the air and landed on its roof, scattering the soldiers in the back out onto the ground.

Artur brought the car to a halt. He and Harry jumped out, opened the rear doors and dragged the king and the crown prince rather unceremoniously up the gangway and onto the ship. Some men had been watching the incident and were quickly on hand to lead the two men and Harry away to safety. Artur ran back down to the car, retrieved his pistol from the front seat and squatted by the car's front wing. The second truck had stopped to attend to some of the wounded from the first one, but they were prevented from doing much as they were being shot at by the group led by the commander that had been involved in the cabin attack.

"Put your hands up or we'll shoot all of you," shouted the commander, as his group came to a standstill some twenty-five yards from the upturned truck, with their rifles at the ready.

Artur walked towards the upturned truck. He saw three men behind the truck – out of sight of the commander – preparing to run around and attack the commander's group. He raised his pistol and fired at the leading man, then at the second one. They both fell to the ground and didn't move. The third man immediately dropped his rifle, raised his hands and walked around in view of the commander.

"Good work, Lieutenant."

The commander walked over to the men on the ground and prodded them. Out of the ten men in the trucks – including the two drivers – five were dead, three were badly injured and two stood with their hands raised.

"Take these two back to our truck," the commander ordered his two leading men. "Bring over our other truck, put the dead and injured in the back and take them to the hospital," he instructed the rest of his group. "Be careful that the injured ones and the other two don't try any funny business. Remember, we are at war; they are the enemy of the state, they will be tried for treason."

Once the trucks had left the quayside, the commander accompanied Artur to the gangway.

"Permission for the commander to come on board?" Artur asked the two officers that had come down onto the quay.

"Permission granted, Lieutenant. A very satisfactory outcome, I would say."

The two walked up onto the ship to be greeted by the captain, his Number 2 and a few other officers that had been watching the exchange.

"Good work, gentlemen. Hopefully we won't get any further interference when the gold arrives. I trust you will be remaining on the quay to await its arrival, Commander?" the captain asked.

"Indeed I shall, Sir. Do you have an ETA?"

"Not exactly," replied the captain as he looked at his watch. "It's nearly 11:30 a.m. so I would expect it to be on the quay quite shortly."

"In that case, is it possible to see the king?" Artur asked.

"Of course, Lieutenant. He is with the admiral. You may not know it, but their royal highnesses will be using my quarters until we reach Britain."

"Before I do, there is some luggage belonging to them in the boot of the car, so I ought to get it, sir."

"Go with the lieutenant to get the luggage," the captain ordered a couple of seamen that were standing nearby.

Artur and the two men collected the three bags, brought them up on deck and followed the captain to his quarters. He knocked and was told to enter by Harry, who had been with the king during the time of the fighting on the quay.

"I understand you were apprehended by a few of Quisling's supporters, Lieutenant?" the king said to Artur. "I hope none of our men was injured?" he said to the commander.

"No, Your Highness; we escaped unscathed, I'm pleased to report. Mission accomplished."

"That's excellent news, isn't it, Olav?"

They all shook hands and smiled at each other.

"Do you think this calls for a celebration, Your Highness?"

"I think that would be a little premature, Captain. We ought to wait until the gold has been safely stowed and we are on our way to England," Artur retorted.

"Some of my men have taken all Quisling's lot away from the quay in our trucks. They will be joining the remainder of my group before the gold arrives," the commander reported. "Hopefully, we can expect an easier entry to the quay than you did, Your Highness."

The men talked amongst themselves for a short while. There was then a knock on the door. A junior officer came into the room and addressed the captain as he saluted:

"Sir, I am told to report that two trucks are at the port's entrance and wish to come onto the quay."

"Lieutenant," the captain said to Artur, "would you go to the port entrance and give the truck drivers permission to enter. Commander, I think it would be prudent if you went with Artur in case any difficulties should arise,"

"Of course, sir." The two men bowed to the king, saluted the officers and left with the junior officer. Once down on the quay, Artur decided to move the car so that the trucks would have better access to the ship. He sent the commander over to the crane, where the driver was waiting for instructions to move towards the ship. After he had parked the car, he went to the port entrance. He spoke to the drivers of the two trucks and asked for the papers detailing the amount of gold they had.

"Did you encounter any problems?" Artur asked the driver of the first truck, slowly in Danish.

"No sir, everything was very straightforward, thank you," the driver replied in Norwegian.

Artur took the papers and spoke slowly to the port's guard in Danish. He explained that the ship's captain was expecting the crates and that he would be signing the papers on his behalf. That done, the trucks drove up to the gangway where the crane had already been positioned. Artur ran up the gangway and presented the papers to the ship's Number 2 who was waiting on deck.

"These papers show the details of the consignment that is to be placed in the hold, near the aft end of the ship. Is everything ready?"

"Yes, Lieutenant, we are ready to receive it."

Artur saluted and returned to the quay, giving the thumbs up to the crane driver. After twenty minutes, the job had been completed. The papers were signed by the Number 2 and a copy was given to Artur to give back to the first truck driver, who in turn would take it to the bank.

"It's been a pleasure working with you, Lieutenant," the commander remarked as they shook hands. "I wish you and all those on board a safe trip back to England. We look forward to the time when the Nazis will have been beaten and our royal family can return safely to our country."

"It might be some time before that can happen; your job in the resistance is far from over. You can rest assured, however, that the free world will do its level best to keep the war as short as possible," Artur replied.

"You may not know it, but our ship will leave the port at 2 o'clock this afternoon. I would like to suggest that you allow a few of your men to be near the port entrance and not let any vehicles in until we have left the harbour. I'm sure word will get back to Quisling's men that they were unsuccessful in capturing either the gold or the king. They might very well try to spring a surprise at any time before our departure."

"I quite understand, Lieutenant. The thought had also crossed my mind. We will keep a platoon of men in or near the port, but we can't prevent the Luftwaffe from having a go."

"Thank you, Commander. Our ship's guns will take care of any Nazi planes," Artur said with a smile as they shook hands and saluted.

Artur waited as the commander marched towards his leading truck where he climbed into the passenger seat. All the trucks left through the port's main gate, leaving the upturned ones belonging to Quisling's men behind them. They disappeared out of sight as Artur reflected on what they all might be involved in next, as servants of their king and country.

Chapter 22
Friday, 7th June 1940

At precisely 2 o'clock, the British battle-cruiser left its moorings. The harbour pilot was at the helm as the tug pulled the ship around so it was facing the port's exit. It sounded its horn making a 'whoop-whoop' noise as it eased its way out of Tromsø harbour. The escort ships were already on their way into the Norwegian Sea.

"Thank you, Captain," the ship's captain said to the pilot, as he left the bridge. "We all wish you and your people every success for the foreseeable future and the continued fight against the Nazis."

"Thank you, Captain. Take good care of our king and his cabinet. Have a safe trip to England," as he saluted all on the bridge and left to scale the ladder down to his tug that was now steaming alongside. They proceeded away from Tromsø on their way to Vanna and out into the Norwegian Sea.

"I need to tell you all," said the captain, to the few senior men on the bridge – including Artur and the admiral – "with our cargo of gold and Norwegian royalty on board, it is a top-secret mission. We are instructed by London to keep radio silence until we enter British waters. We will be on full alert; we will only pick up incoming messages. The order is to proceed at full speed once Vanna is behind us and we're in the Norwegian Sea.

"When can we expect to reach Glasgow, assuming no delays?" the captain asked the navigating officer.

After some careful reckoning, he replied:

"At a sensible speed of 28knots average – barring no mishaps, with a moderate sea – we should be in Glasgow by midday on Sunday 9th, sir."

Just at that moment, one of the junior officers came onto the bridge.

"Excuse me, Captain, gentlemen," he said, "there are three gentlemen on the starboard side of the main deck near the aft end. I think someone should go and see if they are alright."

"Thank you, Lieutenant; someone will be down shortly," the captain replied. He waited to say anything further until the officer had left the bridge.

"I expect they are the king, his son and Mr Ballantyne," said the captain. "I suggest you go and see that all is OK, Lieutenant Selmer."

Artur saluted and left the bridge. Once on the main deck, he looked to his right and saw the three men at the aft end of the ship – just as the junior officer had reported – leaning against the rail. He could see that they were staring out at the land and glancing back at the town of Tromsø.

"It must be a time of many mixed feelings for you, as your beloved country disappears from view," said Artur, as he arrived at the king's elbow.

"I'm still not sure, Lieutenant, that I should have been persuaded by the princess' words. I think I would have been able to pull an army together and fight against the German invaders," the king replied.

"But do consider, Your Highness, just how easily it has been for the Nazis to reach Trondheim with all their equipment, men and machines. I accept you would have put up a good resistance, but I suspect not for very long and all those countrymen you would lose for that cause."

"You are right, of course, Lieutenant, but it is a sad time, leaving my country and my people like this. If you don't mind, I think we should go to our quarters and take some refreshments – it's been a long, few days and I'm feeling rather tired and emotional."

"That's what I was going to suggest, Your Highness," Artur remarked, with a nod of agreement from Harry.

Artur and Harry escorted the two royals from the main deck, took them to the king's quarters and bade them a restful afternoon.

"I'm going to report back to the captain, Harry. Shall I meet you in the officer's mess in ten minutes?"

Harry agreed, as he turned to return to his cabin to freshen up. It seemed a bit strange to Artur that Harry would be using Helena's cabin. On entering the bridge, Artur saluted the captain and took him over to one side. He explained what had transpired and the captain was well pleased with the situation.

"Before you meet Mr Ballantyne in the mess, I need to explain something to you of great significance: we have recently picked up a communication from a Norwegian trawler that two convoys, including the two aircraft carriers, HMS *Ark Royal* and HMS *Glorious,* are due to set sail from Narvik with the last remaining allied troops and planes, heading for the Scapa Flow. A second message from the same source has broadcast that two of Germany's pocket battleships, the *Scharnhorst* and the *Gneisenau,* left Kiel three days ago with orders to bombard the British base near Narvik, but on hearing that the allies are withdrawing from Norway, they will now proceed to look for and intercept the convoys."

"Is it possible, sir, that we might get caught up in this battle? Is it your intention to get involved?" Artur asked.

"As I have said before, our mission is to make haste for Britain; to keep out of trouble, where possible. If necessary, our course will have to take us further out into the Norwegian Sea and well west of the Lofoten Islands where the action could take place."

"I know that will be your decision, sir, but shouldn't we be on standby to pick up any survivors from our ships, should they all engage in a battle?"

"I understand your concern and it is mine also, but unless I'm instructed otherwise, we will follow the instructions given to me and the admiral by London."

The discussion came to a halt as the captain was called away by the navigating officer. Artur thought for a moment about how the two British carriers would deal with the German battleships. After some minutes, he left the bridge to join Harry in the mess.

"Is all OK, Artur? You seemed to take rather longer than I expected?"

"Yes, fine, thank you, Harry," Artur replied, without saying anything about his chat with the captain. He found a few morsels of food, but he didn't really feel hungry; everything seemed rather tasteless and uninteresting. Harry tried speaking to Artur, but he wasn't in any mood to make conversation. After some ten minutes, Artur excused himself and went back to his cabin; Harry said he would join the Norwegian cabinet members.

I have to update Charles with today's events, he said to himself. He sat at his desk, wrote out his message and put it into a coded format. He then remembered that they were under orders from London to keep radio silence until they were in British waters. *Oh well,* he mumbled to himself, *he'll just have to wait a day or so to hear about Helena's demise, won't he,* as he placed his message inside his code book which he then put under the top end of his mattress. He looked around his cabin before leaving for the bridge.

"We're coming around the northerly part of the Vesterålen Islands," the navigating officer remarked to Artur, who had already been there for some fifteen minutes. "We will then be setting a heading that will take us between the Faroes and the Shetland Islands. That said, we should keep an eye out for a possible, and maybe an unlikely, sighting of the British convoys and the German battleships."

"Aye, aye, sir," Artur replied. "Have we received any update on their positions?"

"No, not since we picked up the second message from the Norwegian trawler." Artur took a pair of binoculars, scanned the area to port and then to the starboard side where the escorts were. He noticed the sea was getting rougher and visibility was worsening. He looked at his watch: it was nearly four hours since they left Tromsø.

"Set our speed to 26 knots, now we're nearing the open sea," the captain ordered. "Keep a keen eye out for mines and U-boats, gentlemen, as we set our heading at 230°."

"Could we not send a message to one of the escorts to be ahead of us to watch for mines, sir?" Artur asked.

"Good idea, Lieutenant. The only trouble is that they are not quite as fast as our ship when we are at full speed, but we'll keep steady at our current speed for a couple of hours. Send a message anyway. Number 2; arrange for it to be sent."

"Aye, aye, Captain," he replied and left the bridge for the main deck.

After a few minutes, Artur saw the coded Morse message being flashed using the Aldis lamp to the escort ship on the starboard side, followed not long afterwards by her reply and her gradual move ahead.

The watch had changed at 6 o'clock. Artur told the captain and the admiral that he would like permission to stay on the bridge until they returned, so he could help keeping a look out for anything – friend or foe – he was granted permission. On the ship's current heading, the ship would be taking them slightly away from the line of the Norwegian coast. Artur focussed his binoculars to the port side and ahead. He kept this up for nearly an hour without seeing anything. He hung his glasses down on his chest, rubbed his eyes and relaxed for some twenty minutes, chatting to the others on watch.

"Are you still here, Lieutenant?" the captain asked rather jovially as he returned to the bridge.

"Another half an hour then I'll find something to eat, sir," Artur replied.

"Nothing to report, I'm pleased to say," the navigating officer chipped in, "as we say 'hello' to the start of the Lofoten Islands, some 50 nautical miles to the west of us, sir."

"Send another message using the Aldis lamp to the escorts to say we will be increasing our speed to 28 knots at twenty hundred hours," the captain ordered with a glance at the admiral, who nodded in agreement.

Just after 8:00 p.m., Artur was granted leave of the bridge. He spent half an hour in the mess followed by a period of resting on his bunk in his cabin.

Chapter 23

Saturday, 8th June 1940

Artur suddenly woke up. He looked at his watch: he saw it was 6 o'clock in the morning. He sat up with a start – he couldn't believe the time. He was surprised someone hadn't been to his cabin to find out how he was. He assumed nothing untoward had happened at sea, else he would have heard the 'action stations' alarm going off. He lay back on his bunk with his hands behind his head. He thought about the possible plight of the two aircraft carriers, their convoys and whether or not they would be in danger from the two German battleships.

He got up after a while and readied himself for duty – he couldn't remember changing into his night clothes the evening before. He decided to go to the communications room before going to the bridge.

"Stand easy, gentlemen," Artur said, as most of them got to attention when he entered the room. "Just wondered if you had picked up any more messages from the Nazi battleships or the British aircraft carriers?" he said, to the leading signalman.

"It's strange you should ask that, sir. A few hours ago, we just happened to pick up a communication from HMS *Glorious* on one of our special naval frequencies. They asked command for permission to proceed to Scapa Flow from Narvik independently of HMS *Ark Royal*, citing their being low on fuel. Permission was granted to her; the destroyers, HMS *Ardent* and HMS *Acasta*, would be her escorts."

"Have you informed the captain of this?" Artur asked.

"He was briefed, sir. The captain's only comment was that we should keep our ears open for any further info."

"Was there any indication of when these ships were due to leave Narvik?"

"No, sir, but we did get the impression that *Glorious* would be leaving a good number of hours before *Ark Royal* and the rest of the fleet, but it was rather garbled, so this is only an assumption. They probably didn't want their departure time to be leaked to the Germans."

"I'll go and talk to the captain," Artur replied as he left for the bridge.

"My apologies for not being here earlier, sir," Artur said to the captain on arrival. "What progress have we made?"

"I'll let the navigating officer tell you that."

"We've been going at 30 knots since 10 o'clock last night," the officer mentioned. "We've covered just under 300 nautical miles in that time. By my reckoning, we should be passing Stornoway in less than 14 hours, making our arrival in Glasgow before midday tomorrow. Once we are within sight of the Hebrides, we will come out of radio silence. We will then contact the port authorities in Glasgow and give them an updated ETA."

"Any news about the carriers, sir?"

"Only what we've been given by the senior signalman."

The atmosphere on the bridge seemed tense: nobody saying anything, everybody thinking too much about possible dangers. They felt the situation of their ship might be vulnerable – still a long way to go too.

Artur picked up the spare binoculars, adjusted them and scanned as much of the port side that was in his field of view. He stopped, rubbed his eyes and returned to where he had last been looking.

"Sir," he said, mainly for the captain's ears, "a long way off at about eleven o'clock, I'm certain I can see something in the water. It disappears every now and then as the waves obscure it."

The captain and a few other officers, trained their glasses in the direction that Artur was pointing for a few minutes.

"Sorry, Lieutenant, I can't see anything," the navigating officer remarked. "Nor can I," the captain said.

"If I'm not mistaken, we will be that much nearer in ten to fifteen minutes' time, you'll then see what I saw," Artur explained.

Just at that moment, the leading signalman entered the bridge in rather a hurry. He saluted the captain and presented him with a piece of paper.

"Sir," he said, "we overheard a 'mayday' distress call about fifteen minutes ago. It wasn't very clear so we couldn't say if it was friend or foe. A ship appears to have been hit and was on the point of sinking, calling for assistance. We haven't replied as we're in radio silence, but I thought you ought to know, sir."

"Thanks, Dick," replied the captain as he read the message. "Were you able to get any coordinates?"

"No, sir, we weren't."

"Return to the comms room and immediately report back to the bridge if you hear anything further."

"Aye, aye, sir; will do."

"Seems as though you might well have seen something after all, Lieutenant. Everyone to keep a good look out," the captain ordered the others. "If it's not too far off our course, we'll go and give assistance."

Just at that moment, a flare went up in the direction that Artur had spotted the distant object. The captain ordered a slight change of direction, but no reduction in speed. After fifteen minutes, they all clearly saw a small life raft with the sailors waving wildly at the approaching ship. Artur looked through his glasses and said to the captain that they were waving a Norwegian flag. In next to no time, the ship had slowed right down, the nets were lowered from the railings and men were on the deck shouting at those in the raft.

"Go and give a hand, Lieutenant," the captain ordered Artur. "You might be able to make them understand what we can do for them and where we will be taking them."

Artur left the bridge for the main deck. When he reached the railings, he cupped his hands and shouted to the men in Danish. One of them, to

Artur's great surprise – probably the senior man in the raft – replied in Danish. He explained that their trawler had been attacked by a large German ship about four hours earlier. Artur told them to climb the netting and to attach the raft's ropes to the net. Six men clambered up onto the deck and shook hands with the waiting seamen. The senior man came up last, saluted Artur and thanked everyone for spotting them and rescuing them. Lastly, the raft and the net were hauled up from the sea and stowed on the aft deck.

"Are any of your men injured?" enquired Artur.

"No, sir, but four of our crew were lost at sea as our trawler sank. We are the lucky ones."

"Are you all Danish or Norwegians?" asked Artur, as he told them to follow him to the lower deck where they would be given hammocks and something to eat.

"I am Danish, but the other six are Norwegian, with their families still in Norway. We all are very concerned for their safety, now that the Nazis are overrunning our country."

"Are you aware that the Norwegian king and his cabinet have left Norway?"

"We had heard something, but we haven't been told the full story. By the way, I'm Prince Olav's cousin; my name is Knud." Artur shook Knud's hand and bowed his head slightly. As he did so, he felt the surge of the ship resuming her earlier speed, as well as her change of direction back to the previous heading.

"My goodness, that must make you royalty!"

"It's a bit complicated in the Danish and Norwegian royal families. My father and Olav's were brothers. My father was the elder and he is King of Denmark, whereas Olav's father was made King of Norway when it gained full independence in 1905."

"I sort of understand," said Artur jokingly, "but why were you on the trawler?"

"It's a long story as to why I was in Norway, but we all were trying to escape to the Scottish islands of the Shetlands. Unfortunately, our escape was intercepted by these huge German ships. We were lucky to escape with our lives."

"I need to tell you, Knud, that your uncle, King Haakon, your cousin, Prince Olav, and the Norwegian cabinet are on this boat," he said with a broad smile, when nobody else was within earshot. "They are to be given exile in London." He explained that only a few of the senior officers knew that the royal party were on board.

"It is a secret mission: we are acting on behalf of the British Government. We aim to be in the Port of Glasgow by tomorrow lunchtime," he added.

"Oh. My goodness! What an extraordinary coincidence."

"Now that you know where your quarters are, I'll take you to your royal relatives. I'm certain they'll be very surprised to see you and pleased that you are safe and sound."

Artur left Knud and the other men while some of the ratings went to fetch food from the main mess. He told Knud that he needed to update the captain on the rescue operation and that the king's nephew was on board, together with six other men.

Artur entered the bridge and saluted the captain. In front of the small number of officers, he told him that the rescue operation had been successful – one of the seven men saved was King Haakon's nephew, Knud. He is a prince in the Danish royal family.

"Good Heavens! Does Knud know that we have his close relatives, the Norwegian royalty, on our ship?" the captain asked Artur.

"I have briefed him, sir. He is quite incredulous at the coincidence."

"Then you had better reunite them straight away."

Artur saluted and left the bridge. He found Knud in the cabin with his fellow sailors and suggested he should follow him to the king's quarters. He knocked on the door, but couldn't enter as it was locked. After a few moments, the door was unlocked by Prince Olav.

"I've brought someone to see you, Your Highness."

Artur smiled and went inside with Knud trying to hide behind him. Knud then jumped out and exclaimed to the king and the prince.

"How on earth did you get on this ship, Knud?" the king remarked with a broad grin, reverting to English. He briskly walked over to embrace him. Knud explained everything to his wide-eyed uncle, who then grinned at Artur.

"Was it you who spotted the raft when nobody else could see it?" he asked Artur.

"I was the first to see it, sir, yes. But it was mainly because I just happened to be looking in that direction, that's all."

"But if you hadn't seen them, Lieutenant, this ship would have sailed past and my brother's son and his fellow seamen would have been lost, probably never ever found."

"If you put it like that, sir, that's very likely what would have happened."

"I shall have to speak to the captain and the admiral before too long asking them to write a commendation so I can consider giving a Norwegian decoration to you."

"That's very good of you, sir, but I was only doing my duty as an officer on this ship. As I said a moment ago: I just happened to be looking in that direction at the time and I am also very fortunate to have very good eyesight."

"We'll see what we can do for you. Thank you so very much. Olav, I know it's only 10:30 a.m. in the morning, but we need to celebrate Knud's escape from the sea with six of his fellow sailors, and Lieutenant Selmer's amazing eyesight."

Harry was already in the king's room when Artur had arrived. He beamed broadly as he saw how delighted the king was to see his nephew. He came over and shook Artur's hand strongly and warmly.

Olav rummaged in the cupboard and brought out a bottle and five glasses. He placed them on the table that the king had moved into the centre of the room. As he poured out the liquid, he apologised for it not being ice-cold, but it was the best he could do, under the circumstances.

"*Skol* to us all," said the king, as they clinked glasses. "In traditional style, gentlemen, down in one."

"*Skol*," they all shouted, as they threw the liquid into their mouths, raised their empty glasses and looked into the eyes of each man in turn. They chatted amongst themselves with Knud describing his and the other sailors' ordeal, after being seen by the German ships.

"Your Highnesses, I'm quite certain that you will be enjoying another drink, but I must apologise, for leaving you to celebrate with Knud and Harry," Artur said, as he excused himself to return to the bridge. He shook the hands of each man, bowed his head as he did so to the royal men and went out of the door. He thought he overheard the king saying what a special man that the lieutenant was. He didn't stay to hear any more in case it embarrassed him. He walked away quickly for the bridge.

"Are they well settled, Lieutenant," the captain enquired, "and relieved to see Knud?"

"Absolutely, sir. Any further sightings while I've been away?" Artur asked, trying to change the subject, feeling a bit light-headed after the glass of schnapps.

"Nothing to report, Lieutenant. All seems mysteriously quiet. I just wonder where those Nazi ships are? Have they been seen by *Glorious* and her escorts?"

"One must remember, Lieutenant, that the carriers are very likely to send some of their planes out to do a recce – especially the Swordfish – as they can land back on the deck quite easily, unlike the Hurricanes. That should give our ships plenty of notice of the German ships' intent and be able to put up a good fight."

Chapter 24
Saturday, 8th June 1940

The first three hours of the afternoon went by without any incident, but all on the bridge were keeping a wary eye out for ships – particularly those of the enemy kind. Their concentration was suddenly interrupted by the door of the bridge being opened very fiercely and crashing against the metalwork at the side.

"My apologies, Captain Sir, but we have received a rather garbled message," said the senior signalman, as he got his breath back."

"What is it, Dick? Show me," replied the captain as he took the paper from the signalman's outstretched hand.

"It appears, gentlemen, that one of our carriers has been spotted by the German battleships and they are engaged in battle. Presumably it's *Glorious* as she was intending to leave Norway first. I suggest, Admiral, that we are now in a dilemma: do we brake signal silence and go to her help or continue with our assigned mission in silence?"

There was some discussion amongst a few of the senior officers, including Artur, but they knew that, ultimately, the admiral would make the final decision – the signalman had left the bridge at this point.

"Please go and ask King Haakon and the princes to join us on the bridge, plus Mr Ballantyne, of course. It is of great importance that we alert them of the situation," the captain said to Artur. Within ten minutes, the four men entered the bridge. They all saluted them and bowed their heads to their highnesses. The captain explained the situation which resulted in serious talk between them all.

"Right, Your Highnesses, gentlemen," the admiral said, drawing the discussions to a close after only a few minutes. "The situation is very serious; you've had long enough to make up your minds. I will ask for a show of hands on the two options.

"Firstly, all those in favour of changing course, entering the fray and giving assistance to our ships, please raise your hands." Only the king, Prince Olav and Prince Knud put their hands up.

"All those wishing to continue our mission in silence and on our current course, please put up your hands." Everyone else raised their hands, including the captain.

"Thank you, everyone. It is quite clear to me that we should continue with our mission. I have to say that this decision does not make me a very happy admiral. Here am I, Admiral of the Fleet, being seen to turn my back on *Glorious* and her escorts. They face a battle situation without our support when we are not that far away from their position. Your Highnesses, I understand your preferred action, but we are charged with taking you and your cabinet safely to England. Thank you for your kind attention; you may now return to your quarters."

Harry took the king and the princes from the bridge. The admiral ordered the captain to continue at full speed, to give the order of action stations and to exercise full armament, as the ship was likely to be under a surface threat from enemy ships. The instructions were given to all crew members via the ship's tannoy system. The admiral then retired to a corner of the bridge, lit his first of many cigarettes. He mopped his brow with his handkerchief – he had visibly paled from the decision he had just made. Everyone on the bridge fell silent as the crew raced to their stations and readied their armaments. Artur couldn't help thinking about all those men on the *Glorious* and their two escort ships. So long as they managed to get the Swordfish planes airborne, they might stand a chance. His thoughts were interrupted by the captain calling him to the port side of the bridge.

"You look very pensive, Lieutenant, what seems to be on your mind?"

"As you know, sir, we are under orders from London to safely take their royal highnesses and the Norwegian cabinet to England. I just can't help myself from thinking about all those men taking on the might of the German pocket battleships. In addition, why has *Glorious* and her escorts left Norway without *Ark Royal* and her escorts? With all of them together, they might be able to inflict serious damage on the two German ships, but on their own, it could be a disaster."

"You are quite right, of course. We must just hope and pray for a successful outcome. Those German battleships, however, are a formidable pair, especially as their big guns have a range of over 13 nautical miles. As you say, it will all depend on whether or not they get their planes off the carrier to search for the battleships, or create smoke screens to confuse the enemy."

"If you'll excuse me, Captain, I would like to go to the comms room and find out if they have had any more messages."

Artur left the bridge and, as usual, everyone stood when he entered the wireless office.

"Have you received any further messages, Dick?" he asked.

"I was just about to bring this up to the captain," he said, and passed the paper to Artur.

"This is in German," he exclaimed, "and it doesn't seem to be in any code. It is a message from the *Scharnhorst* to her sister ship the *Gneisenau*. My German isn't up to much, sir, but it appears that a British force has been spotted. I think it says that the *Gneisenau* should go at full speed to intercept the ships. The time of this communication is 1700hrs."

Artur read the text that had been written from the Morse code message. He agreed with the signalman's interpretation. Artur looked at his watch and saw it was 5:15 pm. He assumed the battle must now have started, or was soon to do so. He said he would wait in the main wireless office in case further communications were picked up. Nothing was received, so he left for the bridge at 5:45 p.m. He spoke to the captain and the admiral about the message sent by the *Scharnhorst* and they were dumbstruck at the news.

Artur took a pair of binoculars and scoured the port side horizon.

"It might be a strange request, but I would like to take a better look from the crow's nest. I am aware that someone is up there on look out now we're at battle stations, but, as you well know, my eyesight is better than most people's, and the horizon will be that much further away from that height," Artur explained.

"It isn't really that much higher than the bridge, Lieutenant; maybe thirty feet at most. Just make sure you are wrapped up well; the wind up there will be fresh," the captain commented.

Artur took one of the great coats hanging at the back of the bridge, hung the glasses from his neck, saluted the captain with a smile and went through the door. He found his way to the base of the ladder leading to the crow's nest. He looked up to see a senior rating searching forward and then to port. Artur ascended very carefully as the ship pitched and rolled at each wave. The man above saw Artur coming. He opened the small hatchway and stepped to one side to let Artur up.

"The captain has allowed me to come up here," he said as the rating saluted Artur and helped him up.

"Have you spotted anything of significance?" Artur asked, knowing that if he had, a message would have been sent to the bridge straightaway, together with direction coordinates etc.

"No, sir, nothing yet," the rating replied, as Artur steadied himself. He searched the port horizon. He put down the glasses, looked back at the flags and reckoned the wind was easterly.

"How strong is the wind from the east?" Artur asked.

"According to the gauge, it's about thirty knots, occasionally gusting to forty, sir."

"So, if there was a battle going on between a German battleship and one of our carrier's escorts, would we hear distant gunfire from fifty miles away with this wind?"

"It is unlikely, sir," the rating replied, as Artur continued to look at the port horizon through his glasses.

"I can see nothing and I can hear nothing, so I'll return to deck," Artur said after a further few minutes. The rating opened the hatch for Artur to go down the ladder. Artur thanked him for giving him space. He noticed that his watch said 6:20 p.m., so he decided to go to the comms room again before reporting to the captain on the bridge.

"Sir, sir," said the senior signalman excitedly as he entered the room, "my man is picking up a message on a frequency not often used, from the *Gneisenau*. It's in German, sir." When the message seemed complete, the paper with the decoded Morse message was passed to Artur. *'Congratulations for having sunk the destroyer'*, he read.

"Must be one of *Glorious'* escorts that has been sunk," said Artur, as he left the comms room hot foot for the bridge. He reported to the captain, who ordered the ship to increase to 31 knots and to start a zigzag course for the next hour. No further messages were picked up on any of the frequencies or wavelengths that the comms room operators had been listening in on.

"By my calculations," the navigating officer said to those on the bridge at 1900hrs., "we are only an hour away from being in sight of the northern part of the Shetlands. Under the circumstances, that's very good progress. As I said earlier, it will also mean that we will be able to break radio silence."

On hearing the good news, a few went for some refreshments. Artur decided to go to see how the king was getting on and to tell him of the ship's position. The door was unlocked and he found the three royal men sitting back and talking animatedly and noisily about the situation in Norway. *It must be the schnapps*, Artur said to himself.

"I'm sorry to trouble you, Your Highnesses," Artur said with a slight bow of his head, "but I thought you would like to know that within one hour we shall be looking at the Shetlands and be in British waters. We will then have about seventeen hours at sea before reaching the Port of Glasgow – just before midday tomorrow."

"That is indeed very good news," the king replied. "Have we heard any more about the German ships and the British carriers?" the crown prince asked.

"No, sir, we haven't," Artur lied. "Also, we couldn't send out any messages as we are under orders to be in radio silence."

"I remember," said the prince, "but presumably we might find out more once we're in British waters?"

"Quite so," Artur responded, taking care not to give any further details. "Can we get you anything more to eat or drink?" Artur asked, smiling at all of them.

"No thank you, Lieutenant. Everyone has been very attentive and we've enjoyed the schnapps very much. It might soon be a good time to get some sleep while all is quiet."

"Then I'll wish you all a good night's rest." Artur smiled at each of them individually, bowed and left the cabin for the mess. Once again, he didn't feel very hungry, nor like making polite conversation so, after about twenty minutes, he returned to his cabin to write up his report and get some sleep for himself.

Chapter 25

Sunday, 9th June 1940

Artur was up and on the bridge by 7:00 a.m. to find that they only had four and a half hours still to go. He was told by the captain that the deputy Foreign Minister, together with the Norwegian ambassador, would be at Port Glasgow to greet the Norwegian royal family members – plus the Norwegian cabinet – and to escort them to the train bound for London.

"Please could you tell me if the king has been updated with those in the welcome party, sir?" Artur asked the captain.

"Not yet, as we have only recently received the news. Would you like to be the one, Lieutenant, to speak to him about the arrangements?"

"I should be delighted, sir, but I think I ought to leave it for a half an hour or so, as it's still quite early."

"I don't think there will be a problem as Harry was called by the king to go to see them an hour ago, just before we received confirmation of who would be meeting them at Port Glasgow."

"Fine, I'll go straightaway, sir," Artur responded as he saluted and left the bridge.

"I hope I'm not too early, Your Highnesses, as it's only 7:30 a.m.? Have you been able to enjoy seeing the Scottish countryside as we have sailed down the Lower Hebrides towards our final destination?"

"You are not too early, Lieutenant, and a lot of the scenery very closely resembles some of the landscape in Norway. We are starting to feel quite a bit at home," the king responded.

"That's good to hear, Your Highness. I have come to tell you that there will be a small welcoming party on the quayside at Port Glasgow. The British Government are obviously overjoyed to know that you have accepted their offer of exile in England. They have deliberately scaled down everything, so as not to draw too much attention to you and your cabinet being here. Your ambassador in London, plus a senior member of the British Foreign Office, will welcome you as you step onto British soil. A train has been made available to take you and your cabinet to London. Our king and queen have offered you, and the princes, accommodation at Buckingham Palace until you find somewhere to live. We trust this meets with your approval?"

"My goodness! That is a remarkable offer of considerable generosity by your Royal Family. Thank you also to everyone concerned."

"I will let you prepare for disembarkation. Mr Ballantyne will come to your cabin in about an hour to ask for your permission to receive your parliaments' cabinet members. You will, no doubt, want to discuss the trip from Tromsø, as well as to start discussing the plans for your resistance network. This will help you effectively guide and support your people in Norway during the German occupation."

"Once again, thank you," the king said.

Artur bowed, left the royal cabin and returned to the bridge.

"Not long now," the navigating officer declared as they rounded Arran into the Firth of Clyde. "The last couple of hours always seem to take quite a while to pass. We'll probably be met by the pilot boat before too long, as we pass Dunoon."

"Captain, would you like to join me in paying a visit to the king?" the admiral asked. "We haven't spoken to them since yesterday evening in the captain's mess."

"I would very much like to do that," the captain replied, as the two senior officers left the bridge. "Number 2, you are now in charge."

"Aye, aye, Captain."

The ship started to reduce speed as she came alongside Dunoon. The navigating officer spotted the pilot boat heading towards them. In next to no time, the nets were lowered over the ship's side for the pilot's captain and his mate to climb onto the main deck. The captain must have been aware of what was going on as he and the admiral had come back on deck to welcome the two men from the pilot boat on board; they saluted each other. The four men went straight to the bridge and the pilot boat's captain took over control of the ship.

At 11:30 a.m. sharp, the ship was securely moored to the quay. By this time, Artur had retrieved his kitbag from his cabin and was standing on the starboard side of the main deck next to the Norwegian royalty with the country's cabinet members behind them. Artur took a look over the rails and thought he saw the welcoming party. They walked towards the gangway that was being put in place for disembarkation amidships.

Harry picked up two of the king's cases and Artur the third, after he'd slung his kitbag over his shoulder. Harry led the way off the ship, Artur followed on behind the king and the princes.

"Welcome to Britain, Your Highnesses," said the man from the Foreign Office, but he didn't shake their hands. "My name is Conway-Blythe. Amongst other things, I have recently been appointed to look after Norwegian interests in Britain by the British government." He smiled as he greeted the king in Norwegian, this time shaking his hand and bowing his head just a little in deference.

"We trust you have had a pleasant trip from Tromsø and that you didn't run into any of the enemy?" the ministerial man said with a slight smirk.

"We were well looked after, thank you, but we still think about our poor countrymen that are trying to resist the invading forces from Germany," the king remarked with seriousness.

"Might I suggest we walk to the train that is waiting to take you to London?" Conway-Blythe said, diplomatically evading the king's statement.

"Before we do, I must go and thank the senior officers for taking care of us, as well as some of my senior cabinet ministers that will probably be in a different part of the train," the king mentioned as he disappeared in the crowd surrounding them all.

Artur told Harry to look after the king's bag that he had been carrying and walked quickly after the king. He knew more than anyone that he had been given the responsibility to keep the king safe, at least until he reached London.

After some ten minutes, the king returned with Artur. He picked up the king's bag and nodded to Conway-Blythe to start walking to the train.

"A special first-class carriage has been reserved for your Royal Highnesses plus the three of us – Ballantyne will be in the Norwegian prime minister's carriage – with the cabinet members plus their wives in a separate one," Conway-Blythe explained as they reached the train. "The Norwegian ambassador will escort the cabinet members to their carriage which is the one next to the one we will be using," he continued.

Once everyone was on board and in their seats, there were two whistles from the engine as the train started to move out of the station.

"I take it the carriages are interconnected?" Artur enquired. Conway-Blythe replied that they were. Artur explained to the king, and the others in the compartment, that he was going take a stroll through the carriages to see who else was on the train. He asked some of the cabinet ministers in the next carriage if they were happy to be on British soil and they all answered in the affirmative. After going through six more carriages – plus a buffet car – he eventually reached the guard's compartment. Noticing all the packages, Artur was instantly reminded of the time he was on a train in France in April 1940. At that time, he was escaping from the French police disguised as a Danish businessman. He visibly paled, but stood bolt upright when the guard asked him if he was alright.

"Yes, thank you, I'm fine," Artur replied. "For a short moment, I was just remembering another occasion when I was last in a guard's van. I didn't think it would have affected me like it has."

"The situation must have been a scary one, sir," the guard said.

Artur didn't reply, but smiled and walked out of the guard's compartment. Once in the corridor, he loosened the leather strap to open a window. He wanted some fresh air, but only got smoke from the engine. He was not well pleased.

"Where do we stop on our way to London?" Artur asked Conway-Blythe on his return to his compartment.

"Even though this train has special carriages for the Norwegians and us, we will be stopping at Carlisle, Preston and Crewe. Security has been strengthened at all stations to check that all passengers wanting to catch this train have a reason to do so and have the correct papers. We can't be too careful, Lieutenant."

"I agree entirely," Artur replied. He took his kitbag down from the rack and pushed his hand down to the bottom. He felt for his pistol and was reassured on finding it. He excused himself, went out with his kitbag into the corridor to the lavatory. After locking the door, he took out his pistol, checked it was loaded with a full magazine and slipped it into his jacket's inside pocket. He knew it bulged a bit, but that couldn't be helped. He returned to his compartment and sat down.

During the course of the journey to Carlisle, a few people wandered up to the head of the train, some looking inquisitively at those in the reserved compartments. Artur noticed the train slowing as it entered Carlisle. He went out into the corridor, opened a window and looked at the small number of people standing on the platform as the train went slowly past. He wasn't sure what or who he was looking for, but something in his mind told him that he needed to check.

After seven minutes, the engine's whistle blew and they were on their way again – Artur was back in his seat by this time. He talked casually to the two princes about the times before the outbreak of war. Time passed quickly, but every time someone came past their compartment, Artur gave them a stare. He felt the responsibility of getting the king safely to London rested entirely on his shoulders.

The train slowed once again as it approached Preston. Once again, Artur went out into the corridor and looked out of the window at the waiting passengers. There seemed to be many more people than there were at Carlisle. He hoped they had been properly vetted. After ten minutes, the whistle blew and the train started to move forward. Artur went back to his seat. He smiled at the princes and Conway-Blythe, but the king and the ambassador had fallen asleep.

After a little while, the train reached full speed – everyone in Artur's compartment was sleeping – he also had his eyes closed. For some unknown reason, he woke, looked through the window to the corridor and saw a man staring at them all. Without wishing to make a sudden move, he slowly put his hand into his jacket pocket, grasped his pistol, took off the safety catch and in one swift movement, leapt to his feet. He stood in front of the compartment door so that he shielded the king from the man's view. At this point, everyone woke up, they stared at Artur as he slid the door open and pointed his gun at the man in the corridor. Before he could ask him anything, the man took a shot at the king, who was now half-hidden behind Artur. Instinctively, Artur shot the man twice in the chest, but before he fell to the floor, he took a shot at Artur.

"Stop the train," Artur shouted as he fell to the floor over the man in the corridor. Conway-Blythe jumped up and pulled the communication cord. The train came to a halt after what seemed a very long time to Artur. He looked at his left arm and there was blood seeping through his sleeve below the elbow. He turned around and saw the king was unhurt. There was a bullet hole to the right of the window, just above where the king's head could have been.

"Are you all right, Your Highness?" Artur said to the king very calmly.

"Thanks to you, Lieutenant, I'm unharmed," said the king, as he got up and went over to Artur, who was now on his feet, holding his left arm.

There was a lot of noise as people tried to work out what the problem was and why the train had come to an abrupt halt. The ticket inspector came along the corridor. He saw the man on the floor with blood coming through a gap in his jacket.

"What seems to have happened?" the inspector asked, as he bent down and checked the man's pulse.

"This man attacked us in our compartment with a pistol. This person is the King of Norway," Artur explained, as he pointed to the king, "and we are here to protect him on his way to London. The man shot at us. I had no alternative than to shoot him in self-defence."

Oblivious of his own injury, Artur searched the man's pockets for any means of identification. He pulled out a passport, a ration book, a piece of paper with a phone number written in pencil and a pocket diary.

At that moment, the engine driver appeared. He spoke to the inspector, who explained what he had been told had happened and pointed to the king.

"I was aware that you and other Norwegians were to be on this train," the driver said, as he bowed his head at the king. "I'm very sorry this incident has occurred, but we ought now to be on our way so we can get this man off at Crewe. We are close to a small station so I'll get the station master to phone through to the Crewe station. The police and an ambulance will be waiting for our arrival."

With this, the driver disappeared. After about ten minutes, the whistle blew and the train started moving again. Artur knew the man was dead, so he pulled him into the compartment and closed the door. A few minutes later the train drew into a small station, the driver jumped down from the footplate and went to find the station master in his office. Some minutes later, the driver returned to his cab and the train set off for Crewe.

"Do you really think the man is dead?" Conway-Blythe asked. "If so, shouldn't we put a cover over the man's head?"

Artur and Conway-Blythe managed to take off the man's lightweight rain jacket and laid it over the man's chest and head. Artur took off his own jacket, rolled up his shirt sleeve and tied a handkerchief around his wounded arm, with the help of Conway-Blythe. He thought it more of a graze than anything more serious, but that was what he thought about his leg. He replaced his jacket, sat down and looked through the man's papers. Even though the passport and ration card were British, he was sure they were forgeries. He wasn't an expert, but the name in the passport and the other paper was 'John Smith': *not very original,* he muttered to himself. He found the diary, however, of much more interest: entries for today, one a week ago and others earlier – all in German. He wanted to search his trouser pockets, but he thought he ought to leave that task to the police. He took the man's pistol and placed it in his kitbag.

Artur sat back in his seat to contemplate what might have been, had he not apprehended the man.

Chapter 26

Sunday, 9th June 1940

Artur's arm was starting to throb a bit as the train rattled southwards towards Crewe. His watch told him there were still forty-five minutes to go: he needed a drink.

"Does anyone want to join me for something to drink?" Artur asked. "Conway-Blythe, make sure that nobody else tries to attack the king," as Artur handed over his pistol with a wry smile.

"I'd like something, Lieutenant. I'll follow you," said Knud. Artur was relieved that everyone else turned down his offer, so he didn't ask a second time. He and Knud walked through two carriages to reach the buffet car. With there being a war on, there wasn't a lot of choice.

"It looks like tea or weak orange squash, Knud. Which will it be, although it might not taste like tea?" Artur joked. "There's no coffee, I'm afraid." Artur always preferred black coffee, so they both had to choose tea, with milk. He asked for a brandy, but there wasn't any. They took their tin mugs from the counter and stood looking out at the passing countryside.

"How do you feel, Knud, after that chap attempted to take your uncle's life?"

"It was certainly a big surprise, but we are very pleased that you were so quick to respond. There is no doubt that the man was intent on killing my uncle. I think he must have been hired by someone who knew the king would be on this train. I wonder if he was anything to do with that Quisling man."

"That's a very good point, Knud, but whoever set the assassination up, didn't do it very professionally. I therefore don't believe the German intelligence people in the *Abwehr* were involved." Artur said all this in a whisper, as other people were coming into the buffet car and he didn't want them to hear what they were talking about.

"Tell me, Knud, do you know what sort of ship shot at you when you were all in the trawler?"

"We were made aware that the two German battleships were not far from us, but it was one of their escort destroyers that fired at us and sank our boat. We really had no way of defending ourselves against their fire power. You can't sink a destroyer with six pistols," he said with a smile.

As they were continuing their conversation about the sinking of the trawler, a crackly announcement said they were only six minutes from Crewe. They returned the mugs to the counter and walked back to their compartment.

"Any more disturbances, Your Highnesses?" Artur asked as he entered the king's compartment.

"Fortunately, nobody bothered us, Lieutenant," Conway-Blythe replied on the king's behalf.

"Hopefully, the poor man's body will be removed once we're in Crewe station," he continued.

Artur looked out of the compartment's window. He saw two policemen and three ambulance men standing on the platform. As the train went further along to the end of the station to a stop, the five men walked in the direction of the train and saw Artur looking out at them. He heard the door open at the end of the carriage, so he went down the corridor to meet them. He pointed into the compartment at the man's body. One of the ambulance men turned down the jacket to reveal the man's face.

"Who was it that shot this man?" one of the policemen asked, looking around the compartment.

"I did," Artur replied. "It was in self-defence and we were here to protect the gentleman sitting in the corner."

One of the policemen had taken out his notebook. He licked his pencil and wrote down what Artur had said. He asked Artur to repeat the circumstances and time of the incident, which he also noted. The discussion went on for several minutes after which, two more ambulance men came down the corridor bearing a stretcher and a blanket. They lifted the man onto the stretcher, covered him with the blanket and took him from the train onto the platform. Earlier, one of the policemen had felt in all the man's pockets and had only recovered a few notes, some coins, a train ticket from Preston to Crewe: nothing else.

"It seems odd to me, especially as we are at war, that I can't find any form of identification on him," the policeman said, as he looked around at everyone. "Also, where is the gun that, by all accounts, he fired at the gentleman in the corner seat?"

"I have the gun and his documents, Officer," Artur mentioned in a casual manner, as he took his kitbag down from the rack. "I don't think the documents are real; they look like forgeries to me," he said, as he handed them over plus the gun, but not the diary or the piece of paper with the phone number on it.

"You don't happen to have anything else of this man Smith, do you?" the policeman asked, but Artur shook his head. He knew nobody in the compartment had seen him put the diary and the piece of paper into his kitbag.

"I've written all the details down," said the second policeman, "so perhaps you would be prepared to sign it as a form of a statement. Put down your name and contact number, as we might well need to get in touch with you again. I also need to know the names of all the other people in this compartment."

Artur read the notes, signed the paper as Artur Selmer and put his boss, Charles', phone number down. He wrote down the names of the others present, but gave them all false names. He showed the policeman his passport who flicked through the pages. He refrained from telling him that he'd been in Norway and what he'd been up to over there – it seemed irrelevant. There was no stamp showing that he'd been in and out of Norway anyway.

The train driver appeared at the compartment door; he wondered how much longer they would be as there were many people anxious to get to London. The policemen looked around at everyone, apologised for delaying their journey to London and hoped they wouldn't encounter any more dangerous men. As soon as they all appeared on the platform, the train's whistle blew, setting off for London.

After all the disturbances, everyone in Artur's compartment relaxed, sat back and closed their eyes. Conway-Blythe stood up after some minutes saying that he ought to find out how the prime minister was – he hadn't been to speak to him since leaving Carlisle. He felt he also had to tell him and other cabinet members what had happened – and what nearly happened. Artur asked if he could come along as well.

They spent over twenty minutes with the ministers in the two compartments. One of them noticed that there was blood seeping through Artur's jacket sleeve. He told him that he was a doctor and that he would like to look at the injury. Artur reluctantly agreed. He took off his jacket, rolled up his left shirt sleeve and allowed the minister to move it nearer to him to give a better examination.

"That is a gash that is very nasty, Mr Selmer," he said in broken English. "I clean it, put on disinfectant and cover it properly – not with a kerchief this time," the minister said with a smile.

"That is probably what it needs, sir," Artur remarked. He never liked this sort of fuss, but he was trying to be sensible, for once.

"I really came to find out how you were, rather than my being given treatment for a silly scratch," Artur said with a grin.

The minister smiled at Artur as he stood up to fetch his Gladstone bag down from the luggage rack. He took out the items he needed, pulling Artur's arm around to get it in the right position for him to attend to it properly. He thought the minister was being unnecessarily rough, but he could only try to grin and bear it.

"Well, that might help you till you arrive in London. I recommend you see your doctor tomorrow morning."

Artur thanked the minister, stood up as he put his jacket back on and left for his compartment, leaving Conway-Blythe to continue his discussions with the other ministers. He looked at his watch as he entered his compartment; he hoped they shouldn't be too far from London, but he could be wrong.

Artur took his kitbag down from the rack, sat down and pulled out the dead man's diary. He flicked through the pages, stopping every now and then where there was something written down. He then went to the back pages and found a list of names and associated phone numbers. He reckoned some were in Norway, but there were three London numbers: one was the Norwegian Embassy, the second's name meant nothing to him, but the third was Helena Olsen's.

A scrambled, almost inaudible voice came over the speakers that seemed to suggest they were only eleven minutes away from London. One or two got up to use the facilities at the end of the corridor just as Conway-Blythe came back to the compartment.

"As soon as we arrive at the station, I will phone King George's private secretary at Buckingham Palace to tell him of your arrival. You, the princes and I will then take a taxi to the Palace," Conway-Blythe informed the king.

"What will happen to my prime minister, the cabinet ministers and their wives, Mr Conway?" asked the king, shortening the Foreign Office man's name.

"When I was in Glasgow, I arranged for a bus to take them all to the Ritz Hotel in Piccadilly. I hope that meets with your approval, Your Highness?" Conway-Smythe explained. "After a good night's rest at the Palace, Mr Churchill has invited you and the princes for lunch and talks at his Downing Street address."

"Thank you to everyone for all they are doing to make us feel welcome in London," the king said.

After some minutes, the train came to a halt in Euston Station. Artur recommended that all the people in his compartment stayed where they were until the rest of the other passengers had left the train. Artur had hoped he could go with the king to the Palace, but obviously it wasn't to be. He went into the next compartment to find Harry.

"What do you intend doing, Harry, now that we're in London?" Artur asked.

"I've nothing planned, Artur. As it's early evening, though, why don't we get a cab to one of the Lyons Corner Houses for something to eat? Perhaps after that, we could go to the Windmill Theatre for a bit of light entertainment?" Harry suggested with a wink.

"That sounds a great idea, Harry. I do need to phone my boss, Charles, before I leave the station. He'll want to hear that I'm back more or less in one piece."

Artur returned to his compartment. He told everyone that it was now a good time for them to leave the train. They took down their suitcases, went out into the corridor and stepped onto the station platform. They all walked together to the taxi ranks. After making a phone call, Conway-Blythe returned to the group explaining that King George's private secretary was awaiting their arrival.

"I won't exactly be very presentable to meet the king and queen," King Haakon explained with some concern.

"Don't worry, Your Highness, you won't be seeing them till tomorrow morning after breakfast."

"That's a relief!"

Artur shook hands with the three royal men, bowing his head as he did so.

"Lieutenant Selmer, you have executed your duties in an exemplary manner. We have nothing but heartfelt thanks for all that you have done," the king said. "You have risked your life at our expense. You unfortunately have a couple of wounds to remind you of our time together, but we hope they will quickly heal when properly attended to."

"Thank you, Your Highness. It was all in the line of duty and I've enjoyed being of service to you, your son and Knud."

Artur and Harry waved to them as they drove off. Harry saw the cabinet ministers into their bus as Artur ran off to phone Charles. After he had made the call, he came back to Harry, who had asked a taxi driver to wait for his colleague's return.

"Harry, I must firstly go to my flat to change into some casual clothes before going out on the town."

"OK, that's fine by me."

Artur told the taxi driver to take them to his address, to wait for a few minutes and then go to the Lyons Corner House in Piccadilly, the one on the corner of Coventry Street.

"What did your boss have to say when you called him?" Harry enquired, once they were on their way.

"Not much really, Harry. I have to see him tomorrow morning and give him my reports on everything that's happened since I left on Sunday, 2nd June. I know that's only a week ago, but it seems like a lifetime."

They arrived at Artur's flat. He dashed in with his kitbag and within ten minutes, he reappeared at the taxi.

"Let's go," Harry said to the driver, in a rather excited tone. When they reached Coventry Street, Harry paid the taxi; they went up to the second floor. There were many people chatting, eating, being entertained by the small orchestra playing popular dance music. They both ordered tea and apple tart from the attractive 'Nippy'.

"Considering there's a war on," Artur mentioned, "it's really surprising how many people are in here."

"It's always a popular place to come to, even on a Sunday."

They finished their meal and decided they needed some exercise, so they walked to the Windmill theatre.

"I've been meaning to come here ever since the outbreak of war," Artur commented, "but there just hasn't been enough time. It's great fun. Those girls: they are so elegant and very pretty. It's quite amazing how the manager persuaded those old-fashioned stick-in-the-muds in the Home Office to allow nudes on the stage."

"As I'm sure you already know, they aren't prancing about without their clothes on. They stand still, as though they are statues. They just smile enticingly at the audience that is predominantly male," Harry replied.

"Not just male," Artur retorted, "but service men. They make a bee-line for here almost every time they are back on leave! It's a complete show that changes every two hours; it goes on twenty-four hours a day. 'We're never closed' is the theatre's motto, but it's better known now as 'We're never clothed!'"

Artur was loving every moment of the show. His eyes were almost out on sticks from looking at one of the girls in particular: an auburn-haired woman – probably in her mid-twenties – standing to the left of the other eight that were all in the form of a pyramid. He felt sure she was looking straight at him; even if she weren't, he certainly had eyes for her.

"I wonder if there's any way of meeting some of these beauties?" Artur whispered to Harry. "I certainly wouldn't mind seeing that one on the left."

"As far as I am aware, the manager has very strict rules and looks after all the girls very carefully. Mind you, once they've left the theatre, they have to look after themselves. They usually leave by the rear door and leave in pairs."

"Oh well. I'm certain every man in here is getting a bit carried away with one or the other of those girls. It wouldn't be natural if they didn't."

They decided to leave at 10:30 p.m. They had had a long and very difficult last few days ensuring that the king arrived safely back in London. Spending nearly two hours at the Windmill was a very appropriate way to finish off the week. Harry hailed a taxi, taking Artur back to his flat before going to his own.

"Cheerio, Harry," said Artur, as he got out of the taxi. "Very nice to have met you. Thanks for all your help in bringing King Haakon back from Tromsø. It was quite a memorable trip, wasn't it?"

"It certainly was, Artur. Good luck in whatever else you are involved in during the war. Don't forget to have those wounds looked at tomorrow."

Artur waited till the taxi was out of sight, then went inside to his flat. He now knew he was no longer in agent mode.

Chapter 27
Monday, 10th June 1940

Andrew woke early and knew he had to read through the reports he was to present to Charles later that morning. Once he had completed the reports to his satisfaction, he looked through the diary and at the piece of paper that he had secreted from the dead man. He thought he would try to phone the number on the piece of paper after his meeting – whatever time that was. The diary, however, was a different matter. He wrote down the names and numbers from the back, as well as the entries from the days prior to the date of the shooting, on a separate piece of paper. He knew full well that if he told Charles about the dead man's diary, he would want to keep it, so he put the diary and the piece of paper in his desk drawer.

Andrew tidied himself, put his papers in his briefcase and left the flat at 9:30 a.m. by taxi for St James. It just seemed ages since he had been there, but he realised he must be feeling that way because of all that he'd gone through over the last twelve days. *All your lifetime should you have such excitement*, he said to himself, *and survive!* He was then reminded of his two injuries. He had no intention of telling Charles how he got them, but – knowing him as he did – he was bound to ask, especially after he had read his reports.

He paid the taxi driver, walked the last few yards, knocked on the brass knocker and went inside.

"Nice to see you again, Mr Williams," said Miss Jones, in an unusually jovial manner. "As you will remember, please sign in. I'll call Mr Compton-Browne and tell him that you've arrived."

After a few moments, Miss Jones told Andrew to go upstairs. Andrew knocked on Charles' door. He went straight in, not waiting for an answer.

"Andrew, how good to see you. Congratulations on achieving our objective of bringing King Haakon back to Britain. You remember the head of the Service, C, I'm sure." Andrew went and shook his hand. "And this is the Secretary of State for War, Mr Anthony Eden, who has heard so much about you from Lord Halifax – the Foreign Secretary – as well as from Mr Churchill himself. Mr Eden, sir, please may I introduce you to Mr Andrew Williams."

"My goodness," said Andrew, as he went over to shake Mr Eden's hand, "if I'd known in advance that I was to have the honour of meeting you, sir, I would have put on my new suit!" Everyone smiled; the atmosphere then seemed to become a bit more relaxed.

C went to sit to the left of Charles' desk, Anthony Eden to his right, Andrew in front. Charles, for the moment, hovered around as the lady completed her distribution of tea and biscuits. Charles thanked her and opened the door for her to leave. He moved the sign on the outside of his door to 'ENGAGED' and closed the door behind him. He went to his desk, phoned the receptionist downstairs to tell her they should not be interrupted until he called her again.

Andrew had placed his report on Charles' desk as soon as he had entered his office. He knew he would only read it after the meeting, so Andrew knew he was expected to give a summary of his trip to Norway for everyone's benefit.

Andrew stood up and went through the flight to the Shetlands, the journey to Tromsø, fetching the king and his son to the ship from the cabin outside Tromsø, the rescue operation of the king's nephew, the arrangements at Port Glasgow, the incident on the train, his arrival with Harry Ballantyne at Euston. In no way did he give any details about his two injuries, or about the dead man's diary and the phone number on the piece of paper that was now in his pocket.

"That's certainly quite a mission, Andrew," the Secretary for War remarked. "What do you make of this Miss Olsen? Do you think she was hired by one of Mr Quisling's henchmen? What do you think was the relationship between her and the man that attempted to assassinate King Haakon, Mr John Smith, or whatever his real name was?"

"When I sent a coded message to Charles – sorry, Mr Compton-Browne – after I had found the letters addressed to *Fraulein Olga Schwartz* in her cabin's desk – the Service found out that she was a known member of the *Abwehr*. The Norwegian Embassies in Europe, however, had no record of a Miss Helena Olsen. The plot thickens, gentlemen, when one starts trying to work out why Mr John Smith also wanted to kill King Haakon. I am totally confident that Smith was not the real name of the would-be assassin and that his documents were forgeries. There's no doubt that he – or his handlers – knew that King Haakon had escaped from Norway and that somehow they were aware he was on that very train from Port Glasgow to Euston that I was on."

Discussions went round and round between all three men – with the exception of Andrew, who just remained quiet, but listened very intently – without coming to any conclusion. Andrew was almost 100% certain that the dead man's diary and the piece of paper with the phone number held the key to the whole puzzle.

"Are you sure you've not forgotten to tell us any other details, Andrew?" Charles enquired. "Did you search through all his pockets before the police came on to the train?"

"As I've said in my report, Charles, I didn't go through any of his trouser pockets, just his jacket. The police, however, did examine every pocket and, apart from his ticket, passport and ration book, they found nothing else."

"We seem to be very baffled, Andrew," C exclaimed. "Charles, I believe you need to carry out more enquiries about *Fraulein Schwartz* through the normal Service channels. Do we have any of our agents working in the *Abwehr* that can assist us? Contact the police station in Crewe and get more details about Mr Smith's passport. If necessary, I suggest you get a warrant to have it sent to our boys in the Service *poste haste*. If anybody can get to the bottom of who supplied the passport – and what his real name is – they certainly will."

"You know you mentioned the dilemma that the ship's captain was in when he heard about the German pocket battleships being in his vicinity," Mr Eden mentioned. "I need to tell you that the aircraft carrier HMS *Glorious* and her two escort ships – the destroyers HMS *Acasta* and HMS *Ardent* – were all sunk by the *Scharnhorst* and the *Gneisenau*. More than 1,500 men and sailors were lost. One thing in our favour, however, was that the *Scharnhorst* was so badly holed that she and *Gneisenau* both returned to Trondheim for emergency repairs. What is quite appalling is that they made no attempt to pick up our men that were in the sea or in life rafts. Apparently, *Glorious* was sailing with one third of her boilers shut down. Additionally, for no real accountable reason, none of the planes on *Glorious* was launched to carry out a recce. They all became just sitting ducks to the German battleships. But, because the German ships went back for repairs, HMS *Ark Royal* and her escorts made it safely back to Britain without incident."

Silence fell over the men in Charles' office on hearing the account of the navy's ships as they mulled over Mr Eden's words. After a few moments, C felt he ought to say something:

"Gentlemen, I don't think we need to spend any more time now thinking about the demise of those poor men. I'm sure Mr Churchill will be extremely angry at what has happened. He will no doubt put all our naval forces on the look-out for those Nazi ships in the hope of tracking them down and sinking them.

"I want to thank Andrew Williams, once again, for what he has managed to achieve over the last week or so. For not allowing Miss Olsen to achieve her objective; for apprehending the would-be assassin of King Haakon on the train to London," C mentioned.

"Thanks also to Mr Eden for attending this meeting. I know he is a very busy man and has a meeting this afternoon with Mr Churchill, King Haakon and the royal princes at Downing Street."

They all stood up, shook each other's hands. C said he would escort Mr Eden to his car that was in St James, whereas Charles beckoned Andrew to stay a little while longer.

"That seemed to go very well, Andrew," as they all took their seats again. "You seemed to summarise everything without going into too much detail, all to their satisfaction."

"There are a couple of things I need to talk to you about that are not in my report and I didn't want to say at the meeting," Andrew said. "They both involve the man that was shot on the train. Firstly, I found a pocket diary in his jacket. I didn't tell the police that I had it and I don't think anyone saw me take it. When I looked at it, it had some names and associated phone numbers at the back. Two, I think, were Norwegian names and numbers, another was Miss Olsen with a London number. There were also entries in the diary prior to the date of the shooting, written in German. Secondly, I found a piece of paper with a London phone number on it. I wrote down all the information on this piece of paper," Andrew said, as he passed it to Charles. "What do you think we should make of all this, Charles?"

"What have you done with the originals, Andrew?"

"Don't worry, they're safely stowed away in my flat. In any case, I thought it would be best if we both had the information so we could decide who does what."

Charles looked at the paper. "You ought to be aware that neither King Haakon's escape from Norway nor his arrival in London has deliberately not been reported in any of the British Press or mentioned on the radio.

"So, why don't we try calling the number that doesn't have a name against it, now. I wouldn't be surprised at all if that John Smith chap was supposed to call the number after he had done the deed of assassinating the king."

Charles picked up the red phone's receiver – the one for direct calls – and dialled the number. Charles and Andrew looked at each other as the ringing tone rang for over a minute. Charles listened as someone started to speak. It was a woman, speaking in German. Charles spoke to her in

German, asking for her name and saying that he was John Smith. The woman didn't give her name. Charles thought there must be a coded phrase that Smith was supposed to say if he had successfully killed the king. Charles looked at his piece of paper and the words that had been written in Smith's diary against the day of the assassination. But before he said them, he asked for the name of the person he was speaking to, once again. He said he needed to be absolutely certain that he was speaking to the right person.

"I am *Olga Schwartz*," the woman said, rather hurriedly and in an agitated manner. "Don't you recognise my voice?" she said angrily.

Charles decided to complete the exercise by saying the words from the diary. "That is very good news," the woman responded. The line then went dead.

Charles and Andrew looked at each other in almost total disbelief.

"So, Helena Olsen wasn't *Olga Schwartz*, even though she had letters with that name on them, Artur pointed out."

"I'll give our lads this phone number and they'll find out the address. It shouldn't be too difficult to get it when the code starts with MAI. It could be some smart address in Maida Vale with the possibility of other *Abwehr* personnel living there," Charles said, as he dialled the number of one of the Service's departments. He explained the situation and gave the number of *Olga Schwartz*. He told the person he didn't want them phoning the number, just finding out the address. He should be phoned back with the details as soon as possible as it was of the utmost importance.

"I thought you replied to my message on the boat saying that *Olga Schwartz* was a known member of the *Abwehr*, and now we find she's here in London!" Andrew remarked.

"What about those other numbers?" Andrew enquired, "or will you give them to someone else in the department to do some work on?"

"You came back with Harry Ballantyne, who's in the British Embassy in Oslo, did you not? He might be the man to follow up on the Norwegian numbers, don't you think?"

"Good idea. He would definitely be the right man for that job."

They concluded their discussions. Charles said he would read Andrew's report with great interest; he would get back to him in the next day or two. Andrew left the St James' office. His arm and leg were beginning to give him a bit of pain. He knew there was a nurse – and sometimes a doctor – at the Broadway offices so he took a taxi and arrived just after 12:30 p.m.

"Hello, Mr Williams," the receptionist said as Andrew entered the building. "Do you need to see anyone in particular today, sir?"

"Do you know if nurse Symonds is in today, please? I have been injured a couple of times in the last few days that I believe should be attended to."

The receptionist phoned a number and had a short discussion with someone.

"You are in luck, Mr Williams. The nurse said she was free so please take the lift to the second floor and turn right as you come out of it. The nurses' rooms are down on the left. Please sign in the reception book."

Andrew gave the receptionist one of his appealing smiles, signed in and took the lift to the second floor. He knocked and went in to a waiting room. He gave his name and was told to take a seat for a few minutes.

"Mr Williams? Will you come in, please; nurse Symonds will see you now," The door was closed behind him and he was shown to a seat.

"So, what seems to be the problem, Mr Williams? What have you been getting up to?"

Without getting into too much detail, Andrew told the nurse that he had a scratch on his left lower leg and another – slightly bigger scratch – on his left lower arm. He told her he received the injuries on two separate occasions and each had been given treatment soon after the time of the incidents.

"Please take off your jacket, Mr Williams." He did as he was asked and rolled up his sleeve. She took off the adhesive plaster and revealed the scar.

"That's a very bad scratch, as you call it, Mr Williams. I shall have to clean it properly so I can have a better look at it."

She bathed it with cotton wool and disinfectant. She examined the cut more carefully.

"The injury looks as though it's starting to heal, but I would advise you to have a few stitches to help it knit together better. Let me look at your left leg, please."

Andrew pulled up his trouser, took off his shoe, rolled down his sock and placed his leg on the nurse's lap. She undid the bandage and removed the gauze very carefully.

"This injury is much worse and you must have incurred it a few days before the one on your arm. Who attended to this injury?"

"I gained the injury last Thursday afternoon. The ship's doctor attended to it two days later in the morning."

"He has done a very good job for you, but I recommend some stitches for this injury too," the nurse said. "You have enough time for me to do them now, Mr Williams?"

"Yes, I do, nurse. I'm very grateful to you for being able to attend to my wounds so promptly."

The nurse got down to business. She cleaned off the wounds again, put four stitches in the leg and two in the arm. She applied some iodine and gauze to the leg and his arm, wrapped both with a bandage and fastened each of them with a safety pin.

"That should do for now, Mr Williams, but please be very careful not to knock either of those wounds. I suggest you make an appointment to come back here on Friday afternoon so I can see how they are healing. I don't expect to be able to take the stitches out until sometime next week, but it will very much depend on how much or how little you use your leg. Does either of them give you any pain now?"

"No, they don't, nurse. I am hardly aware that I have done anything to either limb, I'm pleased to say," he said untruthfully.

"I'm glad to hear that. Please be careful how you bath or wash as the bandages ought to be kept dry. In the meantime, if either of them starts to bleed, or you have any severe pain, come back here straight away. Is that understood?"

"Loud and clear, Miss Symonds. Thank you very much for your kind attention," Andrew said, as he put on his sock, shoe and his jacket. He left the building and took a taxi back to his flat. *What a bore*, he said to himself in a disgruntled manner, *I might even have to talk to my flatmates for once.*

Chapter 28

Wednesday, 12th June 1940

Andrew spent the next couple of days resting his wounded leg and arm. He didn't like doing nothing, he was very fed up with the injuries. He was sure they were not nearly as bad as the nurse had made out, but he wanted them to have a chance of healing properly, and quickly. He had thought through the situation with Miss Olsen, *Olga Schwartz* and the man on the train, John Smith, at length. He was wondering if Charles' people had come up with the address for the phone number on the piece of paper when the phone rang. He quickly went downstairs.

"Hello," said Andrew. "Can I help you?"

"Andrew, it's Charles. Can you come to my office at about 4:30 p.m.? I have something I would like to discuss with you."

Andrew looked at his watch – it was 10:30 a.m. – and he agreed to be at the St James' office in six hours' time. After a very light lunch, he took a taxi part of the way. He walked the rest as it was a warm day and he desperately needed some exercise.

"Hello, Mr Williams. How are you? Please sign the register. Mr Compton-Browne is expecting you so go straight up," Miss Jones said, quite cheerfully.

"Thank you, Miss Jones. I am well, I trust you are too?" she nodded and smiled.

Andrew went quickly upstairs, knocked and went in, just as Charles was saying "enter".

"Have you been relaxing since Monday morning or have you been wandering around town?" Charles enquired.

"Not much of either, actually. I've been trying to work out the possible connection between Helena Olsen, *Fraulein Olga Schwartz* and this John Smith bloke."

"I want to say that I found your report of the mission to Norway very interesting. You were very lucky not to have been seriously injured when the plane careered off the runway at Sumburgh. I have put out an enquiry about the hostess' condition, but I wait to hear a response. Quite an exciting business with Miss Olsen and the Quisling gunmen. Pity you felt you had to kill her; she might have been quite useful by giving us an insight into Quisling's thinking and his real relationship with *Herr Hitler* and his mob. It seems you got yourself quite involved in protecting the ship when you manned the anti-aircraft guns. I wouldn't be surprised if the captain submits his report with a commendation for you in it. We'll see what it says when it arrives. And fancy being able to see that life raft in which King Haakon's nephew was, when nobody else could see it. The king must have been so pleased to have him and the six other sailors brought on board the ship.

"Well, I do have some really good news," Charles continued. "Our chaps have located the address of the phone number we rang. Also, Harry Ballantyne has been doing some excellent digging around into the Norwegian numbers that were in the back of Smith's diary. I tried the Maida Vale number again, but, not surprisingly, there was no reply this time. One of my men contacted the police in Crewe and we have been given special permission to receive Smith's passport and his ration book. Because it belongs to an attempted murder enquiry, we will have to return it after we have had it thoroughly examined – even if he is dead."

"I'm very interested to hear all this, but presumably you've called me in to help in some way?"

"Exactly right, Andrew. I have managed to persuade the police in London to issue a warrant to search the premises of the Maida Vale address. Two detectives will be available tomorrow at 10 o'clock; you will go with them."

"Do I meet them here, or somewhere else?"

"You will meet them here and go to the address in their car. OK so far?" Andrew nodded.

"Not sure how much you know about the other theatres of war, but things are getting very desperate in France. Mr Churchill has been flying backwards and forwards to France for meetings. He, Mr Eden and other senior staff officers flew to Briare yesterday; the French army headquarters have been moved to Chateau du Muguet nearby. They are having a two-day meeting with de Gaulle, Pétain and senior French military personnel. They make up the Anglo-French Supreme War Council that has been meeting at various times since the outbreak of war. The French have been appealing to the British for more military support and aircraft as the German army is nearing Paris.

"Not only are we at war with Germany, but Italy declared war on France and Britain yesterday."

"I assume Churchill is standing firm on Pétain and de Gaulle's appeal for more British arms?" Andrew interjected.

"Absolutely. Even if Britain did commit to supplying more men and machines, he is well aware that over 45,000 British and French soldiers have just surrendered to General Rommel at St Valery-en-Caux on the coast."

"So, if France end up surrendering in the next few days, it looks as though Hitler will then set his eyes on invading Britain?"

"That's one of the main reasons why Churchill will not supply more arms – planes, in particular – to France. We will need every pilot and airplane to defend our country against the Luftwaffe."

"That all sounds very bleak, Charles. This war could go on for a good number of years. The only way it could end earlier is if the Americans can be persuaded to join the allies."

"I think we could consider all sorts of scenarios if they don't, but I've heard that the Russians are not exactly standing still. They've had the

Lithuanian government's agreement to allow Soviet forces to occupy their country. No doubt Latvia and Estonia will follow suit in due course. All three countries will then be overrun by the Ruskies.

"I forgot to mention to you when I was mentioning the surrender of the forces to Rommel that German forces have entered the Place de la Concorde. Several million people have now fled Paris."

"As I said earlier, Charles, everything appears to be very bleak. Perhaps we should adjourn our discussions and leave for a drink," Andrew suggested. "It's nearly 6 o'clock anyway and I'm feeling parched."

Charles tidied his desk and they left his office. They decided to go to a pub not too far from the office. They walked as it was a warm evening.

"Are you limping a bit, Andrew? You don't seem to be quite as sprightly as usual?"

"It might be these shoes," Andrew said, not wanting to say anything about the wound in his left leg."

They arrived at the pub. Charles ordered two pints and, as they went to sit by the window looking out onto the street, Andrew knocked his left leg against the table leg. He let out an expletive, but not enough to alert anyone else. *I must remember to keep the appointment with the nurse on Friday*, he mumbled to himself.

"Cheers, Andrew. I hope all goes well tomorrow in Maida Vale. It could be a very interesting visit."

"I'm not sure what I'm supposed to be looking for in this flat. Can you give me some guidance?"

"I'm not sure either, but take great care. The place could be booby-trapped. The two policemen will be the best we can get hold of at present."

"I'm sure that fills me with confidence, Charles!" he said with a smile.

They talked about various areas of the war and whether or not Britain and the Empire could prevail against the might of the Germans.

"As I've got an interesting and different day tomorrow, Charles, I think I ought to be wending my way back to my flat. Do you want me to come and see you after we've completed this detective work?"

"I was going to suggest that to you, so the answer's yes."

They finished their drinks. Charles found a taxi at the end of the road. They went to Andrew's flat first before going on to his own house.

The following morning, Andrew rose early. After some breakfast, he put on some casual clothes, took his pistol from the cupboard and checked he had plenty of rounds of bullets. He was fairly sure he wouldn't need to use it, but *you never really know when you might,* he said to himself. He was ready in good time and arrived at Charles' office just before 10 o'clock. A car was parked outside so he assumed it must belong to the police. He knocked on the door and Miss Jones came and let him in.

"Two young policemen are here, Mr Williams. They have been awaiting your arrival for a full ten minutes."

"Thank you, Miss Jones," Andrew said, without paying any attention to her jibe that he had kept the policemen waiting. The three men introduced themselves and shook hands.

"Shall we be on our way, Mr Williams?"

"Please call me Andrew."

"My name is Pete and my colleague here is Mike."

They said goodbye to Miss Jones as they left the office for the car. Andrew was offered the seat in the back. The streets were not too busy so they made good time to the address in Maida Vale. They pulled up outside and examined the house carefully before getting out of the car.

"Looks like a good house in quite an expensive neighbourhood," Pete said. "Shall I go and have a closer look?"

They all got out of the car. They saw there was a narrow passageway going to the side of the house.

"There are several stories so do you think it's been turned into flats?" Pete asked.

"I don't think so," Andrew said. "My understanding is that the building is all one house. Mike, I suggest you go around the back. Take a good look up at all the windows. See which have their curtains drawn closed and which are open. Have a snoop around the garden. Come back here when you've done that. We'll go and try the door."

Mike disappeared down the passageway, Pete and Andrew walked up the steps to the door. Pete tried the door – it was locked.

"Don't watch what I'm doing, Andrew, as I pick the lock."

Within a couple of minutes, the door was opened and Pete looked inside. He stopped in the doorway, listening intently: no sound from anywhere inside. They closed the door behind them, but put the latch up so that Mike could get in, if he needed to. Andrew said he would make his way up to the first floor. He took his pistol from his jacket pocket; he cocked it.

Pete went in to the room immediately the other side of the hallway. It was a large, square room with a large rug covering most of the floor area. The curtains were closed so he switched on the centre light to see what was in the room more clearly. He walked over to the window, drew back the curtain a little and saw Mike wandering around in the garden, occasionally looking up at the windows. One cream telephone was on a knee-hole desk to the right of the window, positioned across the corner. He took out his handkerchief and lifted the receiver – he heard the dialling tone and replaced it. There was a blotter pad on the desk, a pencil and some loose papers with writing on a few of them.

Andrew stepped very carefully and quietly on the outside of each step as he went up the stairs to the first floor. He saw two doors, one of which was ajar. He opened the door, pushed it so he could see inside, but the curtains were closed. As he stepped inside, he saw that the bed was unmade. He switched on the light and saw there was a body on the bed that seemed to be tied up. He went to the landing and called Pete to come up quickly to the first floor.

"This is more your scene than mine, Pete," as he arrived at the door's entrance. Pete went over to the bed, pulled the sheet back to reveal a woman's face. He put his fingers to her neck and felt for a pulse.

"She's dead, Andrew, but she hasn't been that way for very long as she's still slightly warm. Have a look to see if there's anything in the room that might help us identify her."

Pete lifted the sheet gently, saw that the woman was clothed. "That's a relief," he said to himself, but just loud enough for Andrew to hear what he had said. She had been shot several times in the chest – "It wasn't suicide then," he mumbled. There was no gun in her hand or on the floor near the bed.

Andrew looked in the cupboard. There were some dresses on hangers, several pairs of shoes on the bottom shelf, items of underwear and blouses on shelves to the right, a brown leather suitcase to the right of the shoes.

"Are you happy for me to touch any of the things in this cupboard?" Andrew asked Pete. "Can I have a look in the suitcase?"

Just at that moment, Mike came in to the bedroom and saw the body on the bed.

"Mike, there's a phone downstairs in the lounge that seems to be working. Phone the yard, ask to speak to the super, give him this address and tell him about us finding a woman's body. We need someone over here sharpish together with an ambulance. Hopefully the line hasn't been bugged."

Mike disappeared downstairs. Andrew heard him speaking to someone as he looked through the things in the suitcase. From the mixture of items in the case, he had a sneaking suspicion that the owner of the suitcase was due to be going somewhere, and soon. He started to look in the bedside drawer for any more clues. He found two passports: one French and the other German. The photos in each were identical, as were the names: *Fraulein Olga Schwartz*!

"Take a look at these, Pete," as he handed the passports over to him.

"Who's *Fraulein Olga Schwartz* when she's at home, Andrew?"

"Not sure how much you know from discussions with my boss, Pete, but this woman's name is known by us in the Service. That's assuming, of course, that the passports and this woman are one and the same person!"

Andrew went around to the other side of the bed and opened the second bedside drawer: empty. He then searched the dressing table drawers: nothing.

"Do you think we should go through all the other rooms, Pete, just on the off chance of finding something important: like the gun that was used to shoot this woman?"

"No, I don't think so. We'll leave that to the lads coming from the yard."

At that moment, Mike arrived in the room from downstairs.

"Chaps from the yard and an ambulance are on the way. They should be here in about ten minutes."

Andrew knew that Charles would be very happy with this morning's work, and would be curious to find out who shot the woman. One major thought will be that it was probably an inside job carried out by the *Abwehr*, or one of Quisling's supporters. They could have found out – somehow or another – that King Haakon wasn't dead after all and that the mission to kill him had failed. If the dead woman had been responsible for the success of the mission, she had paid the ultimate price.

Andrew told the two policemen that he was going downstairs to the lounge. He walked over to the desk and picked up the papers. There were some scribblings on the first page, suggesting that someone had been doodling whilst listening to the person on the other end of the line. He wondered if they were *Olga's* from when Charles phoned the number and pretended to be John Smith. Maybe the phone is bugged and a senior *Abwehr* man was listening in and realised Charles was not John Smith, or that the *Abwehr* already knew John Smith was dead? So many questions that needed answering.

The next two pages were much more decipherable. They contained names with numbers against a few of them. He folded them up, put them in his jacket pocket; he would give them to Charles when he saw him later on. He hoped the police wouldn't want them.

There was a knock on the front door, so Andrew went to see who it was. On opening the door, he saw two policemen and two other men – presumably the ambulance men. He saw the ambulance in the street, so he let them all in.

"The body is upstairs in the back bedroom," he said to them. As they went up, he shouted to Pete that they were on their way up. Andrew followed them and went over to speak to Pete as the body was placed on the stretcher and covered with a blanket.

"How much longer do you and Mike want to be here?" he enquired.

"I've just got to brief the lads from the yard and then we can go."

"Will you be needing the woman's passports for the next day or two as I would like to take them to my boss?"

"That should be alright, but we will need them in due course."

After some minutes of discussions between the four policemen, Pete looked over at Andrew:

"I think we're done here now, so if there's nothing else you want to do, we can take you back to your boss' office?"

"Fine by me, Pete." They all shook hands, said their farewells. The three of them went down to the hallway and out to their car.

Chapter 29
Thursday, 13th June 1940

Andrew was dropped off at Charles' office. It was about 1 o'clock so he hoped he hadn't gone to lunch yet. He knocked on the door, went into the reception area and asked Miss Jones if Charles was in.

"You are in luck, Mr Williams. He came back here only twenty minutes ago. Please sign in and I'll call him to say you are here to see him."

After a few seconds, he was told he could go up as he was free. He knocked and, as usual, went straight in.

"So, Andrew, have you had a useful morning in Maida Vale?"

Andrew took the passports from his pocket and handed them over. At the same time, he said they belonged to *Fraulein Olga Schwartz* and he believed it was her body that was in the bedroom of the house. He explained everything to Charles and ended up by handing over the pieces of paper he had taken from the desk.

"That looks like a good morning's work, but who did the police think might have killed her?"

"They have no idea. They didn't even know of *Fraulein Olga Schwartz* let alone who killed her – if that's who she is. We left some senior detectives at the scene carrying out further investigations and searching the house from top to bottom. My theory is that if the *Abwehr* killed one of their own for not fulfilling the mission of killing King Haakon; we might never know the real story."

"I agree," Charles said, as he thumbed his way through the two passports.

"As you say, the two photos are identical, as are the details. The German passport has been used more than the French one. Judging from the visa entry into Britain, however, she came to our country using the French one. It makes sense as she would have been asked fewer questions. It appears she came through immigration in Liverpool from Dublin only one week ago and entered Dublin a few days before that. In both passports, it says she is a teacher."

"**Was** a teacher," said Andrew with a grin.

"Exactly so," Charles replied.

"I think it's going to take quite a lot of time to get to the bottom of this mystery, Andrew. As I knew you would be coming back to my office, I had some sandwiches made. They're nothing special, but it will save us having to go out, like we usually end up by doing. I'll get some tea brought in, so we can relax and talk further in here. There are a couple of ideas that I would like to talk over with you. I've already talked them over with C and he has agreed with what I have in mind."

"Sounds a good idea to me," Andrew replied.

Charles phoned the receptionist asking for some tea to be sent up to his office as he and Mr Williams would be staying in his office over the lunchtime. Charles took the sandwiches from his briefcase, went to the cupboard to the side of the window and brought plates and napkins to the small table next to his desk.

"Not very imaginative, Andrew, but they'll keep the wolf from the door for a while."

After a few minutes, a lady brought the tea in and placed the tray on Charles' desk.

"Thank you, Mary. Please slide the sign on the door to ENGAGED after you go out."

"So, what is it of interest that you want to talk to me about, Charles? I'm very intrigued and all ears," Andrew asked, after having consumed a couple of sandwiches.

"Ever since you joined the Service, one of your identities has been that of a lieutenant in the navy. C and I have been in discussions with Naval Intelligence and the Admiralty for quite some time and we believe it would be highly appropriate for you to go through a significant part of naval officer training. You could then be considered as a real lieutenant," Charles said with a laugh.

"This move is not really meant to help you in the short term, but perhaps more in the longer term. You have occasionally expressed a wish to be in the Royal Navy, so this could help you in that regard. What do you think?"

"That's probably not a bad suggestion. Hopefully, however, while I've been acting as a lieutenant – particularly during the mission to Norway – nobody has questioned my real credentials?"

"On the contrary. You have been praised very highly by both the captain and the rear-admiral. They have even suggested to the Admiralty that you should be considered for command of your own ship. Their reply – as you might imagine – was that, even though they welcomed the recommendation, there was no way they could consider any such appointment at this present time. The captain hadn't been told that you weren't a real lieutenant."

"My goodness, that's praise indeed, especially coming from the rear-admiral. I'm not sure what I did to deserve such a commendation."

"I am not going to go into any details as the final reports from that mission have to be submitted to the Service, but C has received some glowing statements from the captain.

"So, what do you think of the idea?"

"It's certainly come as a bit of a surprise; I have to say. But what alternatives are there within the Service as you see things?"

"That's a very interesting question. As a bit of background – and I must remind you that this is strictly confidential – the SIS, as far back as March 1938, established a section known as Section D. Its primary function was to evaluate the use of sabotage, propaganda and other 'unlawful' means of weakening an enemy. Later in 1938, the War Office expanded an existing research department – known as GS (R) – to conduct research into guerrilla warfare. Early in 1939, the department was renamed MI R. It was SIS and MI R that somehow or other in early 1940, put together the mission, involving you and George, to carry out the successful sabotage of the German railway line back in March.

"I have it on good authority that today the Prime Minister has persuaded Section D and MI R to coordinate their operations."

They each fell silent as they finished their tea and sandwiches. Andrew walked around the room, stopping to look out of the window at the street below. He tried to contemplate what Charles might come up with next for him to be involved in.

"You are probably wondering where this is all leading to, Andrew. As we speak, however, there are serious concerns that the French government are even more strongly considering throwing in the towel and looking at drawing up an armistice agreement with Hitler. The only possible saving grace is if the French Prime Minister, M. Reynaud's, appeal to President Roosevelt for increased American commitment to the allies' struggle against the Nazi regime, is accepted. Mr Churchill has flown to Tours this morning where the French government is now located.

"We will hear of the meeting's outcome in due course, but what I can say, however, is that there seems to me to be a 90% chance of France asking Britain to be released from their joint pledge to continue fighting on. If that happens, M. Reynaud will be forced to resign allowing the elderly Marshall Pétain to be appointed Prime Minister. He is in favour of an armistice agreement with Germany, meaning that France would capitulate. This would leave Britain and her Empire to fight on her own against the Nazis."

"I'm still not sure how I fit in and what role I might be asked to play?"

"C and I have some ideas, but it will depend on what happens in the next few days. Why don't you leave here and think over the alternatives that I'm offering you: do a fast-track naval officer training course or go on another mission for us, the SIS. Come back here on Monday at 3 o'clock with your decision. With things developing so quickly at present, there might even be a few more options I could offer you by that time. Just before you go, I need to tell you that after your killing of Helena Olsen and John Smith – not to mention your knowledge of *Fraulein Olga Schwartz'* demise – you need to take extra care. If, as we think, the *Abwehr* controlled all three of them, you could be a wanted man and be on their hit list. On that salutary note, I wish you a pleasant weekend."

As Andrew walked away from the office, he felt rather concerned for his own life, but this was just about overridden by his pleasure on hearing the comments coming from the captain and the rear-admiral. The other thing he was happy about was not having to see Charles till Monday afternoon; it will at least give him the chance of visiting the nurse about his injuries. He thought they felt better, but he was cross with himself for knocking his leg on Wednesday afternoon.

Andrew slept well that night after a good supper with two of his flatmates, followed by a couple of hours of cards. He looked at his leg to see that it wasn't swollen, nor had it been bleeding after being knocked. He had a light breakfast of toast, decided to go to the SIS main office in Broadway and see if Helen was still working there as C's secretary – he would go to the nurse afterwards at the appointed time of 3:30 p.m.

He walked to the SIS office and went in to the main ground floor reception. He realised he didn't know Helen's surname.

"Please could you tell me if C's secretary is working here today?" Andrew asked the commissioner.

"Yes, she is. Would you like me to contact her? Who shall I say is wanting to speak to her?"

Andrew gave his full name. The man dialled a number and spoke to someone. He passed the phone to Andrew.

"Hello, Helen? This is Andrew Williams. Do you remember me? I used to see you when I came to visit Mr Compton-Browne at his office in St James."

"Yes, I do, Mr Williams."

"I was just passing by your office and was wondering if you would like to come and have some lunch with me today?"

"That's a very nice idea, but I'm quite busy at present. I will be leaving the office at 5 o'clock, so if you would like to, we could go for a drink before I go home?"

Andrew thought her idea was a very much better one, so he agreed to be back just before 5 o'clock. At least he knew he would have plenty of time before hand to visit the nurse. He told her that he was looking forward to seeing her later in the day and rang off. He thanked the commissioner for his help.

Bearing in mind Charles' words about being a wanted man, he decided to go back to his flat via a different route, and not down the main roads. As he turned down a small street, he thought he was aware of being followed. He suddenly dived down an alleyway to his left and stood against a door that was inset from the passageway. He looked carefully to his right and saw two men go past the end of the alleyway. They didn't look his way. He waited for a full five minutes, in case they realised they'd lost him, and turned back. Satisfied that he'd escaped this time, he continued on his way to the flat.

After some lunch and a rest, Andrew set off by taxi for the Broadway office and his appointment with the nurse. He checked in, took the lift to the second floor and sat in the waiting room. Just after 3:30 p.m., he was called in to the nurse's surgery.

"Nice to see you, Mr Williams. Have your wounds been giving you any cause for concern?"

"No, they haven't, thank you," he replied, with his customary engaging smile.

"Let's have a look at the leg first, please."

Andrew removed his shoe and sock, placing his foot on the nurse's lap as before. She took the bandage off, then carefully removed the gauze. She said the stitches were holding the wound together nicely, but they couldn't come out till the middle of the following week. She cleaned the wound, put on some disinfectant and a new piece of gauze. She wrapped a new bandage around the leg and secured it with the safety pin.

"Now, let's look at the arm."

Andrew took off his jacket, rolled up his sleeve. She looked at the wound, once she'd taken the dressings off.

"That is looking much better, Mr Williams. You've obviously taken care not to knock it or get the bandage very damp. I'll definitely take the stitches out next week," she said, as she cleaned the wound and put the bandage back on.

"Your skin obviously heals quickly, Mr Williams. You are a lucky man."

"Thank you, nurse, but some credit must go to you and the way you have attended to the scratches," he said, in his usual charming manner. "Do you want me to come back on Wednesday?"

"Yes, please. Will 10:30 a.m. be alright with you?" Andrew agreed, left the surgery and went out of the building. He took a taxi back to his flat. He thought about where he should take Helen when he meets her at 5 o'clock.

Chapter 30
Friday, 14th June 1940

Andrew changed into his casual jacket and trousers. He saw there was enough time so he decided to walk. After his earlier near-encounter with the men following him, he took a different route to the Broadway offices near St James' underground station – just in case.

Andrew hadn't been on his way for many minutes when he was aware of people walking behind him. He pretended not to notice by not changing his pace or turning to look behind. In his mind, however, he prepared for a possible attack from behind, or in front, or perhaps both. All of a sudden, a man walked quickly passed him, stopped, turned around to face him. Andrew continued to walk. The man in front went to strike Andrew with his fists at the same time as the man behind threw his arms around Andrew's neck. In two swift movements, before the men knew what was happening, Andrew kneed the one in front very hard in the crutch. He fell to the ground writhing and clutching himself. Andrew grasped the man's arms that were around Andrew's neck, bent his legs pulling him over his right shoulder. He threw him to the ground whilst still holding the man's right arm. He heard the arm go 'crack' as it broke at the shoulder.

"Whoever you are, don't ever try to attack me again or I'll kill you both." They said nothing, just groaned.

He knelt down, searching their jackets for some form of identification. They struggled and tried to get up, but Andrew was on top of them both. He held them down by kneeling on them. He retrieved a brown identity card from each, found a few other documents, plus some pieces of paper with handwriting on. He put them all in his jacket pocket. He looked around for any possible assistance or eye-witnesses, but there was nobody. He stood up as they stared at him. He kicked each of them again very hard in the stomach – more in anger than anything else. They shouted and grasped themselves. Andrew felt pleased that he had at least remembered something from his short course on unarmed combat almost a year ago, else he might have been in real trouble.

He straightened his hair and jacket and walked on; he was pleased with his efforts; the injuries on his arm and leg didn't seem to have been affected. He looked at his watch; he saw it was already past 5 o'clock. He swore to himself for being late. He hoped Helen would wait for some minutes before giving up and leaving for home – wherever that was.

He reached the SIS office in Broadway at 5:20 p.m. He was sure she would have left by now. He went to the receptionist, asked if Helen had been waiting, only to be told that she had left the building ten minutes earlier.

"I don't suppose you can let me have Helen's home address, can you?" Andrew asked the receptionist.

"I'm sorry, sir, but it would be a breach of security if I did that; sorry, no."

"I thought so," Andrew replied. "Thank you."

Andrew left the building and stood outside for a few minutes, wondering what he should do now. He suddenly had a brainwave. *As I'm so close, I'll go and see if my mother is in. The Ritz is only along the road,* he mumbled to himself. *I might even get a free meal.*

He couldn't believe he had made the decision to see his mother, when there was so much else to do in London – even in war time.

She was a woman who only really thought about what she wanted to do. She hadn't even bothered to attend his son's Baptism or his first birthday party in May when he was away. Nevertheless, he felt he should try and rebuild a few bridges.

He went up the steps to the hotel's entrance, wandered over to the reception counter, smiled at the attractive brunette receptionist.

"I don't suppose Mrs. Anna Williams is in her rooms by any chance?" The receptionist looked around at where the keys were hanging. She turned back to Andrew.

"She should be, sir. Shall I call her? Who shall I say wishes to visit her?"

"Please say her son, Andrew, is in reception and would like to see her in her room."

The receptionist dialled the room's number. Andrew heard her speak. She replaced the handset.

"She told me to tell you to go up to her room. Do you know which room she's in?"

"Thank you. I know her room number."

He took the lift to the fourth floor. He turned left and knocked on the door. He heard a noise, turned the handle and walked into the suite's lounge area.

"Darling Andrew. What a nice surprise," his mother said in Danish. She nearly always spoke to him in her native language. He also enjoyed the chance to keep practicing the language.

"Hello, Mummy," he replied, also in Danish.

"I thought you were supposed to be in the British Royal Navy fighting against our enemy, the Nazis?"

He knew he had to say something to her, but she wouldn't really be too interested in his answer.

"I have some time off, I thought I would come and pay you a visit to see how you are."

"I'm fine. I have many kind visitors here in London. How's that wife of yours? I can't understand why she hasn't been here with your son. He must be fourteen months old by now."

Andrew knew the conversation was going to go down the same old path. His choice of a wife was never liked by most of his close family members.

"You had the opportunity to attend Alfred's first birthday party," Andrew explained, "but you thought it would be better to have dinner with Lord Fontleroy instead – or whatever his name was."

"Oh, don't be like that, darling. Anyway, you weren't going to be there, so I would have had to be looked after by that wife of yours."

"But you had arranged to stay at the local hotel which would have kept your contact with her to a minimum."

He needed to change the subject onto something of more interest and enjoyable to his mother.

"Have you had much news from our relatives in Denmark since the German invasion in early April?"

"Nothing very specific recently, but I do get the occasional call from the Danish Ambassador, who keeps me in the picture as best he can – security permitting."

Andrew thought the conversation was getting a bit flat and he was feeling rather thirsty, especially after his ordeal with the two men that attacked him.

"Have you got anything to drink in your room for your dear son?" he asked.

"I don't have any aquavit, darling, but I've got some gin. What I think might be better is if I ask room service to bring something up for us. You'd like a gin 'n' tonic and I'll have a large sweet sherry?" Andrew nodded in agreement.

She went over to the phone and gave her drinks order. She also asked for some canapés.

In what seemed next to no time, there was a knock on the door. The waiter entered, placed the tray on the table, gave a chitty to his mother to sign and left the room. Andrew saw that there were two small carafes: one of gin and another of sherry. He poured out the measures, adding ice and lemon to his gin.

"*Skol,*" they said to each other as they touched glasses and took a sip of their drink.

"This is indeed a nice surprise, Andrew darling. You must come around more often. I do suggest, however, that you phone next time just in case I already have a visitor."

They chatted for well over half an hour covering various topics. They were both well in to their second drinks; Andrew thought his mother was starting to slur her words, whereas his second drink was deliberately just straight tonic.

"Are you going to treat me to a meal tonight, Mummy, or do I have to go to a nearby restaurant, on my own?" he tried to rub his solitary position in as much as he could.

"Do you mean you haven't got some attractive young lady to meet tonight?" his mother asked, with a wink and a smile.

"I am here to be with you. Let's go to the restaurant and indulge ourselves?" he said, as smarmily as he thought he would get away with, seeing that it was now well after 7 o'clock.

His mother agreed. She rang the reception and reserved a table for 7:40 p.m. They went down to the main restaurant, once they had finished their drinks.

"We've reserved the usual table for you Mrs. Williams," said the head waiter, as he walked towards the far window. They enjoyed their meal with a bottle of red, although the selection of food was far less with the war on.

"Are you quite comfortable in that new house, Andrew? I know it's quite old, but it's not nearly as large as your first one?"

"It's alright, Mummy, I suppose. I'm still not sure why you reduced my allowance, as it forced me to move into something smaller. Anyway, it's over a year ago since we moved, so we've sort of got used to it. With my being away at war, I still don't understand why you can't go and see my wife and your grandson, at least once in a while?

"Do you ever get to hear from my brother? Where is he now? He joined the Army, didn't he?"

"He came and saw me in January, I think it was. He's a commissioned officer in the Army. I like his wife a lot."

Andrew believed he was starting to walk on dodgy ground, especially regarding a suggested visit to his wife. He, therefore, felt it was time to leave before the conversation got completely out of hand. His mother signed the bill and they walked out to the reception area. She asked the hotel's commissioner to get him a taxi. He certainly didn't fancy walking back to his flat this evening and giving the opportunity to someone else to attack him again.

Chapter 31
Monday, 17th June 1940

Even though Andrew did very little over the weekend, it did give him a chance to think over the options that Charles had spelt out to him. Unless he was persuaded otherwise, he had made up his mind over what he wanted to do.

He arrived at Charles' office just before 3 o'clock, signed in and went upstairs. He knocked, heard Charles' voice and went in.

"How have the last few days been for you, Andrew?" as they moved towards each other and shook hands. "Not got up to any mischief, have you?"

"I should have had such luck. But I have to tell you that I was attacked late Friday afternoon," Andrew mentioned. He took some things out of his jacket packet and placed them on Charles' desk.

"As I said a moment ago, I was viciously attacked, but I managed to do some damage to them and these are the items I took from them."

"Did you go to the police?"

"No. I thought you might be more interested in this stuff than the police. Have a look through their identity cards. I haven't spent too much time going through the other papers, but your chaps will have a real field day locating these two. You had warned me about possible reprisals, but I didn't expect to be the centre of attention quite so soon after your warning."

"With your history of killings over the last few weeks, you can't be too careful. Were you injured at all? You said you did some damage to the men that attacked you, but what specifically did you do to them?"

"What would you expect me to do?" Andrew said rather irritably. "One attacked me from behind, the other from the front. I kicked one of them hard in the crutch, the other I pulled over my shoulder and threw to the ground. I'm certain I broke his arm."

"They are not likely to make a complaint to anyone, so, as long as you're alright, that's what really matters. I'll look at all these papers later with a great deal of interest, but I need to talk to you about some extremely important, and extraordinary, recent events.

"General de Gaulle has been a very active person over the last couple of days, or even weeks. He came for a meeting with Churchill on Saturday afternoon, having flown into Heston aerodrome. The two of them had already met each other at various meetings in France, together with M. Reynaud, the French Prime Minister.

"Churchill and de Gaulle were due to meet for lunch at Chequers yesterday. Early that morning, however, Churchill received Reynaud's telegram asking for armistice terms. He called for a cabinet meeting in order to draft a reply and moved his lunch with de Gaulle to the Carlton Club. His communique was sent to Reynaud in Bordeaux clearly forbidding the entering of armistice negotiations with Hitler. He also said that His Majesty's government were resolved to continue the war – not wishing to be party to any armistice."

"My goodness! What was Reynaud's response to that?" Andrew enquired.

"There was no reply from Reynaud at this stage. Churchill and de Gaulle spoke at length during and after their lunch, focussing on the position of the French Fleet, and the possibility of it falling into the hands of the Germans. Quite extraordinarily, they drew up a proposal to establish a single Franco-British government, with Reynaud as *le président*. The main purpose being to prevent France capitulating to the Germans.

"Churchill then went to seek affirmation from the War Cabinet. De Gaulle phoned Reynaud to tell him of what was afoot only for Reynaud to tell him that he needed to inform the Council of Ministers of the proposal before the end of the afternoon.

"After much discussion and with Churchill's very persuasive words, the draft proposal was approved by the War Cabinet. De Gaulle, who was in a nearby room in Downing Street, was immediately informed of the decision; he was told to phone Reynaud. He dictated the document's contents to him, just in time for Reynaud's meeting."

"I can hardly believe what you are telling me, Charles; and all this happened yesterday?"

"Don't think it's over yet, Andrew. Yesterday evening, de Gaulle flew to Bordeaux by plane – lent to him by Churchill – to discuss the Declaration of Union with Reynaud. On his arrival, he heard that the Council had unanimously rejected the proposal. Reynaud felt he had no option, but to submit his resignation. This resulted in Marshall Pétain being asked by the President to form a new government."

"So, where does this leave Britain and de Gaulle?"

"When Mr Churchill heard the news, he decided to phone Marshall Pétain, in the middle of last night, would you believe? He tried to persuade the Marshall in no uncertain terms not to seek for an armistice, but it was all in vain. He told Churchill that he would contact Hitler at his headquarters, near Sedan, to draw up peace negotiations.

"I am reliably informed that, early this morning, de Gaulle stopped at the General Staff Headquarters, in the rue Vital-Carles in Bordeaux, on his way back to the airport. He told everyone that they must keep on fighting, if for no other reason than for France's honour – they had not lost the war. He said that with Britain's fighting spirit and America's resources, France could not and should not accept defeat. With those words – and his thoughts of continuing the fight – he told them he was leaving France to join his powerful ally: Mr Winston Churchill. He said he would act on behalf of France to the best of his ability in self-imposed exile: in England, until the Germans are beaten."

"It appears to me, Charles, that we really are now on our own. How does de Gaulle hope to rally French support from London?"

"Everyone in the War Cabinet knows that Hitler will accept Marshall Pétain's proposal for an armistice. It could well be drawn up and signed within a few days. As for de Gaulle, he arrived back in England by plane this morning. General Spears accompanied him as he had been appointed earlier in the month by Churchill as his personal representative in France. He had attended every meeting in Briare, Tours and Bordeaux. He had also become an ally and a friend of de Gaulle's.

"It is expected that de Gaulle will live in London for some while and that Spears is very likely to head up the British Government's mission to de Gaulle. Until these developments had occurred, I was going to suggest that you go through Naval Officer training. I now have a more important job for you. General Spears has been in touch with C. He is looking for one or two bilingual people to join his small team supporting de Gaulle. And before you try to argue your way out of it, I know that many senior people – within and outside the War Cabinet – will see your involvement as a very appropriate and positive move."

"Charles, I am humbled by your suggestion and your faith in my ability to provide support to such a group. When are you likely to receive confirmation of my appointment?"

"Possibly tomorrow, but more likely to be on Wednesday. Unless you have any further questions, I suggest we meet again here on Thursday at 4 o'clock."

"I do have one more question: how long do you expect me to be working for General Spears?"

"It will very much depend on what de Gaulle has in mind, but it won't be for less than two weeks. I can't be any more specific than that at present, I'm sorry to say. Anything more?"

Andrew shook his head, stood up, shook Charles' hand and told him he would be back in three days' time. He left the St James' office and felt he was desperately in need of a drink. He remembered there was the Buckingham pub not far from Charles' office; he hadn't been in there for many months. He knew he would get a good pint. He wandered into the saloon bar that was quite crowded. He looked at his watch to see it was after 5:30 p.m., so he guessed that some office workers were there on their way home. He paid for a pint of bitter, turned towards the window at the front of the pub only to find he was face-to-face with Helen: the secretary from the Broadway office.

"Well, what a nice surprise to see you in here, Helen."

Andrew was just about to apologise for not arriving on time for their previous meeting, when she interrupted his thoughts:

"Can I introduce you to my brother, Jack? Jack, this is Mr Williams. He works at an office where I used to be a secretary."

Andrew and Jack shook hands. Andrew then smiled at Helen.

"Please call me Andrew. What will you have to drink?"

Jack ordered a pint of bitter, Helen asked for a dry vermouth. Andrew gave Helen his pint to hold, went back to the bar and returned to the table by the window.

"So, what do you do with yourself, Jack? Do you work in London or are you just visiting?"

"I'm a doctor in a practice in Sussex, but I used to be at University College Hospital a couple of years ago. I've come up to have lunch with a few of my friends that I trained with. It's also an opportunity to see how my lovely sister is getting on. How about you, Andrew?"

Andrew always knew he should have a prepared answer for this sort of question, but with Helen knowing his boss, it made his reply a bit difficult.

"I'm in the Royal Navy," he said. "I'm on extended leave for the moment as I damaged my arm and leg."

"Oh, that's very unfortunate for you. I'd offer to examine the injuries, but you're probably already being looked after by some nursing staff," Jack said with a grin.

Silence came over the three of them for a few moments as they raised their glasses to each other and took a couple of mouthfuls of their drinks. They started chatting about the situation of the war and what was likely to happen in France, but Andrew contributed very little. He knew when he needed to say very little.

"Do you think Germany will invade us?" Jack asked. "And what is Italy up to?"

"It's hard to tell what the Nazis will do," Andrew replied. "It very much depends on whether or not France can hold on, but they certainly don't show any stomach for a continuation of the fight at present."

They lapsed into further conversation of relative insignificance. Jack offered to buy another round, but said he ought really to catch a train back to his home in Sussex.

"Nice to have met you, Andrew. All the best with your injuries." He embraced Helen and left the pub. Helen and Andrew looked at each other. They both started to speak at the same time, but Andrew let Helen continue.

"Please go and buy us another drink, Andrew," as she pulled out a ten bob note from her purse. Andrew tried to resist, but she insisted.

He returned to the table with the drinks. Andrew knew he now had a chance to explain why he hadn't turned up for their previous meeting.

"I am so very sorry about last time. You will probably not believe it, but I was attacked on my way to the Broadway office." He explained in detail what had happened, he pulled up his left trouser leg to show her the bandaging.

"Oh, my goodness. That's dreadful," she said, as she gently placed her hand on his right arm, after he had stood up straight.

"I'm teasing you a bit," he said, as he smiled.

"Those injuries were not really inflicted by the attackers. Those occurred on other occasions, and not in London. But those attackers did delay me by a full twenty minutes, so my sincere apologies," as he looked into her eyes and gave one of his engaging smiles. She blushed a bit, just as she had done when he first met her at the St James' office reception. She was the first to break the gaze, as she took a large sip of her drink.

"Are you enjoying your new job, Helen?" he enquired, careful not to mention the name of the office in public.

"Yes, I'm liking it a lot. My boss is very pleasant too, although he's not in his office much at present."

They had nearly finished their drinks and the pub was starting to clear.

"Do you have to leave soon, or have you got time to have some supper with me?"

"I'd like that very much, Andrew," as she looked at her watch.

"I really ought to phone home first to tell my sister that I won't be home for supper."

"They finished their drinks, left the pub and Andrew hailed a taxi to the outside of Victoria Station. He pointed to the phone box nearby and Helen went off to make her call. Within a few minutes, she returned to Andrew. He took her hand and they walked to the restaurant that he had last been to with Charles.

"I'm so sorry, I forgot to ask you where you live, Victoria Station might not be of any use to you later on?"

"It's alright, I can change at Clapham Junction."

They arrived at the restaurant and the waiter showed them to a table by the window. He brought the menus, apologising that a few items were not available. Andrew saw, however, that there was still quite a lot of choice.

"Would you like some wine, Helen, or some other drink?"

"Red wine will be fine for me. Thank you," she said, without raising her eyes from the menu.

There wasn't much choice on offer, but Andrew ordered a bottle anyway. They gave their main course choices to the waiter just as he arrived with the wine. Andrew tasted it and he thought it was acceptable. Their conversation flowed very freely, so before they really knew it, their meals arrived. Andrew was enjoying Helen's company, as it helped him to forget the next mission that Charles had planned for him. She was a very engaging young woman; he hoped he might have further opportunities to entertain her.

After the rather simple dessert had been eaten, Andrew asked for the bill, while Helen went to powder her nose. They thanked the waiter for his kind attention as they left the restaurant. She took Andrew's arm.

"You really need to go to Waterloo, don't you?" Andrew asked. She looked up at him as she answered 'yes please'; he waved a taxi down. As the taxi drove away, Andrew turned his head towards Helen. They kissed amorously without Helen giving any indication of wanting to pull away. They seemed to arrive at the station in next to no time. Andrew got out and helped Helen to the pavement.

"I hope we might get the chance to do something like this again before too long," Andrew remarked, to which she agreed.

Andrew waited for Helen to go out of sight, got back into the taxi and asked to be taken to his flat address. He felt he was on cloud nine.

Chapter 32
Wednesday, 19th June 1940

Andrew relaxed for most of Tuesday, except for a walk up to St James' Park and back. He was keen to let his injuries have the best chance of recovery before seeing the nurse again. He knew he had to be in good shape for his next mission.

He arrived at the Broadway offices in good time for his appointment at 10:30 a.m. He signed in and went up to the second floor. He knocked on the waiting room door and went in.

"Good morning, my name is Williams. I am here to see the nurse, Miss Symonds." The receptionist looked down her list.

"Ah, yes. Please take a seat Mr Williams, you won't be kept waiting very long."

Within five minutes, the nurse called him in to her surgery.

"Hello Mr Williams. How have you been getting on with your injuries? You haven't knocked them or been taking too much exercise, have you? Let me look at the leg first." Andrew said nothing. He rolled up his trouser leg, took off his shoe and placed his leg on the nurse's lap. She very carefully took off the bandage, removed the gauze and dabbed the wound with some cotton wool.

"I am very pleased at what I see, Mr Williams. The stitches have really done the trick. I think they could come out, but you will still require some protection for a few days."

The nurse took out her scissors and eased the stitches from Andrew's leg. She dabbed the scar with disinfectant, put on a small piece of cotton wool and wrapped a new bandage around his leg.

"How does that feel?" she asked, as she indicated to him to stand up and walk around the room.

"It seems fine, nurse, thank you."

"You must still be careful not to knock it for the next few days, as it is still looking rather tender."

Andrew replaced his sock and shoe, took off his jacket and rolled up his sleeve. She took off the bandage plus the dressing and examined the wound through a small magnifying glass.

"This wound is not healing as well as the leg. Did you tell me how you got it?"

"It's a long story. A person I was trying to guard was shot at by someone. My arm was in the way, so I received a glancing blow from the bullet. I thought it was just a graze?"

"Oh, I see. That might account for it healing rather slowly. You should have told me how you received the wound when you first came to me," she said rather sternly. "I'm just wondering if there are any bone fragments still lodged in the flesh, or the muscle, or even some pieces of cloth. I cleaned it well initially, but I'll have to poke around a bit to double check."

After some minutes, the nurse proclaimed that she had taken out a very tiny piece of cloth with her tweezers; she couldn't locate anything else. She cleaned the gash with TCP, put on a new gauze plus a new bandage.

"I will need to see you again next Monday. Please make an appointment with the secretary outside. I say again, treat it with great care. You've been very lucky that it hasn't turned sceptic."

"Yes, nurse, I certainly will. Thank you," Andrew said as he stood up and put on his jacket. He left the surgery – smiling broadly at the nurse as he went out of the door. He made an appointment for 10 o'clock the following Monday and left the building.

Andrew was not very good at just whiling away the time, he much preferred to be doing something, but his hands were tied to staying in London. In the afternoon, he decided to take a bus to Regents Park and go to the zoo for a couple of hours. He wandered around looking at all the animals, birds and snakes. He couldn't help thinking that it all looked so similar to how Hitler would be viewing the people of western Europe: everyone caged up with nowhere to go.

He returned to his flat by 6:15 a.m. finding that two of his flatmates were there. Nothing was ever said between them about their missions or tasks within the Service. Only very occasionally would two of the six living in the same flat be in involved in the same operation. They had a light meal together, but one of them happened to mention de Gaulle and his broadcast on the wireless to the French people the evening before at 6 o'clock on the wireless.

"Did you hear it, Andrew?" one of them mentioned.

"No, I didn't. What did he have to say?" he knew he should have listened to it, particularly if he might be working with the general and Spears.

"It was a call to arms. It was an explicit reproach to Marshall Pétain and his new French government for negotiating with the Germans before the battle was lost. He emphasised that France was not alone: she has a vast empire and she can work alongside the British Empire, which commands the seas and is continuing the struggle; both of us will benefit from the immense industrial resources of the United States. He remarked that because France had lost a battle, it had not lost the war. He said he was now in London calling on all French officers and men, engineers and skilled workmen in Britain to get in touch with him. He said the French resistance must not die."

"Sounds like strong stuff," Andrew remarked. "Do you think many people in France heard this broadcast? Will many in Britain respond to his appeal?"

"Probably not on both counts," one of them said.

Andrew pondered over the brief summary of de Gaulle's words. He wondered if the mission he will be asked to be involved in is anything to do with the French resistance, as the general called it. He excused himself from the others saying he had an important meeting to prepare for the next day. Nobody questioned what he said; they had all been in a similar position one time or another.

The following morning, Andrew went for a walk in St James' Park as the weather was dry and warm. He was very unsure about his possible mission to be working with de Gaulle and General Spears. He couldn't see what he could bring to any discussions, how he could be used to protect them, or even be an interpreter of French when Spears was so fluent in the language from birth.

He went to a nearby pub at lunch time, had a pint of beer plus a very unappetising cheese sandwich. He knew Charles was unlikely to see his point of view, especially as so many more senior people than Charles had agreed with his appointment. He thought there must be something more to it that Charles had not told him about. He went back to his flat to change into his suit with a mixed feeling of elation and concern. He knew he could probably do any job assigned to him, but perhaps the last three weeks were beginning to take a toll on his usual confidence.

At 3:15 p.m., Andrew started out from his flat for Charles' office. In view of his encounters a few days ago, he took yet another different route. He was relieved to arrive without anyone attacking him. As usual, he signed in and was told that Charles was waiting for him. He wondered who else would be in the room this time, as he knocked on the door and went into the office.

"Good afternoon, Andrew. Nice to see you again," Charles said as Andrew looked around the room to find nobody else there to his surprise and relief.

"Hello, Charles," he said, as he was shown to the chair in front of the desk.

"You will no doubt be interested to know that our people have been very clever and have identified the real name of our Mr John Smith – the fellow you shot on the train. As you rightly guessed, his papers were forgeries, and not very good ones at that. He was in fact *Fraulein Schwartz's* brother, *Heinrich*! They both were working for the *Abwehr*, based in London. You may well be aware, there has been no German Embassy in London since we declared war with Germany last September. All German residents in Britain were instructed to leave immediately. Some ignored that order and, because of their connections with senior Nazi members back in Germany, it was felt that they could be of more use staying low in Britain – most of them moved to London. The house in Maida Vale was the *Abwehr's* main operation centre for the spy network. The police have done sterling work for the Service by providing the names of some ten other spies working for the Nazi regime in London, four of whom lived in the house with the *Schwartz's*."

"That is quite amazing news, Charles. Presumably those ten people – once they are all captured – will be interrogated, perhaps by Service personnel as well as the police?"

"That's right. Three of them are already in captivity while the others are still at large. We will start questioning the three spies very soon – we may have more by then. It is imperative that we waste no time, just in case they have plans to carry out even worse atrocities than assassinating King Haakon and his son.

"Reverting to what we were going to get you involved in, we in the Service, plus the Admiralty, believe you could be very usefully employed in this interrogation process. You speak German like a native and we believe you could be very helpful to us in a few weeks' time. For the time being, however, we have decided to have you spend some weeks working with General de Gaulle, plus General Spears and his small team. The French general has many ideas about setting up a resistance movement while he is in voluntary exile in London; your command of the French language will be very useful."

"I would very much enjoy doing that. Has he obtained any accommodation in London yet?"

"We are working closely with Spears on that, but for the moment, he is living in a hotel. De Gaulle is still fuming at Pétain's offer of an armistice with Germany, as well as Italy. I'm pleased you are happy to be involved, Andrew. There's no mad rush on this, but I will get a message to Spears to tell him you are interested. Please come here next Monday at 10 o'clock and I'll tell you more."

They talked for some while about the position Britain would find herself in, now that she's on her own. Andrew left the building and decided he'd go via the nurse's surgery on his way back to the flat, as he needed to bring his appointment forward from Monday. He signed in at the Broadway office, went up to the second floor and entered the waiting room, hoping he wasn't too late to see the secretary.

"Ah! I'm very glad to see you are still here," Andrew said, as he got his breath back.

"I'm very sorry to trouble you, but I have an appointment to see the nurse on Monday and I need to bring it forward as I will not be able to keep the Monday appointment."

"Just let me see," she said, as she looked down the entries in the diary. "You are in luck, Mr Williams, the nurse is going to be working all day Saturday. She has space in the morning and the afternoon. Which would you prefer?"

"As late as possible in the afternoon, please."

"How would 4:30 p.m. suite you?"

"That would be excellent, thank you."

The entry was made in the diary and she gave him a card with the date and time on, as a reminder. Andrew thanked her very much as he left the office. He thought he had been very lucky getting an appointment so close to the one originally set for Monday.

Chapter 33
Saturday, 22nd June 1940

Andrew arrived at the Broadway offices on time. He went into the waiting room on the second floor to see that there was only one other person before him. Within ten minutes, he was called in to the nurse's surgery.

"So, Mr Williams, what has prompted you to bring your appointment forward?"

"I do appreciate your being able to fit me in today. As I said to the receptionist when I phoned, I have to attend an important meeting on Monday. I might be very busy for the next three weeks, so I'm hoping my arm will have recovered enough for the stitches to be taken out."

"Let me take a look," the nurse said, as Andrew took off his jacket and rolled up his shirt sleeve.

"It looks a lot better than it did; probably because I took the fragment of cloth out." She gently prodded around the outside of the scar.

"Now, be honest with me, Mr Williams, does it hurt when I press the flesh around the injured area?"

"No, it doesn't, surprisingly. That must surely be a good sign, nurse?"

"Yes, it is. Under the circumstances, I'm going to take a slight risk and remove the stitches. Once I've done that, I'll put some more iodine on, plus new gauze and a bandage. I'm going to give you two lots of replacement dressings which you should apply on Wednesday and next Saturday. I'm sure you will find someone to help you to change the dressing. Please remember, however, that you have had a very bad injury;

it needs looking after with the right care for it to heal properly. You will, unfortunately, be left with a scar, but it will reduce with time."

Andrew felt like hugging the nurse after what she had said, but he thought better of it. The nurse attended to the wound, put the extra dressings in a small surgical bag that he passed to Andrew.

"I can't thank you enough, nurse. I will take good care of my arm and do what you have advised." He unrolled his shirt sleeve, put on his jacket, stood up and shook her hand gently, giving her one of his most endearing smiles.

Once out of the building, he skipped like a young boy down the road for a short way, clutching the bag, before getting a taxi back to his flat. He relaxed for the rest of the weekend.

As arranged, Andrew went to Charles' office on Monday morning. They greeted each other warmly, then sat down at opposite sides of Charles' desk.

"I'm pleased to tell you that I've had confirmation from Spears via C for you to work with his team in support of de Gaulle. I thought our meeting today would give me the opportunity to update you with what's happening in France.

"An armistice has been drawn up and it will be signed later today. The full text of the armistice was supposed to have been sent to the War Cabinet, but the French government in Bordeaux has not complied with this request. Can you believe it, the signing will be at Compiègne, the site of the 1918 armistice? Foch's railway carriage used in 1918, has been returned to the forest site for this signing to inflict revenge over the French.

"The British Government has denounced the armistice and ceased to recognise Pétain's government as having authority over all French people and its Empire.

"I am reliably informed that France will be split into two areas: one to be under the command of the Germans covering the north plus all the coastline from Calais to the Spanish border; the second – most of the rest of France – to be governed relatively freely by a French administration based in Vichy under Marshall Pétain."

"I'm assuming there's a good chance that Germany will now put all its efforts into attacking Britain? What happens to France's naval ships and its land forces?"

"We expect the land forces to be taken as prisoners of war, perhaps leaving the Vichy government with a token force for keeping law and order. What happens to her ships is a very interesting question. If Germany ordered them to be placed in the hands of the *Kriegsmarine,* it would alter the balance of power away from our fleets in favour of the German's; they would then rule the waves, not us. It would put the protection of the convoys from Canada and America in considerable danger, to put it mildly."

"How does de Gaulle view the armistice?"

"He wants to broadcast for a second time, but he is facing huge resistance from the British establishment and the Foreign Office of Lord Halifax. Additionally, there is the deep unwillingness of French people to accept his undertaking as no more than a Fascist coup or a Communist plot against Marshall Pétain's position. De Gaulle, however, is made of sterner stuff and will no doubt be, in due course, successful in building a resistance movement to support what he calls the Free French. Sorry, Andrew, I have gone on rather a long time, but it's important for your own sake that you understand the broader picture of our current situation."

"No, problem, Charles; it was very useful. I have to admit, however, that I missed de Gaulle's speech last week and its repeat on Saturday. One of my flatmates gave me a brief summary and it was apparently a very strong message calling on all French officers and men on British soil to get in touch with him. French resistance must not die, he said."

"What the Service wants you to do, in support of Spears and his team, is to convince de Gaulle of the importance of not letting the French Fleet – whether in Mers-el-Kabir in French North Africa, or southern France – to fall under German or Italian control. It must either become part of the British fleet or be sunk by the RAF."

"My goodness, a tough couple of alternatives for de Gaulle to grapple with. Have you been given a start date for me?"

"General Spears knows we are meeting today, so he would like you to meet him tomorrow at his office at 10:30 a.m." Charles passed a piece of paper over his desk with the address on.

"He would like you to meet him in his rooms at the House of Commons – he is MP for Carlisle. Here is his card with a message inviting you to the committee room he will be working in. This should help with security. You will use your real name, not your agent name. He is a strong supporter of the PM and has always held the policies of Mr Chamberlain's government with suspicion. As I have probably mentioned to you before, Spears was appointed as Mr Churchill's representative in May. He has accompanied the PM, or been sent instead, on numerous occasions. He is much respected by Mr Churchill and his opinions are listened to with great interest by the War Cabinet. The reason why you have been selected is that you will be representing the Intelligence Service and you speak French."

"Phew! I hope I live up to your expectations. I shall be in very senior and experienced company."

"I have written a few words about General Spears' life, how and when he made an impression on Mr Churchill plus his various roles between the wars." Charles pushed two pages of A4 paper across his desk to Andrew, who attached Spears card to the pages with a paper clip.

"You won't be questioned on anything about Spears, but at least you will have a good idea of who you will be working with."

"Thanks, Charles. That will be very useful."

"Do you have any questions?"

"No, I don't, but I'm sure some will come to me when I'm on my way back to the flat," he said, with a big smile.

They got up, shook hands, with Charles wishing him 'good luck' as he went out of the door. He thought he would be better off walking back to his flat so he could get some fresh air, but as it was getting towards lunchtime, he took a small diversion to the pub where he'd seen Helen with her brother. He ordered a pint, went to the same table near the window; he wondered if he would have the chance to see her again before too long. He pulled out the papers with the notes about General Spears. After some minutes, he exclaimed to himself: *what a man, what a life for just a fifty-four-year-old: amazing.* He placed the papers back in his jacket pocket and wondered what contribution he could make to the meetings and the discussions. *Obviously, people more senior than Charles think I am up to the job,* he thought to himself. He finished his beer and walked in a contemplative mood back to his flat.

Andrew was up early on Tuesday. He put on his suit, white shirt and old school tie. He picked up his briefcase, left the flat at 9:45 a.m. and took a taxi to the Houses of Parliament. On arrival, he showed his letter and General Spears card to the policeman outside who told him where to find a visitor's assistant to take him to the Central Lobby. One of the attendants took him from the lobby to the room that Spears was using. He knocked on the door and waited for a reply.

"Come in," said a strong male voice from inside.

Andrew entered the rather large room. Spears got up, went over to Andrew, greeted him and shook his hand, as he ushered him to a chair on the opposite side of the table to where the general had sat.

"Very glad you can join our team, Andrew. As you probably know, I am Winston Churchill's representative when dealing with General de Gaulle. By the way, please help yourself to tea if you would like some.

"This afternoon, the Prime Minister will address the Commons on the current situation of the new French government under Pétain, as well as the arrangements for the disposition of the French Fleet. The general has been invited to attend this afternoon's session and will be in the Visitors' Gallery. You and I will escort him there, but not stay to hear the speeches. We will return to this room to discuss the completion of Operation Cycle. Have you heard about this exercise, Andrew?"

"I have very little knowledge of it, General."

Spears passed him a sheaf of papers and suggested he brought himself up to speed with this significant rescue operation from the French port of

Le Havre. This kept him busy for the next two hours while Spears was writing copiously and making many phone calls.

"Right," said Spears, "we had better have a light lunch." He phoned for some sandwiches and liquid refreshments. Andrew was pleased to get a break from reading. Before too long, a lady arrived with their lunch. Spears and Andrew sat in more comfortable chairs for their snack. Spears asked him to tell him about some of the missions he had been involved in. Before too long, Spears saw it was 2 o'clock. He walked Andrew out to the Central Lobby where the tall figure of de Gaulle stood, looking about him at the splendour of the architecture and statues.

Spears welcomed the general and introduced him to Andrew, who would be working with them for the next few weeks. De Gaulle appeared to look surprised at Andrew's command of French, saying that he looked forward to knowing him better over the weeks ahead. Spears gave the general a ticket and led them up the stairs to the Gallery, where they left him saying they would be back at 4:30 p.m.

During the afternoon, they talked about where de Gaulle should stay in London.

"He first lived in a friend's flat in Seamore Grove, but as it became too inconvenient for him, he moved into a hotel. This again is temporary. We will need to take a trip around the central parts of London to help him find something a bit more permanent: perhaps tomorrow?"

"Fine by me, sir. Do you think the general will be joining us?"

"No, I'm sure not. He has so many other things to deal with. It's the least we can do for him.

"It's after 4 o'clock, Andrew, so would you like to fetch the general from the Visitors' Gallery? I'll meet both of you in the Central Lobby, so wait for me there."

Andrew put his papers in his brief case, went to the Gallery and easily saw the unmistakable figure of de Gaulle, who was looking intently at the proceedings. He asked him if he found the debate interesting. He told Andrew that his English was not so good, but he thought he got the gist of what had been said. He also told him that Mr Churchill looked up and saw that he was there.

They left after several minutes; Spears was waiting for them in the Lobby. He led the general and Andrew out of the building to a waiting car.

"Are you happy for us to take you back to your hotel or do you have some questions?" Spears said, as they arrived at the car.

"I have a number of things I need to do, so please take me back to the hotel."

On their arrival at the hotel, they all got out of the car. De Gaulle thanked them for a very interesting day.

"So, Andrew, what do you think of the general?"

"He looks as though he has much on his mind."

Spears agreed.

"I think we've done enough for today. I'll take you back to your flat for some rest; I'll collect you tomorrow at 10:30 a.m."

Chapter 34
Wednesday, 26th June 1940

Andrew had finished his light breakfast by 8:30 a.m. He thought he would have enough time to go and contact Helen, find out when they could meet up, and get back to the flat by 10 o'clock.

He walked quickly to the Broadway offices and into the reception hall. As before, he asked to speak to the Service Chief's secretary.

"Who shall I say is wanting to speak to her?"

Andrew gave his name. The receptionist passed the phone to him, he heard her sweet voice say 'hello'.

"Good morning Helen. It's Andrew here. I'm in a bit of a hurry, but I wondered if you would be free for supper on Friday?"

"It's good to hear from you, Andrew. That should be fine. Do you want to meet me here?"

"It might be best if we meet at the pub where I saw you with your brother. Shall we say 6 o'clock?"

"That would be lovely, Andrew. I look forward to it. I must ring off as C needs me for some dictation. Bye for now."

Andrew thanked the receptionist for her help, walked quickly out of the building back to his flat. He changed into his suit and was ready well ahead of schedule. It was an easy morning and afternoon. Spears had a list of possible houses and flats: probably about ten, Andrew thought. One of them in the morning looked very promising, the last one in the afternoon also looked a possibility. Spears said he didn't want to rush through all the options as he wanted to find the right place and not to spend another day searching around London, when he could be more usefully occupied.

Spears suggested they should have lunch at his Club in Pall Mall. Once again, Andrew noticed he was in no real hurry to get back to driving around London. He met quite a few of his fellow Army officers at the bar and talked to a few more who were seated at adjacent tables. They talked about the properties they had seen and they agreed on the appropriateness of the one in the morning.

Spears got up from the table just before 2:30 p.m., signed the chitty and went to the club's entrance just as the car drove up. They spent the next two hours visiting more possible premises, but – in their mind – nothing came near to their favourite from the morning: the flat in Carlton Gardens. They hoped de Gaulle would approve of their choice. It was now nearly 5 o'clock. Spears thanked Andrew for being with him, saying that he enjoyed his company driving around inner London and agreeing with his choice for de Gaulle's new residence. He asked the driver to drop Andrew back at his flat and to return for him at 10:30 a.m. the following day.

The car arrived at Andrew's flat just before 10:30 a.m., but he was ready and outside on the step.

"Where are we going today?" he asked the driver.

"I am instructed to collect General Spears from the House of Commons and drive you both to the hotel where General de Gaulle's staying."

They picked up Spears and, on the way to the Rubens hotel, he told Andrew that Mr Churchill had received a letter from de Gaulle. He outlined a proposal to set up a Council of Liberation and asked Mr Churchill, on behalf of the British government, to recognise it.

"But surely the government, and in particular the Foreign Secretary, will object to de Gaulle's proposal. Don't they want to slow down the withdrawal of recognising Pétain's government?"

"That's quite right, Andrew; very perceptive of you. So, what do you expect Mr Churchill to do next?"

Andrew left his reply for later, as they had arrived at de Gaulle's hotel. They registered at the reception. The lady phoned de Gaulle's number and they were told to go to his suite on the third floor.

When they entered the room, they tried to complete their pleasantries to de Gaulle, but he was pacing up and down, hardly paying any attention to them. Andrew thought he would be bold, so he went over to the table where the coffee and water was.

"Would you like some coffee, General de Gaulle, sir?"

To Andrew's and Spears' surprise, de Gaulle stopped, turned to face Andrew with a smile and said he would. Andrew was told he would like it black with a small amount of sugar. He did as he was asked, taking it over to de Gaulle, who was now seated in one of the chairs near the window.

"You do realise, Spears," said de Gaulle, in an accentuated French accent, "that even though I enjoy my family being in this hotel with me, I shall have to send them to somewhere safer, away from London, before too long."

"Did you have a place in mind?" Spears asked.

"Not yet, but I've got someone at the French Embassy helping me."

"We think we've found a place suitable for you; we saw it yesterday morning and it's in Carlton Gardens. When you have some spare time, we could take you there."

"We can discuss that early next week. For the moment, I have more pressing things to think about: what the government of Pétain will do with the French Fleet and how I – plus the few supporters that I have – will be recognised as leader of the Free French by the British government. It is very disappointing for me that so few officers and men – both in Britain and France – have come forward to support my notion of continuing the fight against the Nazis: for the honour and interests of France."

They all continued to discuss de Gaulle's huge disappointment in response to his appeal from the BBC, even after it had been repeated several times. Spears interrupted the meeting and asked the general if he could order some light refreshments from room service, to which he agreed, especially as it was now after 1 o'clock.

The snacks arrived about twenty minutes later. After they had been eating and drinking for some fifteen minutes, the phone rang. De Gaulle answered it. Spears was nearer to him than Andrew and he heard it was the PM's secretary. In quite good French, she said that Mr Churchill is inviting him to Downing Street for a meeting at 7:30 p.m. De Gaulle told her that he was pleased to accept the offer. He wandered around the room for a full ten minutes; he was deep in thought.

"Mr Churchill's secretary did not give any indication about what we will discuss tonight. Why do you think he has asked to see me, Spears? You know him as well as anybody?"

"He is not an easy person to read, General. My thoughts are that he's much impressed with your stance against the Vichy government of Marshall Pétain. Also, your wholehearted support for the continuation of the war against the Nazis with the Free French. But, sir, you will have to be prepared for his views concerning the French Fleet."

They talked at length about the two main topics, as well as others close to de Gaulle's heart: the likely collaboration of the Vichy government with the German occupiers of northern and western France; his proposals in a letter to Churchill for de Gaulle to set up a Council of Liberation and for it to be recognised by the British government.

These discussions concluded at 5 o'clock as de Gaulle wanted to prepare himself for his meeting with the PM. Spears and Andrew said their farewells, saying they would be back at 10:30 a.m. the following morning to hear how he had got on at his meeting.

Andrew was up early. His mind was not on his meeting with de Gaulle, but more on his seeing Helen. Spears collected him at 10:10 a.m.

"I think this morning will be very interesting," Spears remarked. "I'm looking forward to hearing his view on how the meeting went yesterday evening. I had a call from Winston early this morning about publishing a communiqué concerning de Gaulle. He wouldn't give me the details, but no doubt the General will know the text."

"Did it seem to show de Gaulle in a positive light?" Andrew asked.

"We'll soon find out," replied Spears, as they arrived at the hotel's entrance on time. They took the lift, knocked on the door and heard him say *"entrée, s'il vous plaît"*. They exchanged pleasantries, poured their coffee and sat facing the General.

"So, how are you this morning after your meeting with Mr Churchill?" Spears asked.

"Very long," de Gaulle replied with a smile. "I don't think he sleeps very much. He seems to be trying to run the free world entirely on his own! He had some good things to say to me and some not so good. By now," as de Gaulle looked at his watch, "he will have issued a statement that 'His Majesty's government recognises General de Gaulle as leader of all Free French people, wherever they may be, who rally to him in support of the Allied cause'. He told me," de Gaulle continued, "it was a personal act of faith in me that gave a basis of my relations with the British government. But he turned down my proposal to set up a Council of Liberation; Churchill thought it was not necessary."

"That sounds very satisfactory for you," Spears stated. "And what of the other issues that you discussed?"

"I got very angry about what should happen to the French Fleet. We had quite a heated argument, but he was adamant that his view was the right one. His ideas about the Vichy government were as mine are: they are not to be trusted."

"So, sir, you had an interesting evening with our Prime Minister."

"Yes, I think so, but Mr Churchill's French is not always very expressive and quite difficult to understand, so I might have misunderstood some of the details just a little."

"What I suggest is that I make an appointment to see the PM and ask him to repeat to me what he told you. I can then return to you and tell you what I have heard, so I could clarify any details. Does that sound like a good idea?"

"I suppose that might be helpful," de Gaulle said, rather half-heartedly, and without much enthusiasm.

Spears didn't pursue things any further. He suggested they might go to the restaurant and have some lunch, and that he would foot the bill. The others agreed. They talked easily over lunch. At the end, de Gaulle said he would not be needing Andrew and Spears during the afternoon as he would like to spend some time with his wife and family. They understood very well his position and would return on Monday morning; perhaps take him to visit the accommodation in Carlton Gardens? The general just grunted.

De Gaulle went upstairs to his family that were in a separate suite of rooms; Andrew and Spears went to the smaller lounge to have a coffee and to talk for a while. Andrew knew he was only half concentrating on what Spears was saying – he hoped it didn't notice. After about an hour, Spears said he would take him back to his flat, but Andrew politely declined, as he needed some air and exercise.

Chapter 35

Friday, 28th June 1940

On his return to the flat, he decided to have a bath, but he felt he needed to check his injured leg first, as he forgot to do it on Wednesday. He undressed, took off the bandage and all the dressing and looked carefully at the wound. He put on his dressing gown, went to the bathroom and ran his bath. He dabbed his injured leg with a wet flannel and it didn't feel sore. After the bath, he made sure his leg injury was dry. Back in his room he applied one of the new dressings and wound the new bandage around it all, securing it with a safety pin. He wasn't sure if he should arrive early or a little late, but he decided to be a bit early – especially after the disappointment of the first time.

Andrew wandered into the pub a few minutes before 6 o'clock. He looked around, but couldn't see her, so went to the bar to order a pint of bitter. As he turned around, he saw Helen walk in. Most of the people in the Saloon bar were men; there was an eerie silence as they turned to see her float towards Andrew.

"Hello, Helen. You look fantastic. Did you go to the office in those clothes?"

"Thank you. No, I didn't. I have a cupboard in my office in which I keep some different clothes, in case I'm asked by my boss to accompany him somewhere."

The noise in the bar returned to normal as Andrew kissed her on the cheek. He asked her if she would like what he bought her last time they met: a dry vermouth.

"That's very clever of you to remember, so yes please," she replied, with an amazing smile.

Andrew returned with her drink; they pushed their way to the same table by the window as before. It seemed as though everybody's eyes were on the two of them, especially Andrew's. They talked easily together. He asked about her brother Jack, his sister and parents.

"So, your brother lives in Crawley? Whereabouts?"

"If you know the village, you go over the crossing at the railway station out of the village, he lives up the road on the right. His surgery is on the right just before you get to his road."

They had nearly finished their first drink when Andrew asked where she would like to go for a meal, and maybe somewhere they could dance afterwards.

"Oh, that sounds fun. I'll leave you to say where."

"I believe there's a good dance band playing at the Café de Paris. We should have a meal first, then go to the Club."

"Wow, Andrew; now you're really spoiling me!"

"I certainly think you are worth it," he said with a broad grin.

They finished their drinks, went out of the pub and walked to a restaurant he had been to with Charles about a year ago. She took his arm as they walked along. The restaurant was quite busy, but the waiter found them a table. They took more than two hours over their meal, but Andrew didn't feel it had taken that long. He looked at his watch: to his surprise it was 10 o'clock. He paid the bill and they went out into the street to get a taxi to the Café de Paris.

"Good evening, sir, madam. Will you be dining tonight?" the attendant enquired.

"Not tonight, thank you," Andrew replied as the attendant took Helen's light weight coat and hung it in the closet.

"A table for two, I presume? Please follow me."

Andrew took Helen's hand and followed the attendant to a table by the side of the dance floor. He pulled out the chair for her, then came around to do the same for Andrew.

"Shall I call the waiter over with the drinks menu, sir?" Andrew looked at the attendant and nodded in agreement.

"Is this alright for you, Helen?" as the band started to play another number.

"Just wonderful, thank you."

Andrew looked around to see if he saw anyone he might know or recognise, but all he saw were men in dinner jackets or tails. He felt rather underdressed.in his blue blazer and his old school tie. *Oh well*, he said to himself, *they let me in, so I must look reasonably alright*. The drinks list arrived.

"Shall we splash out and have some champagne?"

"That would be lovely, Andrew."

He ordered a bottle that wasn't too expensive. He moved his chair closer to her, putting his hand on hers. The waiter interrupted their conversation, as he brought the champagne for Andrew to see. He opened the bottle without letting any of the liquid burst out and poured some into each of the two glasses, placed the bottle in the ice bucket, nodded and left them.

"To your health," they both said together, and laughed at coming out with the same statement.

After a few minutes, Andrew asked Helen if she would like to dance, to which she agreed. He took her hand as they went to the dance floor, slipping in to a fox trot without any difficulty. Andrew thought she floated across the floor as he held her close. She was only a few inches shorter than him in her moderately heeled shoes. They smiled at each other as they moved around to yet another tune: this time a waltz. At the end of the third dance, the band announced there would be a brief interval; the dancers applauded the band and returned to their tables.

"This is a well-earned drink, don't you think, Helen?" Andrew stated as they touched glasses before taking another mouthful of the sparkling liquid.

The time seemed to fly by as they danced, chatted and just enjoyed the band's music.

"Oh, I nearly forgot to ask you, Helen: what time train do you need to catch to get back home?"

"I'm not really under any pressure, as my boss has allowed me to stay at one of the Service's flats tonight. Anyway, as tomorrow's Saturday, I can go back home sometime in the late morning."

"That's a very generous gesture of the old man," Andrew remarked with a wink.

"The very first time you winked at me, Andrew, was when I was receptionist at your boss' office. Do you remember; I blushed?" she said, and they laughed.

"My goodness, that was a year ago, and I do remember, very vividly." He remembered very clearly her silky brunette hair, as he looked into her hazel eyes and smiled. They didn't think they would stay for the cabaret, so they decided to have one more dance before it started. Andrew led Helen from the dance floor to collect her shawl and handbag from her chair. They went to the entrance for her coat as a taxi was called by the very attentive door man, who bade them a very pleasant evening.

"Where to now, young lady?" Andrew asked, as the taxi driver waited for instructions.

"I ought to go back to the flat," she said, and gave the driver her address. Andrew held her hand, nestling up to her and looking her in the eyes.

"You are some exceptional lady; you know that? I don't think I have met anyone quite like you." Andrew looked away from her for a moment and recognised some of the buildings that were near his flat, as the taxi drew to a halt. *At least it won't take me long to walk home,* he thought to himself.

Helen paid the driver, as she got out of the cab first and thanked him. Andrew followed and went to her side.

"Would you like to come up for some coffee?" she asked.

"Are you sure it's not too late for you?"

"I don't have to go to the office tomorrow – it being Saturday – so it's not too late for me."

Andrew was very keen, but he thought he should not agree too eagerly. Helen led the way up to the second floor, apologising for the lack of comforts as they reached the lounge area. She went to the cupboard for the coffee and mugs, and as she was filling the kettle, Andrew quietly came up behind her. He put his arms around her waist and drew her to him, as he kissed her gently on her neck. She brought her hands behind her and rubbed them gently against his enlarged swelling.

"My goodness, do you always get so excited about coffee?" she said, with a chuckle, but without turning to face him. He slowly moved his hands from her waist upwards to cup her adequately sized breasts. He pushed himself against her, kissed her ear lobe and put his tongue into her ear.

"The kettle's boiling, Andrew. Do you really want coffee or shall we leave it for later?" as she released his grip and turned to face him.

He made no reply, but took her head in his hands, kissing her on the lips with his tongue penetrating deep into her mouth. She placed her hands behind his buttocks and pulled him ever closer to her. She could feel his arousal pressing against the lower part of her stomach. At this point, she knew she wouldn't be able to resist his advances.

He unbuttoned her dress, letting it fall to the floor. She took off his jacket and tie, undid his shirt and threw them on to the floor. He took off her bra, cupped his hands around her breasts and kissed her again on the mouth. She unfastened his belt, undid his fly buttons and allowed his trousers to drop to the ground, with a little assistance of her foot. As they were standing just in their underwear and he still with his shoes on, she giggled as she looked at him. He bent down, unlaced his shoes and took them off with his socks. She led him from the kitchen into the bedroom. She pulled back the eiderdown and top sheet. A faint light was coming from the lounge as they removed their underwear. She slid on to the bed and pulled him on top of her.

For many minutes, they kissed and teased each other until she reached down and directed his erection into her. In the dim light, he could just make out that her eyes were half open. She was smiling at him, seemingly wanting him to penetrate deeper inside her. He rocked backwards and forwards to increase her excitement. She held on to his buttocks and tried to take more of him with each stroke. Suddenly, he had no more to give as he let out a long, low moan at the same time as she made a strange squeaking sound. His body was wet with perspiration from each of them. He lay still on top of her for many minutes, trying to read her thoughts from her eyes as she stroked his back; they both fell asleep.

Helen woke first to find him facing away from her. She had no idea what time it was, but she thought it must be after 4 o'clock as there was a faint hint of light coming in through the window. Andrew then stirred, turned to face her as they smiled and embraced each other. There was no more love making as they reckoned that the first time could not be surpassed. They fell asleep again.

Sometime later, Andrew was aware that he was the only one in the bed as he felt around with his hands, but heard noises coming from the kitchen. As he lay on his back, the door quietly opened; Helen came in with a tray of coffee and toast.

"You are awake at last, lover boy," she remarked as she put the tray down on the side of the bed.

"I thought it was time I made that black coffee for you that you were expecting last night," she said, with a smile.

"What time is it, Helen?"

"It's 8:15 a.m.," as she looked at her watch.

"Do you need to go somewhere in a hurry?"

"No, I don't, but haven't you to be out of here by midday?"

Andrew sat up with his back against the pillow and drank his coffee. He looked at Helen to see her hair was brushed. She wore a floral dressing gown that was just open enough to reveal the 'V' between her breasts.

"No more today, young man," as she noticed how he was looking at her and closed the top of her gown.

"You have bandages on your leg and arm, Andrew. You mentioned something the last time we met; are the injuries healing alright? We haven't knocked them at all during our love making?"

"No, thanks for asking; they are fine."

Chapter 36
Saturday, 29th June 1940

Andrew arrived back at his flat at 11:30 a.m. After all the activity in Helen's bed, he was worried about his injured leg, even if he had told Helen it was alright. In his room, he took off his trousers, undid the safety pin and unwrapped the bandage. To his concern, the cotton wool and the gauze had stuck to the wound. He squeezed his damp flannel over the wounded area and then gently moved the moistened coverings away from his leg. The wound looked red and rather raw. He took out the TCP ointment given to him by the nurse, dabbing some around the scar with fresh cotton wool. He placed a new strip of gauze plus a small piece of cotton wool over the wound and wrapped a new bandage around his leg. He stood up and walked around his room. He was satisfied with the result, so put his trousers back on.

The rest of Saturday, he went for a couple of walks, as the weather was reasonably fine. On the Sunday, he walked past the Service flat where he and Helen had stayed the night, remembering very vividly that night they had spent in bed together.

On Monday morning, he had a phone call from Spears at 8 o'clock, telling him he would be arriving earlier than usual: 9:15 a.m. There had been some important developments that they needed to talk to de Gaulle about.

They arrived at de Gaulle's hotel, checked in at reception and went straight to his room. *"Entrée"*, a voice said from inside. They entered the rooms to be greeted not only by de Gaulle, but also his ADC. The usual pleasantries were completed, but there was a very serious air to their demeanour.

"I suppose you have heard, General Spears, that the Germans have invaded the Channel Islands; they have taken total control of them and killed over forty people in the process? There appeared to be no military personnel defending the islanders. I remember landing on Jersey's airfield on my way from Bordeaux to Heston about two weeks ago; all seemed very calm. Do you think the British government will do anything to help the people of these islands?"

"Thank you, General, I was aware of the invasion. To the best of my knowledge, the government decided that the Islands were of no strategic importance – they would not be defended – even though we would be giving up one of the oldest possessions of the Crown to the Germans."

"*Mon dieu*," de Gaulle replied, "*peut-être c'est la vie, n'est ce pas?*" He said no more, but he was obviously very confused by Spears words and the lack of interest by the British government in the Islands; he shrugged his shoulders in disbelief.

They continued to discuss various topics of interest – particularly to the two Frenchmen – when there was a knock on the door. De Gaulle's ADC opened it to find two waiters with refreshments, so they were told to place everything on the table in the middle of the room. Towards the end of the morning, Spears asked the general if he would be ready to visit the apartment that they had found for him in Carlton Gardens in the afternoon, to which he agreed. They set a time for 2:30 p.m.; everyone except de Gaulle's ADC went. De Gaulle found it to be in a very pleasing location and the size of the flat more than adequate for his needs for the duration of the war.

They returned to join de Gaulle's ADC, spending the rest of the afternoon discussing what Hitler might do next and when.

The following morning, when Spears and Andrew were at de Gaulle's hotel, Churchill phoned. He asked de Gaulle and his ADC to meet him at 10 Downing Street at 4 o'clock and to be brought by Spears. Andrew – from earlier conversations – was fairly sure the subject for discussion would be the French Fleet, but he didn't want to mention it to any of them. The car to take them to the meeting arrived at 3:30 p.m., so Andrew said he would walk back to his flat.

The next day, Wednesday, Andrew was phoned by Spears at just after 8:30 a.m. He told him that a car would collect him at 10:30 a.m. to take him to his office at the House of Commons. He didn't want to talk about the previous day's meeting with Churchill until he saw him.

Andrew arrived at the entrance to the House and was shown to Spears' rooms.

"Good to see you, Andrew. Please help yourself to tea or coffee. You were lucky not to have been at yesterday's meeting; it was very fiery, to say the least. It concerned Churchill's views about the French Fleet."

"I guessed as much, sir, but I didn't wish to say anything before your meeting in case I was wrong."

"Quite so, Andrew. Churchill and de Gaulle were not exactly at each other's throats, but a lot of heated exchanges did take place over the course of some three hours. Churchill reminded de Gaulle that the Armistice Agreement contained an article that provided for the demolishing and disarming of French warships by the Axis countries. The Germans also declared that the ships would not be used for their purposes during the war. Churchill did not trust the Nazi regime to adhere to the words in the agreement and therefore submitted an ultimatum to the Vichy leaders.

"Early this morning, Churchill sent a message to Pétain: they should either hand over all their fleet to the British, or scuttle their ships in harbour or be neutralised to prevent the ships from falling into Axis hands. If Admiral Dalan and the Vichy government didn't respond to any of these choices, Churchill would have no option other than to give orders to the Royal Navy to sink those in the French Algeria and Alexandria ports. De Gaulle was outraged; it severely tested his commitment to the British government's fight against Germany, as well as his commitment to stand alongside Churchill until the Nazis were overcome."

"Do you know if Churchill has heard anything yet?"

"Not that I'm aware of, Andrew, no."

"So, when will the order be given by the PM?"

"If nothing is heard, the order is likely to be given this afternoon."

"Where is General de Gaulle today?"

"He's discussing last night's meeting with the few senior people who have agreed to provide support to his view of having a Free French Force. It would be very prudent of us at this juncture to leave him alone until tomorrow. I will phone him in the morning to see what the atmosphere is like and whether or not we have anything in common to discuss with him."

They continued to talk over various situations until Spears offered to take Andrew to lunch just before 1 o'clock.

"Is it possible," Andrew asked, after lunch, "if you could phone me at my flat later on, once you've heard if Churchill has given the order?"

"Of course. I'll try to call you around 6 o'clock, but it will have to be in code in case your line at the flat is bugged. I'll get a car to take you to your flat."

"That time will be fine, thank you, but how will I understand the coded message?"

"If Churchill gives the order, I will say the car will come at 10 o'clock precisely to collect you. If I mention any other time, it will indicate that Admiral Dalan chose one of the options."

Andrew understood. They shook hands as he was taken out of the House to the waiting car.

"Please don't take me to my flat address," he said, "but to this address in St James," as he handed the driver a piece of paper. He felt he had to speak to Charles; hopefully he would be in.

He arrived at the end of the road and walked up to where Charles' office was, knocked and went inside.

"I don't suppose Mr Compton-Browne is available, is he?" he asked Miss Jones.

"No, I'm afraid he isn't, Mr Williams, but he is due back any moment now. Please take a seat until he arrives."

After some ten minutes, Charles flew in through the door. He saw Andrew and he was rather surprised to see him.

"Hello, Andrew. What brings you here a bit unexpectedly? Come up to my office so we can talk."

Andrew closed the door as he followed Charles in to his office; they both sat down.

"Is everything alright between you and Spears? How are you getting on with de Gaulle?"

"As it happens, I'm not quite sure how much I'm contributing to all the discussions we're having? Also, are you aware of what Mr Churchill is planning for the French Fleet, if Admiral Dalan doesn't choose one of the options presented to the Vichy government?"

"Hang on a bit, old chap; you're a bit ahead of me."

Andrew explained the options given to the Vichy government, the consequences of not choosing one of them, the meeting of Spears plus de Gaulle with the PM the evening before, the heated arguments between de Gaulle and Churchill.

"I'd heard there was a rather lively meeting at Downing Street, but I didn't know the details. Thank you for updating me. But regarding what you feel you are contributing to the discussions, Spears has spoken to me in glowing terms about your involvement and guidance, particularly with de Gaulle. I realise this work with Spears and de Gaulle is not your usual forté, but I think you are under estimating the value of your input. So much so that, if you and Spears agree, I would like you to stay working with him until the end of next week. By the way, General de Gaulle is particularly impressed with your command of French, and he's usually very difficult to please in that regard."

"I just needed to bounce it off you, but if that's what is being said, then I'm very happy to continue till 12th July."

"Do you have anything else to discuss as I need to make a few phone calls?"

"No, that's all. Thank you."

They shook hands as Andrew left the room. He signed out and made swift progress to his flat so that he was there in good time to take Spears' call. He was in his room when he heard the phone ring. He raced downstairs to answer it.

"Andrew, is that you?"

"Yes, sir."

"Just to let you know," said Spears, "that the car will come to collect you at 10 o'clock precisely tomorrow." The line went dead.

Andrew put the phone down. He went in to the kitchen to get himself a drink. He fancied a coffee and perhaps a brandy, if he could find one. He took his drinks up to his room and sat by his desk. He thought long and hard about how de Gaulle would react to the plight of the French Fleet. He would only know for sure after meeting him with Spears the following morning.

Andrew was ready by 10 o'clock for the car. He asked the driver where he was being taken to; he had replied that he was instructed to go to de Gaulle's hotel.

"Ah, good morning, Andrew," said Spears as he entered de Gaulle's suite. The general is in the other room talking to his ADC. Help yourself to some coffee."

Spears mouthed to Andrew, as he approached the table, that the atmosphere between the Frenchmen and him was a bit tense. Andrew just nodded.

"Good morning, Andrew," said de Gaulle, as he came into the lounge area. I see you have some coffee. Please take a seat, gentlemen. As you may be aware, the British Prime Minister gave the order yesterday for the Royal Navy's ships to attack the French Fleet – plus many smaller ships – moored in the port of Mers-el-Kabir, near Oran in French Algeria; many French sailors died. A French force of some five large ships was immobilised at Alexandria. All French ships in Portsmouth and Plymouth were brought under British control. My initial reaction was of great anger, but I have since done a lot of thinking; I have now recovered my composure.

"General Spears, I wish you to tell Mr Churchill it was inevitable that he made the decision that he did. It would have been a disaster for the

British Empire and the free world if the French ships had been taken over by the Axis countries. For me, I shall be seen by the Vichy government – and many French people living in all of France – as the one who gave Mr Churchill the go-ahead. It will probably be seen as a treasonable act and I may well be condemned to death."

There was a solemn air of silence in the room as de Gaulle walked slowly round and round, looking straight ahead of himself, thinking about what he had just said.

Spears thought he ought to say something to break the ice:

"General de Gaulle, sir, you might well have been quite right to display anger yesterday with Mr Churchill, but I shall tell him that you have displayed great dignity and soul-searching in coming to this position."

"What I need to do – with Andrew's and your help, General Spears – is to prepare a speech that I must give to the whole of France. I will explain the current situation and, in particular, the demise of the French Fleet."

Once again there was a hush in the room, but it was a different one from earlier: there was a certain calmness rather than an angry air. Even if de Gaulle still felt great anger underneath about the loss of so many French sailors, he was outwardly in control of his emotions.

Over the next few days, Andrew and Spears worked hard with de Gaulle and his ADC on his speech. There were occasions when Spears took drafts to the PM for his consideration – translated by Spears, of course – but he felt it was inappropriate of him to make any major changes. It was after all, de Gaulle talking to his people.

Chapter 37
Monday, 8ᵗʰ July 1940

Everyone involved in helping de Gaulle with the final draft of his speech was full of praise for his frankness on the destruction of the French Fleet by the British Navy. His broadcast was from the BBC at 6 o'clock in the evening and it lasted for just over six minutes.

Churchill was magnanimous in his praise of de Gaulle's words. He firmly believed it gave him proof of his trustworthiness as an ally and that he was a true friend of England. It was not a surprise to anyone that the Vichy government had broken off diplomatic relations with Britain following the demise of the French Fleet and the death of so many of their sailors.

In the British press, the image of de Gaulle as a lonely man refusing defeat and joining Britain in her fight against the Nazis, brought a strong feeling of support for him.

The morning after his broadcast, they all got together in de Gaulle's rooms. There was an air of relief and expectation from de Gaulle, as he hoped it would result in more Frenchmen and women joining his cause. For almost the first time, he was enthusiastic to start planning his move to the flat in Carlton Gardens. In addition, as he strongly expected the Germans to start the invasion of Britain in the next few weeks, he wanted his wife and family moved out of London to somewhere that would be safer for them all.

Spears knew people who would help him to identify suitable places for de Gaulle's family; they would get back to him by the end of the week and work with those who supported de Gaulle at the French embassy. Andrew was tasked with arranging for a lease on the Carlton Gardens flat plus getting quotations for the purchase of items he would require in the flat.

At the end of Wednesday, most things were in hand or under control. In appreciation of everyone's efforts, de Gaulle invited them to join him at the French House, in Soho. He ordered a taxi for them all and they joined the many people at the bar. It was obvious to Spears and Andrew that this was the place that was mostly frequented by French people; they either lived in London or had escaped after the threat of the Germans taking over their country.

De Gaulle seemed to be a different person. He talked to as many people as possible, as well as buying them drinks. Most of them had heard his broadcast – some expressed an interest in joining the Free French Force – so their names and contact details were taken down by Andrew. He appeared to be relaxed after his speech, now having a real purpose in his life to giving his beloved France back for his people.

By 9:15 p.m., Spears thought de Gaulle needed to eat something. He suggested they went to the Lyons Corner House in Piccadilly: he agreed. It took a further ten minutes to get him and his ADC away and into a taxi. They had a light snack and some coffee before Spears got a taxi to take them back to the hotel. De Gaulle thanked everybody for their kindness and help. He said he would see them all again in the morning.

After a busy Thursday – organising things for de Gaulle's flat – Andrew was collected, as usual, to take him to the hotel. This would be his last day working for Spears; he felt it was a bit like the end of term at school.

General de Gaulle had set his mind on how he should celebrate Bastille Day on Sunday the 14th. He came to the conclusion that he would lay a wreath – with any other French servicemen and others that wanted to – at the statue of Ferdinand Foch, in Grosvenor Gardens. He had mentioned to many of the people he had met at the French House that he would be in Grosvenor Gardens on Sunday and hoped some would join him. When

Spears and Andrew heard about the wreath laying, they decided also to be present.

Over the last two days, Andrew had managed to arrange for de Gaulle to move into the Carlton Gardens flat on Monday, 22nd July. All he now needed to do was to make sure that any of his items in the hotel be moved to the flat on that day, as well as the delivery of the things he had already purchased. If any extra things were required, Spears would deal with them during the next week, or after de Gaulle had moved in.

At the end of Friday, Andrew thanked de Gaulle for allowing him to work with him over the last two weeks. He told him that he very much enjoyed the experience. He concluded that he would be at Foch's statue on Sunday to support him; he hoped many people would be there. He saluted de Gaulle and shook hands with the other two men as he left the room.

On his way back to his flat, he was in need of a drink, so he called in to the pub he'd last been to with Helen. He knew it was unrealistic, but he half wondered if she might be there. Of course, she wasn't, but he did enjoy his two pints and some brief discussions with a few of the people in there.

Over most of Saturday and Sunday afternoon, Andrew wrote up a report of his time with General Spears so he could present it to Charles on Monday morning. He was pleased to have been at the wreath laying on Sunday at 11 o'clock. He was surprised there were so many French servicemen – and other French nationals – at the statue who clearly were there supporting de Gaulle. A small band had played the Marseillaise as de Gaulle, and others, saluted the statue that was shrouded with the French Tri-couleur.

On Monday morning, Andrew walked to Charles' office, looking very smart in his suit and carrying his brief case. He signed in as requested and was told by Miss Jones that Mr Compton-Browne was expecting him.

"Good morning," they said to each other.

"I understand from General Spears that you seemed to enjoy your time working with him and de Gaulle; you have made significant contributions to the meetings. After you came to see me nearly two weeks ago, suggesting that you were not giving them much help, that was not Spears perception at all."

"The situation seemed to improve over time," Andrew remarked, as he placed his report on Charles' desk. "I have a great deal of respect for de Gaulle; I admire his tenacity and his desire to get France back together again as a single nation."

"As I may have said to you before, it's time we sent you on some naval officer training courses. Combined Operations have set up shore establishments in Southern England and North West Scotland. At the end of the courses, you will be given the position of Temporary Sub Lieutenant in the RNVR. I have already enrolled you on the first of your courses that starts on Monday, 22nd July. You will be a resident at an establishment called HMS *Tormentor* which is at Warsash on the River Hamble in Hampshire. You could be down there for as long as five months. Knowing you as I do, I don't think you will need to be there that long. The second course will be in Scotland that could last a further seven months. Once again, I don't think you will need that long."

"So, you mean I could be undergoing training for almost a year before I gain a commission?" Andrew said with a great deal of surprise in his voice.

"As I said, it is very likely you won't need as long as that, particularly because of your experience on the ship bringing King Haakon from Norway."

"It very much sounds that I don't have any other option," Andrew said, raising his hands in the air.

"What I will say to you is that the war between Germany and Britain is only just beginning. The PM and his cabinet are preparing for the invasion of our islands, either from the air or sea or both. General de Gaulle is going to set up a Free French Force that will be supported by Britain. Most of the European nations' royal families and governments are exiled in London and are starting to set up resistance campaigns in their own countries.

"France is divided into a German occupied sector and one managed by the Vichy government. With all these things happening, it is very likely that the Service will need to call you back from the training course to carry out specific duties."

"I had better go and prepare myself. Do I travel down by train on Sunday afternoon?"

"Yes. Collect some money on the way out. Good luck, Andrew."